She needed him to kiss her...

...to let her lose herself in his passion. His mouth came down on hers, soft and tender, surprising her.

"Don't ever scare me like that again," he muttered, his warm breath feathering her lips.

Her eyes widened at the tremor in his voice. She tried to ignore the delicious heat that ran through her when he kissed her, but couldn't deny the satisfaction that he wanted her. Her lips parted in a sigh.

He didn't hold back as he had last summer. It was as if the dam had burst during their separation, annihilating the restraints around his emotions. She strained closer, angling her head to receive him, to taste him deeply, to remember.

"Stay," he whispered. "Just for tonight..."

ABOUT THE AUTHOR

Tina Vasilos has successfully written romantic suspense for many years. She has traveled widely around the world, and she uses her trips to research her novels. Tina and her husband live with their son in Clearbrook, British Columbia.

Books by Tina Vasilos

HARLEQUIN INTRIGUE

Don't miss any of our special offers. Write to us at the following address for information on our newest releases.

Harlequin Reader Service
U.S.: 3010 Walden Ave., P.O. Box 1325, Buffalo, NY 14269
Canadian: P.O. Box 609, Fort Erie, Ont. L2A 5X3

Nick's Child
Tina Vasilos

Harlequin Books

TORONTO • NEW YORK • LONDON
AMSTERDAM • PARIS • SYDNEY • HAMBURG
STOCKHOLM • ATHENS • TOKYO • MILAN
MADRID • WARSAW • BUDAPEST • AUCKLAND

ISBN 0-373-22463-X

NICK'S CHILD

Copyright © 1998 by Freda Vasilopoulos

This edition published by arrangement with Harlequin Books S.A.

® and TM are trademarks of the publisher. Trademarks indicated with ® are registered in the United States Patent and Trademark Office, the Canadian Trade Marks Office and in other countries.

Printed in U.S.A.

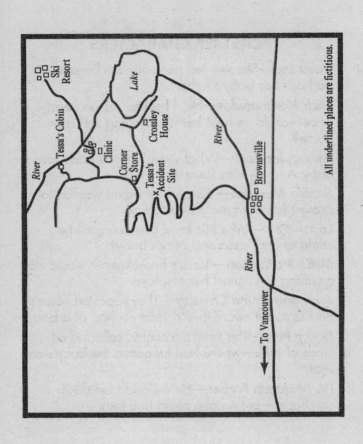

All underlined places are fictitious.

CAST OF CHARACTERS

Tessa Lee—She wanted her baby back—and perhaps her baby's father....

Nick Marcopoulos—He'd broken Tessa's heart once—could he heal her by bringing their son home?

Alexander Roth—What would Tessa's uncle lose if baby Andrew was found?

Sophie Marsden—Tessa's best friend wanted to protect her from more heartbreak.

Larry West—Was this local cop doing all he could to find Tessa and Nick's baby?

Millie McPherson—Tessa's housekeeper would do anything to comfort her employer.

John and Emma Crossley—They reported Tessa's accident, but swore they'd seen no sign of a baby.

Dorky Pete—The town's eccentric collected all kinds of junk—where had he gotten the baby's car seat?

Dr. Benjamin Forbes—He'd signed the death certificate—but no one could find him.

Chapter One

The crash of the car slamming into a tree reverberated through her head. Needles lanced her temples. She forced her eyes open, blinking against a warm trickle of liquid that ran down into them. A dense darkness surrounded her. Her heart pounded in her ears, a deafening clamor. She couldn't see anything.

Had she been blinded? She rolled her head to one side. A pale blob swam into her line of vision. Twisting her head farther, she saw a red light glowing. On the dash that had somehow moved from where it usually was.

She suddenly became aware of the pressure against her shoulders. It struck her why the dash lights were in such an odd position. The car was upside down, or at least tilted on its side so far that she was hanging by the fastened seat belt. The white object in front of her was the deflated air-bag.

A thicker blackness than the surrounding night filled her head. She fought the darkness, blinking again to clear the sticky film from her eyes.

A faint whimper penetrated the deadly fog in her brain. Her baby. She cried out, struggling to free the seat belt. The buckle wasn't where it should be. Her hands didn't seem connected to her brain; she couldn't move them.

The smell of raw gasoline stung her nostrils. She lifted

her head, sniffing. Small particles of glass scattered from her hair and shoulders. Forcing the pain and the encroaching darkness away, she managed to free one hand, twisting it around to turn off the key. The red light disappeared.

Wind rustled the trees overhead, driving rain through the broken windows. She shivered, realizing her clothes were wet. Water dripped on her hands, her face. She welcomed the discomfort. The ground must be soaked, she thought with a sense of relief, reducing the danger of fire from spilled gasoline.

Cold seeped into her extremities, alarming her. Was she dying? She stirred, fighting to stay awake. Her eyelids seemed weighted, falling closed. She forced them up, focusing blearily on the twisted mass of metal surrounding her. The seat belt buckle—it was half under her. She would have to move in order to unclip it.

The baby cried again, a plaintive wail. Tessa turned her head, tears mixing with the blood in her eyes as excruciating pain shot through her temples. She couldn't move. Her legs were numb, trapped by the crumpled metal of the car.

"Andrew." She tried to say his name but all that came out was a weak moan.

She pushed frantically against the restraint of the webbing. She had to get to him. She had to save her baby. Her right arm, caught between the seats, tingled with pins and needles. She pulled at it, biting her lip as the tingling turned to searing pain. If she could reach down to press the seat belt release—

Suddenly a bright light raked the wrecked car. Tessa squeezed her eyes shut, praying frantically. Help?

She heard a metallic sound behind her. A voice. "Damn, it's stuck right at the edge of the ravine."

Ravine? Tessa struggled to make sense of the words, but her head felt as if the high school band were marching through it. She couldn't open her eyes. A heavy copper smell filled her nose. Blood. Her stomach heaved and she swallowed down the nausea, fighting the rolling darkness that threatened to engulf her mind.

"My baby," she whispered raggedly. "Save my baby."

More noises, something scraping along the car, someone muttering. The light bobbed up and down but never steadied long enough for her to see anything.

Ominously, the baby was silent. What was wrong with him? He should have been screaming his head off. She was hanging almost upside down; his car seat must also be tilted at the same precarious angle.

The voice came closer. "Don't worry. Everything will be all right."

The car shifted. Tessa's stomach lurched sickeningly as she slid forward, the safety belt unwinding and no longer supporting her body. She braced her left hand on the strangely crooked dash. Too late. Her neck jerked toward the steering wheel. Pain shot through her temple and the world turned black and cold.

"NO, IT CAN'T BE. You're lying. It's not true." Tessa pounded her fist on the rail at the edge of the bed. She gripped the cold metal and struggled to sit up. The room swirled around her.

Gritting her teeth, she pushed at the rail. The IV in the back of her hand ripped free, the small sting negligible compared to the agony tearing through her heart. She yanked the end of the tape loose and tossed the needle aside. It dangled from the IV pole, swinging gently.

"Tessa, dear, you'll hurt yourself." Alexander stood by the bed, his face creased, his hands twisting together as if he wanted to console her but didn't know how.

There was no consolation. Not from this. "You're lying." Her voice rose to a scream. "He's not dead. My baby's not dead." She hammered her clenched hand on the bed rail that trapped her. "He's not! He's not! He's not!"

A nurse rushed in, a young woman who'd graduated from the same high school class as Tessa. "Tessa, I'm so sorry. We didn't know how to tell you."

Tessa fixed her with an accusing stare. "So you knew, did you?"

"I'm sorry." Tears filled her eyes. She looked at the deflated bag on the IV pole. "I guess you won't need it anymore. I can get you a sedative, if you want. Let you rest until you're feeling better."

"I'll never feel better." The pain spread through her body, lacerating nerve endings. An icy chill enveloped her. She shuddered, her teeth clattering together. "No, he's not dead. You're all lying. He's not." Her voice faded into a husky croak, and she collapsed back onto the pillows, gasping for breath.

"It's hard now," the nurse said soothingly. "But time heals everything."

"It won't bring my baby back." Exhausted, Tessa stared up at the ceiling, her eyes tracing an old yellowed water mark on the white plaster. "Please go. I want to be alone."

The nurse hovered, making worried noises. Tessa wished she'd just leave. She didn't want a sedative. She'd been unconscious long enough. Too long, not knowing.

Alexander spoke to the nurse in a low voice. "I can handle it. I'll call you if we need anything."

"Okay. That might be best, for her to have family with her." Rubber soles squeaked faintly across the floor and the door swished closed.

Alexander touched Tessa's hand. She jerked it out of his reach. His face etched with lines of concern, he sat down, folding his hands in his lap. "Dear Tessa, please let me help you. I know how you must feel—"

"How can you know how I feel? You've never had a child. Never lost a child." She choked on the words, the lump of tears she couldn't shed closing her throat. "Then why did they take my milk, let me believe my baby was alive and in another room? Why?''

"Because you were so ill we feared you'd die unless you had something to hope for. And you insisted."

She shook her head. Mistake. Her stomach heaved and she took a deep breath, afraid she would throw up. Agony, only slightly muted by the residue of painkillers, ripped through her skull. Wasn't it her heart that should be racked by pain? She closed her eyes. Her heart was gone, leaving a gaping, empty hole. It couldn't hurt anymore.

She shifted heavily on the bed until she faced the wall. A sharp pain in her ribs reminded her to move slowly. Every muscle ached as if she'd been beaten. It was too much. First Nick, then her father, and now her baby. There was nothing left. Nothing and no one.

"Please go. Just leave me alone."

Alexander put his hand awkwardly on her shoulder. "If you're sure that's what you want…"

"I want my baby back."

Alexander made a choking sound. "We all do, Tessa. I'd give anything if this hadn't happened."

Dimly she heard him prepare to leave, clothes rustling as he pulled on his raincoat. Still raining then. It had been raining when the car crashed. Water mixing with the blood on her face. It could go on raining forever as far as she was concerned. The sky weeping for her child.

Weeping, as she couldn't.

Alexander patted her shoulder again. "Sleep now, Tessa. I'll come back later."

She must have dozed. She woke when a nurse came in. A different one from earlier, older, with a comfortable, motherly face, someone she didn't recognize. Must have been a change in shift.

Rain spat against the window next to her bed. Tessa shivered and moved her head experimentally. Her temples ached dully, an intermittent thudding rather than the searing pain that had sapped her strength earlier. She felt numb inside, with the uneasy feeling that there was something she should remember, something bad.

She moved her legs under the sheet, wincing as cuts and bruises smarted. "I don't have any broken bones, do I?" she asked with an oddly detached curiosity.

"Nothing broken. You were lucky," the nurse said cheerfully.

Pain exploded inside her, memory sweeping in. My baby wasn't so lucky, Tessa thought, taking a deep, agonizing breath. What were broken bones? She would give up her very life, if she could bring Andrew back.

The nurse's eyes were warm and sympathetic. "Just let me check your temp and blood pressure," she said gently. "It'll soon be supper time."

"I'm not hungry," Tessa mumbled around the thermometer stuck in her mouth. "I need the breast pump."

The nurse took the thermometer, read it and noted down the results on Tessa's chart. She cranked up the head of the bed and wrapped the blood pressure cuff around Tessa's arm.

"The breast pump," Tessa said.

Frowning, the nurse pumped up the cuff. "No talking until I've got the reading."

Tessa bit her lip. As soon as the nurse whipped off the cuff, she said in a tone of exaggerated patience, "Could I have the breast pump when you're finished, please?"

The nurse folded her equipment and perched on the edge of the bed, taking Tessa's hand in hers. Her eyes were soft and kind when she smiled. "I know it's hard for you. Mr. Roth explained that he's told you about the baby. Expressing your milk will only prolong your discomfort. I can give you medication to dry it up."

"No." Tessa's voice echoed around the room, startlingly loud. "No," she repeated more softly in deference to the renewed pounding in her head. "I need to do this. Please."

The nurse looked down at her. "All right. Just once more."

An hour later Tessa lay back, exhausted. The hiss of trolley wheels and the rattle of dishes outside the door told her supper was being served. Her stomach roiled sickeningly at the thought of food. She willed it to subside. She would need the food, the bland liquid diet that was all they fed her at the moment. She had to eat to keep the milk coming in.

She gritted her teeth as pain knifed through her. Her baby was dead. He would never need her milk again.

"No," she cried to the empty room. He couldn't be dead. It was all a mistake.

A curly dark head poked around the doorway. "Did you call?"

Tessa shook her head wearily. "No, I didn't call. Did Mr. Roth say when he'd be back?"

"Seven, I believe. Shall I bring in your tray?"

"Fine."

The young student nurse withdrew, returning five minutes later with a tray. "Just the usual, I'm afraid. Tomorrow you'll be getting something more solid."

As if it mattered, Tessa thought dismally, lifting the cover from a bowl of chicken broth. The student nurse still lingered, straightening the edge of the blanket. "Bed okay? Shall I crank it up a little?"

"A little," Tessa said, picking up her spoon. She searched her mind for the girl's name, remembering vaguely that she'd helped her with the breast pump yesterday or the day before. When they'd all been lying to her.

Wendy—that was it. "Thank you, Wendy. I'm okay now."

"Okay." Wendy reached the door, then paused, turning. Her concern sat uncomfortably on her youthful face. "Uh, Ms. Lee, I'm really sorry about your baby. But the doctor thought it best not to tell you. We were really worried about you."

Tessa gestured with her hand, the lump in her throat choking her. After a moment, she managed to say, "What day is it?"

The girl's smooth forehead wrinkled. "Don't you know?"

Tessa shook her head, grimacing at the pain. Her brain must have really smashed itself against her skull. "No, I don't seem to have my watch."

"I think it was broken in the accident. It's Tuesday. The ambulance brought you in on Friday night or rather, early Saturday morning."

Tessa's tired mind worked to digest this piece of information. Four days. "Was I unconscious all that time?" No, not all the time. She faintly remembered people around her, Alexander soothing her, the nurses whispering.

"You were unconscious most of Saturday and Sunday. You kept asking about the baby whenever you woke a little. Monday you slept most of the day but you probably don't remember much. That's the way it is with head injuries. Today..." She shrugged, going over to the window to pull down the blind, shutting out the rain. "I'm really sorry."

"Thank you," Tessa said, her voice expressionless. How could she say anything else when she was dead inside?

She was just finishing the tasteless yellow jelly when Alexander strode in. A tall, spare man in his early fifties, he wore his clothes with elegant grace. His pale gray hair lay smoothly combed back from a tanned face. He smiled tentatively. "Feeling a bit better, dear?" he asked, shrugging off his damp rain coat and laying it on the back of a chair.

Tessa set down her spoon and fixed a level gaze at him. "How should I be feeling?"

He looked momentarily flustered, the hand he had extended toward her dropping at his side. He rubbed his hand over his perfectly tailored pants, then stuck it into his pocket. "I'm sorry, Tessa. I can't begin to tell you. I know how much the baby meant to you."

"Andrew. His name is Andrew."

Alexander stepped back, as if she'd slapped him. Guilt flooded up in her. Tessa dropped her gaze and began to pleat the edge of the sheet between trembling fingers. "Oh, Uncle Alex, I'm sorry. It's not your fault. I'm sure you did what you thought was best."

"What the doctors thought best, my dear. I had to go along with them. You had a severe concussion. We were afraid there might be brain damage."

Brain damage? Maybe that was why she felt so numb. Maybe she'd lost her mind completely and was dreaming all this. "Was there?" she asked quietly.

"Not as far as they can tell. There may be more tests but so far everything looks fine." He reached for the tray. "Shall I take that away?"

She shrugged. "I'm finished with it."

He set it on the straight chair near the door. Coming back, he drew the armchair close to the bed and sat down, crossing one leg over the other. He plucked at the crease in his pants and cleared his throat several times, clearly ill at ease. Tessa watched him, the thin edge of compassion cutting through her pain.

Alexander didn't handle emotion well. When her father had died, he'd stood stoically at the graveside, his face expressionless. After the funeral, although he'd offered his condolences to Tessa, she had seen how awkward the gesture was.

He must have felt grief since he was her father's distant cousin and they'd worked together in Lee Enterprises for years. He just didn't know how to show it, hiding behind a stoic mask.

"Thank you for coming," she said tentatively.

Alexander cleared his throat. "I'm just happy to see you feeling better."

"Have they said when I'll be able to go home? I asked the nurse but she says it's up to the doctor."

"Yes. I imagine he'll let you know tomorrow morning."

She'd had time to think while she was using the breast pump but the past four days remained a confused jumble in her mind. Pain and cold and voices, none of which made sense. She remembered waking up flat on her back in a moving vehicle with bright lights shining in her eyes. She'd wanted to ask about the baby but someone adjusted an oxygen mask over her face and she couldn't speak. After that, she must have passed out again, because the rest was a blank until she'd woken up in the hospital bed where she now lay.

"Why was I on that road at night in a rainstorm? And in your car?"

Alexander shrugged. "You called me earlier in the day. The weather was good then. You said you wanted to spend the weekend at the cottage. I'd lent you my car because yours had a problem with the electrical system."

Tessa frowned. "Do they have any idea what caused the car to go off the road?"

"The weather, most likely," Alexander said. "It was raining heavily and you know how treacherous curves on that road can be. Maybe you swerved to avoid an animal and the car skidded."

Tessa clenched her fingers together, pain knifing through her temples. The blank space in her memory haunted her. Was the accident her fault? Had she been instrumental in killing her own baby? A silent scream seized her throat. She swallowed to dislodge the suffocating fear. If she thought about it, she would go insane.

She pried her fingers apart and thrust one hand through her hair. Although someone had obviously cleaned the glass and blood out of it, the thick strands felt sticky and matted. Briefly she closed her eyes. If only her head felt better, she'd get up and take a long hot shower. And be done with the humiliating business of the bedpan.

But when she tried to sit upright, the room spun around her and she felt weak and dizzy. Nausea rolled in her stomach, aftereffects of concussion, the nurse had told her. Tessa had no intention of getting up and falling on the floor. Her bones and muscles ached enough as it was, without adding more bruises.

"You're lucky you weren't more seriously hurt," Alexander said. "Only surface abrasions except for the cut on your temple."

Lucky? When her baby was dead? If one more person said that, she'd scream and never stop.

To distract herself, she gingerly probed the thick bandage on her head. It was healing, the nurse had assured her. And would not likely leave a scar. Stifling a cry of pain, she pressed her hand over her mouth. A scar. It would be a cheap price to pay if only her baby lay in her arms.

"How—?" Her throat constricted and she couldn't go on. Eyes burning, she summoned strength, blurting out the words in a tortured whisper. "How did he die?"

Alexander's narrow brows drew together. His fist clenched on his knee until the knuckles turned white. "Please, Tessa," he said in a strained voice. "We can talk about it later."

Alarm skittered through her, quickly turning to panic. Cold sweat enveloped her body. "Later? What do you mean, later?"

"When you're stronger."

He winced under her angry glare, and sighed heavily. "Head injury. He was apparently thrown from the car after it hit the trees."

"What?" She bolted upright in bed. "That's not possible. He was in his car seat. I never went anywhere without putting him in the car seat."

"Nevertheless, something must have given way. He was probably killed instantly."

Killed. The ugly word echoed through her mind. The adrenaline rush subsided, and she collapsed onto the pillows. A memory flitted through her tired brain, gone before she could grasp it. Guilt flooded her. It was her fault. She had gone up to the cottage in a storm, in the dark. Whatever had possessed her to expose her child to that danger? Even in clear, sunny weather, she hated that road, winding and twisting through the mountains.

Her fault. Her fault. She should have gotten a better infant seat. She should have checked the consumer reports more carefully. She should have stayed home, not gone out at all.

She had failed miserably as a mother, letting her baby die.

The faint squeak of the door hinges interrupted her self-recrimination. The young woman who entered hesitated inside the doorway, her eyes dark with concern. A fragile thread of warmth penetrated Tessa's despair.

Unable to speak, Tessa held out her hand.

Sophie ran to the bed and threw her arms around Tessa. Tessa inhaled the familiar scent of Chanel No. 5 and for the first time since she'd been in the hospital, tears stung her eyes.

"Tessa, are you all right?" Sophie asked.

"Yes. No." Choking on the words, Tessa dimly recalled that Sophie had been to see her before. Yesterday, she thought. She remembered the soothing sound of her voice. Had Sophie known Andrew was dead? Was she part of the cover-up? No, she couldn't blame Sophie. Not her best friend. Sisters forever, they'd sworn in kindergarten.

"I'm so sorry about Andrew." Sophie loosened one arm and groped for a tissue to mop up her tears. "I just can't believe it. That poor little baby."

"I can't believe it either," Tessa said painfully, her voice muffled against Sophie's shoulder. "I keep thinking they'll bring him in."

Sophie gave another sob. Tessa, her eyes dry and aching, envied her the easy tears. Like any godmother, Sophie had loved Andrew, doted on him. She gave Tessa another hug and drew away, blowing her nose.

Alexander rose to his feet, arranging his raincoat over his arm. He squeezed Tessa's hand briefly. "Now that Sophie's here, I'll leave you in her capable hands. Take care of yourself, Tessa. I'll drop by again tomorrow."

"Alexander hardly left your bedside when you were unconscious," Sophie said when the door had closed after him. "I never saw a man so worried."

Tessa nodded. "Yes, he's been very supportive." She sighed, agony blossoming anew. "But it won't bring Andrew back." Her voice broke.

Dabbing at fresh tears, Sophie pulled her close. "It's all right to cry, Tessa. Let it go. You'll feel better."

Tessa hiccuped. "I can't. I can feel the tears but I can't."

"Are you going to tell Nick now?"

A pang speared Tessa's heart. Nick, her lover for a brief, summer interlude. Nick, the father of her child. Nick, the man with whom she'd shared a deep, overwhelming passion before he'd vanished off the face of the earth. "Tell him what?" she asked stonily. "It's too late now. Besides, I don't know where he is."

"You could try to find him again. You never know. Maybe some disaster happened and he couldn't contact you."

"Yeah, like amnesia," Tessa retorted. "No, he didn't want a commitment. We had an awful fight and he just disappeared."

"You tried to call his office in Montreal, didn't you?"

"Number disconnected," Tessa said tersely. "No listing in the phone book. It's like he never existed."

"He existed, all right," Sophie was very definite. "He got you with child. Not very responsible, I'd say."

"It wasn't just his fault. I should have been more careful."

Sophie made a dismissive gesture. "You were on the rebound from that rat Scott. You had an excuse for getting carried away." She paused. "Maybe it's just as well he doesn't know. You know how possessive some men can be about children, especially sons."

"Not Nick," Tessa said firmly. "He didn't want children."

"More fool he," Sophie said. "He doesn't know what he missed." She wiped away another tear. "Those gorgeous blue eyes Andrew had, and the way they sparkled when he smiled."

"Nick's eyes," Tessa whispered, wishing she could cry. Wishing she could find release from the bottled-up grief and bitterness.

Her breasts were beginning to hurt again. Would the reminders never end? How long would it take before she stopped speaking as if Andrew were merely asleep in another room, and then got slapped in the face by the truth? The truth she still wanted to deny.

Sophie sat silently, holding Tessa's hands tightly between her own. Tears streamed down her rounded cheeks and she made no effort to stop them. Yes, Tessa thought, cry. Cry for Andrew. And cry for me.

ONCE VISITING HOURS were over and Sophie left, Wendy came in and straightened the bed to settle Tessa for the night. Tessa closed her eyes but thoughts kept spinning through her exhausted brain like demented mice in a maze.

If only her head would stop aching. If only Andrew lay next to her, nursing contentedly.

She had fallen into a fitful doze when a commotion in

the hall jolted her to full wakefulness. The room was dark except for a sliver of light under the door.

"Sir, you can't go in there," the night nurse said firmly just outside her door. "Come back tomorrow. Sir!"

The door swung open, so hard it bounced off the rubber door stop. The silhouette of a man appeared in the doorway, followed by the bulky figure of the night nurse pulling at his jacket. "Sir, I can't allow this. I'm calling security."

"Be my guest," the man stated in a voice that sent shivers up Tessa's spine. Her heart hammered against her ribs in a mixture of dread, denial and helpless elation.

Nick Marcopoulos flicked on the overhead light and strode to the bed. "Hello, Tessa. Would you mind telling me what you've done with my child?"

Chapter Two

Blinded by the fluorescent glare and the pain that shafted through her head, Tessa squeezed her eyes shut. Nick. He couldn't be here. Not now. Not ever. She must have fallen deeply asleep and this was a nightmare. He couldn't have come.

Her heartbeat thundered in her ears but not loudly enough to drown out his deep voice. If this was a dream, it was the noisiest one she'd ever had.

"How did you know?"

"Someone told me." His voice seemed to catch in his throat. "No thanks to you. I had to find out from some anonymous stranger."

The words washed through her, as if they were pebbles tossed into a lake, sinking without a trace. He knew. She couldn't blame him for being angry. But it didn't matter now.

The silence stretched, the room filling with an ominous threat. Unable to bear the tension, Tessa pried her eyes open. He hadn't disappeared. He stood next to the bed, silently staring down at her, his hands at his sides. His fingers were opening and closing compulsively, as if he wanted to strangle something. Or someone.

Inwardly she trembled. She had only seen him angry once before, on the last day of that fateful holiday, nearly a year ago. She'd worked hard to banish the image but now it rushed back with painful clarity.

Nick, the handsome architect from Montreal on holiday in Victoria, where she'd gone to recuperate from her broken engagement. She wanted to remember him as he'd been during the four weeks they'd spent together, tender, thoughtful. Even enigmatic, when he'd seemed to be lost in a world she couldn't share. His smile when he saw her watching him was enough to reassure her. For a month they'd shared their thoughts, their bodies, their souls. It had been the happiest time of her life. And his, he'd assured her. Later she'd wondered if that had been a dream.

It certainly hadn't been reality.

Only the baby had been real.

She moaned inaudibly as a new thought struck her. Had he come to take his child? The bitter truth slammed into her and she stifled a dry sob. He couldn't take Andrew. Andrew was dead, lost to both of them.

An anguished little hiccup shook her body and, unable to meet his gaze, she let her eyelids drop again. In the sea blue depths of his eyes, she saw Andrew. It was too much to bear.

NICK DUG HIS NAILS into his palms and embraced the pain. It was small compared to the agony tearing his soul apart.

He'd thought he'd excised her memory, cut it out of his heart and brain with the finality of a laser eradicating a tumor. Even as he'd charged into the room, he thought he could do it, treat her with indifference, as if she were a casual acquaintance who hadn't made much of an impression. He'd used his harsh words to keep up the pretense, but in fact he wasn't even sure what he'd said. Some mindless stupidity, no doubt.

She lay there, her face as white as the pillow behind her head and the bandage stuck on her temple. Her hair was tangled and matted, a sure sign of the severity of her injuries. The sunny blond color looked dull, dark and lifeless. And she'd hidden her eyes, smoky blue like summer storm clouds, from him behind the delicate, violet-veined lids. Only the sight of her long dark lashes fanned on her pale cheekbones struck him as familiar.

Her body, under the knitted blanket, looked fragile, thinner than he remembered. He couldn't stop the protective feeling that flooded him, any more than he could stop himself from breathing. If he had been there, if he hadn't allowed stubborn pride to take over, she wouldn't be lying hurting in a hospital bed.

Of course he wasn't making any sense; it was guilt nagging him. He felt suddenly old and tired.

He became aware that the nurse had moved around him to Tessa's side. "Are you all right?" She straightened Tessa's pillow, casting a glare over her shoulder at Nick. "I can get an orderly to put him out if you don't want to see him."

Without opening her eyes, Tessa gestured with one hand. "No, let him stay for now. Don't worry. Please."

Uncertain, the nurse glanced at him again. "Well, if you're sure." She placed the call button next to Tessa's hand. "Ring if you need me."

With a final glare at him, the nurse walked out, leaving the door pointedly open. Letting his tense fingers relax, Nick took a step forward to turn on the small lamp next to the bed. He swung around and switched off the overhead light, closing the door at the same time.

When he faced her again, Tessa's eyes were open, warily fixed on him. "Who told you about the baby?"

Whatever he'd expected her to say, that wasn't it. Baby or not—how did he know that muffled voice on the phone hadn't been lying—he would have thought that her first words to him would be a severe tongue-lashing for the way they'd parted.

"Never mind that. We'll get to it. First, tell me how you

are.'' He strove to keep his voice steady, impersonal, even though he knew he'd already blown it by his outburst when he'd entered the room. He'd been determined to be cool and collected, rational, but around her, just as it had been last summer, emotion spilled from his every pore. Emotions he'd vowed never to feel again.

Eleven months and twenty-three days. He stifled a laugh. If he checked it, he could probably calculate the hours and minutes since that first sight of her crying on a bench under a weeping willow. He'd offered her a handkerchief and she'd taken it without a word, not even a trace of embarrassment. She'd mopped her eyes and blown her nose. She crumpled the handkerchief in her fist and looked at him as if she didn't know what to do with it. He'd told her to keep it.

He wondered if she still had it. Or if she'd thrown it out after their stormy parting a scant month later.

She said nothing, her eyes dark and shadowed—with pain, or memories she'd rather not relive, or was it something else? He couldn't tell, had no right to ask.

The silence became oppressive and he shifted his feet, stuffing his hands into his pockets. Awkwardly he cleared his throat. "So, Tessa, how are you?"

Inane. Witless. However he'd envisioned this meeting, he hadn't planned for it to be in a hospital. Nor had he expected to confront her again with the phone caller's words echoing in his brain: You have a child. He'd replayed the caller's faint, muffled voice in his mind a thousand times and still didn't know whether it was a man or a woman. Could have been either.

"I'm fine," she said. Only the faint quiver in her voice betrayed the turmoil he could still see in her eyes. Was it because she was happy to see him and not sure how to react? Or was it residual anger?

Whatever. He didn't much care because at least it wasn't indifference.

He rocked back on his heels. "If you don't mind my saying so, you don't look all that fine. And with the current bed shortages everywhere, they wouldn't keep you in the hospital unless there was a reason."

"Thanks," she said dryly. "I didn't expect to see you again. How long has it been now? Let's see, it's July now. Almost a year. My, the time flies."

"Yeah, doesn't it?" He wasn't fooled for an instant by her flippant tone.

The brief return of liveliness to her demeanor drained away. She seemed to shrink before his eyes. Her fingers plucked nervously at a loose thread in the blanket. "Nick, why are you here? After all this time, I can't believe you just came to inquire about my health."

He glanced around, fixing his gaze on the door for an instant, gauging whether the nurse was about to return to kick him out. It was a private room, though, and even he knew hospitals were liberal with visiting hours in a private room. "Mind if I sit down?"

She shook her head, her eyes deep blue-gray pools.

He shrugged out of the battered leather jacket he wore, hung it on the back of the chair before sitting down. He braced his hands on the arms of the chair, loosening his grip only when he saw his knuckles turn white. "Okay, I had a phone call."

A frown appeared above her nose when he paused. He shifted restlessly. The phone call, rushing here even though he'd had no way to confirm the startling information—it all seemed bizarre and impulsive. Why hadn't he simply phoned her from Montreal and asked her, or called Alexander Roth, who would have been able to give him a simple answer and not put him through this wringer of regret, anxiety, and the recognition of broken dreams?

"A phone call?" Her brows arched questioningly. "How did they get your number when I tried and couldn't find it?"

The news that she'd tried to get hold of him startled him so that for an instant he couldn't speak. He swallowed hard to clear the lump from his throat. "Couldn't find it? How long ago?"

Her fingers gripped the edge of the blanket. "What do you think? After I got home, I tried to reach you in Montreal. Isn't that where you said you lived? They had no listing for anyone with your name."

He closed his eyes, might-have-beens clamoring through his mind. "I'm sorry. I've been out of the country for a while. I got a new number in May."

"Oh." She was silent for a moment, then added, "I presume this phone call you mentioned was something significant."

"You might say that." He turned in the chair so that he could look straight into her eyes. "The caller said I had a son and I'd better get down here."

He wouldn't have thought it was possible but her face grew whiter, drained of color until he thought she would fade away completely against the white bedding. "Your son." Her voice was a bare breath of sound.

"I can see it must have been a hoax," he went on briskly. "Or maybe they had the wrong Marcopoulos. You're here because of a car accident. You're not in either maternity or in pediatrics."

"I wouldn't likely be in maternity unless I'd just given birth, would I?" Her voice seemed a little stronger, strengthening his belief that he'd been the victim of a cruel joke. There was no baby.

He half rose from his chair, extending his hand toward her. "I'm sorry. I see it's all a mistake. I'll leave and let you get some sleep." He took her hand in his, lifting it from the blanket. Her fingers were icy cold, her hand as bony and delicate as a bird's claws. ¹s heart lurched in his chest. She wasn't well at all. S 'dn't a doctor be looking after her?

"Shall I call the nurse? Are you in severe pain?" he asked worriedly.

Slowly, her eyes swimming with tears that didn't fall, she shook her head. "They can't do anything about the pain. They can't bring him back." Her voice broke and she swallowed before she could go on. He had to bend down to hear her next words. "Nick, your caller was right. I had a baby, your son. He's four months old."

His knees gave way. Her hand slid out of his as he sat down heavily. Luckily the chair hadn't moved. He would have collapsed onto the floor. He pushed the heels of his hands into his eye sockets, trying to absorb the words. He was a father. Again. He had a son.

But after a moment the numbness fled. "Four months old?" he said, anger making his voice harsh. "I met you just a year ago."

"Nick—"

He couldn't bring himself to look at her. "We made— had sex the third day after we met. The next morning you started your period. So you couldn't have gotten pregnant until at least a couple of weeks later. I know we were careless about birth control once or twice but if he's four months old, he can't be mine. What were you trying to do, find a handy father for your ex-fiancé's child?"

"Nick, shut up!" The anger in her voice finally cut into his tirade. Tears again swam in her eyes but her mouth was set in a determined line. "Nick, if you saw him, you'd know how unfair that is. He's your son and I can explain."

"So explain," he said coldly.

"He was premature, born six weeks early. There were complications." She choked on the word. Her throat moved as she swallowed. "But it's not important now."

He stared at her, dread making an icy knot in his chest. "What do you mean?"

Tessa raised her eyes to meet his, her expression taut with anguish. "I'm sorry, Nick. He died in the accident."

Strangely, her tears still didn't overflow. She closed her eyes and her lashes grew spiky with moisture but none of it escaped to wet her cheeks. Agony burned through him, icy and hot at the same time. A baby. He'd had another baby, one he'd denied before he knew of its existence. And he'd lost him, just as he'd lost his little girl.

"No," he moaned, burying his face in his hands and rocking back and forth. "No, it can't be."

He jumped when he felt a light touch on his shoulder. Tessa's hand. She hung over the edge of the bed at a precarious angle so that she could reach him. "You believe me, then."

Numbly, he nodded. "I believe you. I'm sorry." Standing up, he felt curiously light-headed, her image swimming before his gaze. He blinked to clear his eyes as he moved closer to the bed.

He tucked her back under the blanket, and stood there, his hands hanging at his sides. "He died in the accident?" His voice was an unfamiliar, husky whisper. "I won't ever get to know him."

"Go outside and shout and scream," Tessa said tiredly. "That's what I wanted to do when I heard. Only I can't, as long as I'm in here. They say it upsets the other patients."

He would have laughed if his laugh muscles hadn't been paralyzed. "And we can't have that, can we?" He laid his hand on her shoulder, then jerked it back. If he touched her now— "Tessa, will you be all right? I think I have to be alone."

She turned her head toward the wall, closing him out. Not that he blamed her. In some corner of his mind, where shreds of sanity still prevailed, he knew he was a coward to leave her. They should mourn the baby's death together. The baby's death. He'd come a long way in facing the bitter truth. With Andrea, he'd never used the term death.

"Go," she said, her voice muffled by the blanket she

pulled up around her chin. "I'd like to be alone, too. And I can call the nurse if I need anything. Goodbye, Nick. Thanks for stopping in."

Dismissal.

He stumbled out to his rented car and drove back through the unfamiliar streets. Brownsville, a little-nothing town in the upper Fraser Valley. Probably pretty enough, but at the moment the world seemed painted in shades of gray. And the dismal hues owed nothing to the rainy night.

By the time he found himself staring through the third story window of his hotel at the street lamps reflected in the wet pavement, he had no memory of how he'd gotten there. Rain washed the window, drops sliding down like silent tears.

His face felt cold, and he rubbed his hand over his cheeks. To his surprise, his fingers came away wet. He could cry for a child he'd never known, within an hour of hearing of his life and death. It had taken him more than a year to cry for his little angel, Andrea, to finally make himself say goodbye to her.

He hugged his arms around his chest, his shirt sleeves clammy against his cold skin. He'd left his leather jacket in the hospital room.

Tessa had said goodbye, not good night. Did that mean she didn't expect him back? Or that she didn't want him back?

And what about him? Could he stand to see her again, knowing she'd kept the baby's existence from him? Or had she tried to contact him as soon as she'd discovered herself pregnant, and failed to reach him because he'd already left the country?

He had to know. He couldn't doubt her word that the baby had been his. She hadn't had sex with her damned fiancé for a long time before she'd met Nick, if ever. She'd told him herself, and if she hadn't, he would have known from the physical manifestations he'd dimly noticed.

He had to talk to her again. Then he would decide whether to stay. Or to leave, never seeing her again.

The thought filled him with despair.

The last year had been hell, but it was over. So he'd thought. Now it appeared he'd been tossed into a greater emotional turmoil.

Tomorrow. He'd see her again tomorrow. She would answer his questions. Then he would decide.

TESSA LISTENED to the faint sound of voices at the nursing station in the hall. Her head felt as if there were a demolition derby going on in her brain. She swallowed, her mouth dry. She didn't want any more painkillers—she hated the fuzzy way they made her feel—but she could do with a drink of water.

She leaned toward the bedside stand, grasping the handle of the plastic jug. Ice clinked inside it as she tipped it over the glass. Her hand shook and water slopped beside the glass. A wave of dizziness overcame her and the jug slipped out of her lax fingers to crash to the floor.

The night nurse burst through the door. "Ms. Lee, why didn't you ring?" She glanced around as if she feared Nick might be lurking in a corner, waiting to pounce. "Did that man go?"

"Yes, he went." Tessa subsided against the pillow, cursing her weakness.

The nurse laid a cool hand on Tessa's brow. "Just hang tough, love. I'll fetch you another jug of water. Sure you don't want anything for pain?"

Tessa shook her head, a mistake, as the hammering in her temples increased. "No, thanks. Just some water. Or juice, if you have it."

"Coming right up."

Tessa sipped gratefully at the tart grapefruit juice while the nurse wiped up the spilled water and replaced the jug with a fresh one. "There, I'll put the straw right in it and you won't have to worry about pouring. Want the light off?"

Tessa nodded. "Thank you."

The nurse nodded. "Sleep now, love. You'll feel better in the morning." She frowned at the chair. "I see he left his jacket. So I suppose he'll be back."

He'd better not have the nerve, Tessa thought dismally. She'd mail the jacket if necessary. If she could find out where he was staying. Or living.

On the heels of that depressing thought, sleep mercifully claimed her.

SHE HEARD ANDREW CRYING. Hungry. She knew that half plaintive, half angry wail he made when he wanted to nurse. Her breasts stung with their weight of milk, distended nipples tingling as drops spurted out, moistening her gown. She had to go to him.

She struggled to sit up, but her arms and legs were numb. Her tongue felt parched and swollen, her vocal cords paralyzed.

The crying beat against her brain as she lay helpless. Inwardly she screamed but no sound emerged from her mouth. Gathering all her strength, she tensed to heave her body over the side of the bed. On the floor, she could crawl to him.

But she couldn't move. She felt as if she were floating, looking down at her inert body on the bed.

The crying grew fainter. She strained her ears but it faded altogether. She hung suspended near the ceiling, and it suddenly occurred to her that she was dead.

She shut out the image of her body lying there, letting the darkness take her away. What did it matter whether she lived or died? Andrew was dead and it was her fault for taking him out in the dark and the rain. He was gone. He didn't need her anymore.

No one needed her anymore.

SHE WOKE TO THE SIGHT of lemon yellow sunlight flooding the room and Nick Marcopoulos slumped in the chair next to her bed.

"Why didn't you tell me, Tessa?" he said in a subdued voice.

"You might let me wake up first." Tessa raked her hair back from her face, grimacing at the sticky feel of it. Sweating all night. Faint nausea sat uneasily in her stomach but the pain in her head had diminished to a dull ache. She cheered up slightly. Maybe they'd let her up for a real bath today.

"Tessa, please."

Compassion at the desperation in his voice tightened her chest. She took a look at him for the first time. His eyes were black holes of pain. He clearly hadn't gotten any sleep last night. Even his tan did nothing to hide the pallor of his skin. Beard stubble shadowed his jaw. He wore the same rumpled oxford-cloth shirt as last night. Hadn't he even gone to bed?

"Tessa, why didn't you tell me?"

"I told you last night. I couldn't find you." Remembered anger and desolation sharpened her tone. "And I didn't think you'd care, in any case. You'd made your feelings about commitment and children clear enough. Not for you, not ever again."

"Still, if you were pregnant, I had a right to know." The dispirited stillness dropped away from him and anger flashed in his eyes.

"By whose standards?" she demanded, her own anger flaring to life. "You told me it was over. You never gave a thought to consequences." Her voice rose. "And you never told me why."

ECHOES OF THEIR FINAL argument rang in her head.

Nick's implacable voice. "I'm sorry, but this is all I can

give you. I'm not going through that again, not for any woman.''

''I thought I was more to you than just any woman.'' She'd drawn on every particle of self-control to keep her voice steady.

''You were. You are. But this is it. You have your family to go back to. I have my work. That's the way it has to be. We never made any promises to each other. You told me you were going into this with your eyes open.''

''Things changed,'' she'd muttered.

He'd closed his eyes. She'd wondered afterward whether it was to hide his feelings? To make it easier to tell the truth, or to lie? She'd never figured it out. Not in all the weeks she'd lain in bed during her difficult pregnancy. Not during the nights of soul-searching when Andrew lay sleeping, a sweet, heavy weight in her arms.

''No promises.'' He'd turned to stare out the window at the storm-tossed sea. ''You agreed,'' he added, his tone accusatory as if it was her fault for breaking the rules.

''That doesn't mean I couldn't change my mind.'' She'd pulled in a deep breath that hurt her chest. ''But if that's the way it has to be, I can't hold you. Goodbye, Nick. It was fun.''

She'd picked up her suitcase and walked out of the hotel room. That was the last time she'd seen him until last night.

''WHEN I MET YOU, I never gave a thought to anything,'' Nick said now with a wry note in his voice. His face changed, becoming bleak and drawn. ''Tell me about him, Tessa. Please.''

She closed her eyes, tears again clogging her throat as she remembered Andrew's drooly, toothless smile, the smile she'd never see again. ''He was small when he was born, but such a fighter. And he grew faster than you can believe. He smiled when he was less than a month old. He was the happiest baby. So smart.''

He made a heartrending sound. She looked at him, amazed to see tears squeezing out from under his tightly closed eyelids. "Nick, I'm sorry." Her voice hitched in her throat. "I'm so sorry."

"I never had a chance to know him," he said in a strangled voice. "To hold him."

How could she say that that had been his own fault? But ultimately hadn't she often been glad she had Andrew to herself without the complication of his father? Hadn't she selfishly hugged him to her, glad he was hers alone? "He had your eyes, the most gorgeous blue, and masses of black curls. Yours again."

Nick pushed his spread fingers through his hair, pressing them against his skull as if his head ached. "I'm sorry, Tessa. I should have been here."

"Would you have come, if you'd known?" she asked. "I got the impression our goodbyes were pretty final."

"A baby would have changed things."

Tessa shook her head. "Not the way I heard it. In fact, it would have done the opposite, driven you away faster. You said it yourself, no kids, ever again. Why?"

For a second a dark, dangerous emotion crossed his lean face. When his gaze softened at once, she wondered if she'd imagined it.

"You lost a child, didn't you?" Tessa added, wondering why it hadn't occurred to her before. It would explain so much.

A muscle ticked in his tightly clamped jaw. "I had a little girl once. Someday, I'll tell you. I know I owe it to you."

"I'm glad we agree on one thing."

He smiled wistfully. "We used to agree on a lot of things."

She couldn't stop a blush from climbing up her cheeks. Yes, they'd agreed all right, mostly in bed. "But not on the important stuff," she said. Like love and loyalty and commitment.

He averted his face, looking out the window as if he found something fascinating about the heat waves rising from the parking lot. "I wasn't ready," he muttered.

"What about now?" she asked with rash curiosity.

"What?" Obviously his low words hadn't been meant for her ears. "Now?" He laughed bitterly. "I don't know. Damn it, Tessa, I just don't know." He stood up, grabbed his jacket, and walked out of the room.

Tessa lay deep in thought after he left. It was obvious to her that he was a different man from the one she'd met a year ago. The man she'd spent a month with had been a tender lover, but out of bed, he'd kept up a wall of reserve, never sharing his feelings.

Cool and composed at all times, he'd only shown genuine emotion on that last day when she'd told him her holiday was over and that she had to go home. And then the emotion had been anger, as if he were outraged that she didn't want to continue their affair. Without strings, a situation intolerable to her after she'd fallen in love with him.

He knew that her work as a technical writer could be carried on anywhere there were telephones and modems. Through the magic of electronics she had access to any information she needed and could present the finished product easily and efficiently without ever setting foot in her employer's office. He'd asked her to come back to Montreal with him and she had refused, wanting more than the affair he offered. No promises, he'd said. They didn't need them.

Trouble was, she did. Not that she believed them entirely after Scott had broken every extravagant promise he'd ever made to her. She'd honestly thought Nick was different. A man who made no promises couldn't break them. But she'd discovered she needed them after all, when she gave her heart.

He hadn't known that, of course, hadn't known how devastated she was, how tempted she'd been to accept the crumbs if she couldn't have the whole loaf. In the end, she'd at least kept her pride. Not that that had warmed her during the long winter when she'd been too sick to get out of bed, and too fearful for the child she carried. Nor had pride kept her from crying endless tears.

The tears that seemed permanently dammed now.

NICK WALKED OUT of the hospital into the blinding sunlight. He was about to unlock his rented car when a man's voice stopped his hand in midair. He turned slowly. The voice was oddly familiar but the face attached to it wasn't.

Fiftyish, graying hair, tall, in good condition, the man stepped across the street after locking a sleek pearl gray Jaguar. He wore a double-breasted, pin-striped suit, a white silk shirt and a tie with a discreet paisley pattern. Power clothes, Nick thought wryly, somewhat incongruous in this town of jeans and lumberjack shirts.

"You are Nick Marcopoulos, aren't you?"

"Guilty," Nick said.

The tall man in front of him made a grimace of distaste, taking in Nick's rumpled jeans and battered leather jacket. Definitely not power clothes. Nick dealt with this type all the time and he could conform to their rules when he wanted to. Most of the time he didn't. His building designs were good enough to stand on their own. "And you are?" he added bluntly.

"Alexander Roth." He didn't offer his hand.

Oh, oh, Nick thought. The Alexander Roth. The man in charge of Lee Enterprises.

"We've talked on the phone," Roth added unnecessarily.

Which explained why his voice was familiar. Nick had phoned the company last fall to ask about Tessa. Obviously Roth hadn't bothered to tell Tessa about the call, or she'd ignored the message. He hadn't had a number to leave so she couldn't have called back in any case. "I'm surprised you remember my name," Nick said.

The man's pale green eyes turned into ice chips. "Oh, I remember your name. And how you used Tessa. So let me give you a piece of advice. The last thing Tessa needs is something else to upset her. We don't want you here. So get out of town."

The hair on Nick's nape bristled. "Is that a threat?"

If anything, Roth's eyes grew colder. He shrugged one shoulder. "If you want to take it that way—" Turning, he stalked toward the hospital entrance.

Nick stared after him until he disappeared inside. Thoughtfully, he got into the car, but he didn't immediately start the engine. Roth practically threatening him? He shook his head. From what Tessa had told him, Roth was an honorary uncle to her, nothing more, a distant relative of her father's and the CEO of Lee Enterprises.

Tessa's father was dead. The hotel desk clerk had given him that piece of news when he'd inquired about Tessa's address. That would explain his veiled threat. Roth had taken over the father role, appointing himself Tessa's protector.

Well, Tessa didn't need protection, not from him. She'd been hurt enough; he would rather cut off his arm than add to her pain.

He wondered if she now had a bigger hand in running the business. She was bright, well educated and capable, but he knew from last summer that she didn't want the daily grind of running a large corporation. She was well established in a career she enjoyed, and her assignments let her set her own working hours. Especially with the baby, her job was perfect. She could work and stay home with him at the same time.

Only she'd lost the baby. That would change everything.

He turned sideways and spread out the map he'd left on

the passenger seat. Brownsville was a town situated at the eastern end of the Fraser Valley, about a two-hour drive from Vancouver. Its major employers were the lumber mill, with its associated industries, and a ski resort forty-five minutes away. Both were owned or controlled by Lee Enterprises. He frowned. If Tessa inherited from her father, she would be a well-off woman.

But would she inherit? Norma, the talkative waitress at Grandma's Diner, where he'd had breakfast this morning, had had a few words to say about her father. How much was true, and how much only typical small-town gossip, he couldn't begin to guess.

"Oh, Joseph Lee nearly had a heart attack when Tessa turned up pregnant," Norma had confided as she refilled his coffee cup. "Him the biggest businessman in town, said he couldn't hold his head up anymore. But after the baby came, he turned right around. He loved that child. I mean, who wouldn't? And Tessa went home to nurse the old man when he got sick." She'd shrugged. "I wouldn't want to call it. Old Joe might have left the business to Tessa but he could just as easily have left it to Roth. He's a distant cousin, after all."

So Roth might be the one who ended up with the company. Nick wondered if Tessa cared.

One thing he knew for certain, right now she would have traded all of her father's estate and more to have her baby back.

Running one finger over the map he found what he was looking for. He twisted the key and started the car.

THE CEMETERY could have been a park, a hilly expanse of green surrounded by tall hemlock trees. Old-fashioned upright gravestones dotted half of the area. On the other, newer half, the markers were flat stone or brass plaques.

No one seemed to be about although the grass looked

well kept, recently cut. Wind stirred the tops of the hemlocks, a gentle sighing.

He sat for a moment, his thoughts in a turmoil. Maybe this was crazy, coming here, but he assumed they must have had the funeral, even with Tessa in the hospital. Her head injury would have made the time of her recovery uncertain.

Clutching a dozen pink roses he'd bought on the way, Nick left the car and stepped through the wrought iron gates which stood ajar. His eyes scanned the new section and dismissed it. The Lee family had been Brownsville pioneers, Tessa had told him last summer. There must be a family plot.

He headed toward one of the fenced enclosures near a gigantic weeping willow. The first one belonged to a family named Braun. But the second turned out to be the final resting place of various Lees over the past hundred years. He walked past stones marking an Agatha who had lived to be a hundred and five and died in 1914, and a Winston who had died in Vietnam.

A broad granite stone carved with the name Joseph Bartholemew Lee stopped him in his tracks. Born 1920, died three months ago. Safe in the arms of God. Tessa's father. Had he really almost disowned Tessa over the baby and the circumstances of his birth, and then made up again?

So much he had to talk to Tessa about. And he might never have the chance, if she decided she didn't want to see him.

To be reminded.

He walked around the fenced plot, studying the stones. Belatedly he realized he didn't know his son's name. Still, his grave shouldn't be hard to find since it would be the most recent one in the family plot.

He found nothing. Several children were buried but they had died more than fifty years ago. David Edward Lee, died

1926, aged five years. He wondered if the child had been Joseph's brother.

He took a final look around but there were no fresh graves. The funeral must have been delayed after all, waiting for Tessa's recovery. He would find out when it was scheduled.

He laid the roses on the long-dead David Edward's grave, standing there for a contemplative moment. Someone must have mourned this child. Someone must have cried out at the injustice of a child dying so young.

The scent of cut grass and roses settled around him like a benediction and he finally found a measure of peace.

But with that peace came determination. He knew what he had to do. He made the sign of the cross, right to left in the Greek fashion. "Peace, little one," he murmured.

He drove back to the town center and bought a newspaper. At least it was out today. He'd asked about one yesterday and been told that the local paper only published on Wednesdays and Saturdays. He leafed through it, finding the obituary notices. Only one. Lee, Andrew Joseph Nicholas, aged four months. Mourned by his mother Tessa, his uncle Alexander, godmother Sophie.

Numb, Nick clenched his fist around the edge of the paper. Last night he'd wept but today his eyes were dry. He understood Tessa's deep grief now, the inability to cry. He realized that, at a gut level, he hadn't believed his child was dead until this moment. Confronted with the printed evidence, he could no longer deny it.

Why, God? Why? His soul cried out the lament of all humans who mourned. He got back into the car and sat staring through the windshield at the sunlit street in front of him. Traffic crept by, people going about their lives, not knowing or caring that his child was dead. The child he hadn't known.

Inwardly he raged at the injustice of it, but outwardly he kept an icy calm. He looked at the newspaper again.

Andrew, he thought, with a jolt. She'd named the baby Andrew. He cast his thoughts back to last summer. Had he mentioned Andrea? No, he was sure he hadn't. He never talked about her. At least he hadn't until this morning when he'd admitted he'd had a little girl. Two years since he'd lost her.

How had Tessa come to name their son Andrew, the masculine equivalent of Andrea? Coincidence? Or had their minds made some sort of psychic link last summer, which had never broken?

One more thing he'd have to ask her.

He ran his eye down to the bottom of the notice. Funeral services would be held in the chapel of Shady Rest Funeral Home on Monday at two in the afternoon.

A vital necessity crystallized in his mind. He had to see his son.

THE FUNERAL HOME was a small building with two somber gray limousines parked in the lot. The door was locked. A sign said that if their services were required, clients were requested to call the number below.

A tight smile playing about his lips, Nick used a pay phone down the street to call the funeral home number. A recording came on. ''Mr. Faversham is presently away. If funeral services are required, please contact our head office at—''

Clenching his jaw in frustration, Nick slammed down the phone. This could only happen in a small town. Of course it was possible that Andrew hadn't been removed from the hospital—where did they keep the deceased? The morgue, he supposed, shuddering.

He ground his teeth in frustration. No way would they let him in there. He wasn't even listed as a relative.

And he couldn't very well ask Tessa. The last thing he wanted to do was upset her further. He would have to wait.

At the hotel, the desk clerk handed him his room key

and a sealed envelope. Nick ran up the stairs and unlocked his door. He tossed his jacket on the bed and ripped open the envelope.

"What?" A chill ran through him as he took in the short message: *Get out of town before it's too late.*

Abruptly he laughed aloud, and tossed it into the waste basket. Let them try to drive him away. He leafed through the phone book he found in the nightstand drawer.

Picking up the phone, he dialed a real estate agency.

Chapter Three

"Why did you name him Andrew?"

Tessa jumped as Nick's voice startled her out of a half doze. She squinted at the light coming in the window. Around three o'clock in the afternoon, she guessed.

Dr. Ivers had taken a look at her pallor late in the morning, listened to her chest, examined the cut on her head and the less serious cuts and bruises on her legs and chest, and ordered her to stay in bed for another day. "A bath?" she'd begged, disappointed but too tired and depressed to argue.

"Maybe in the afternoon, if you feel up to it," he'd said, frowning as he wrote on her chart. "You're not recovering as quickly as you should because of Andrew. Understandable. I can give you something to take the edge off, but I don't normally recommend medication for that kind of thing."

Tessa had shaken her head. "No, I have to learn to accept it."

Dr. Ivers regarded her keenly, his own face somber. "He was a lovely baby. It's such a bloody shame. But you know that it does get easier."

She forced herself to smile at him. "I know. It's just that I'm still at the stage where I think he's only in the next room."

"Hang in there, Tessa. Call me if you need anything."

"I will. Thank you." Dr. Ivers had delivered her and been her physician all her life. She had no secrets from him. He'd seen her through her pregnancy, boosting her low spirits and never asking her any questions beyond the obvious one: did her child's father have any known health problems?

What would he say when he learned the man standing next to her bed at this moment was Andrew's father?

It occurred to her that no one knew, except Sophie. And Sophie hadn't been in today, so she didn't know Nick had shown up.

"Why the name Andrew?" Nick repeated in a tone impossible to ignore.

"I liked the name. And it's sort of Greek."

"Andrea," he murmured, the accent on the second syllable. "She liked me to call her Andy."

"Was that your little girl?" Tessa hardly dared to breathe. Was he finally going to let her into that deep place he'd walled off from her even during their most intimate moments?

"Yes."

She waited for the space of several breaths. When she realized he wasn't going to elaborate without prompting, she said, "What happened to her?"

He fixed those disconcertingly blue eyes on her. "What happened to her, Tessa? Wouldn't the logical question be, where is she?" He dropped his gaze and rubbed his palm over his face. "She died."

Shock ran through her. Dead? The worst she'd thought was that he had lost custody in a bitter divorce. "Her mother?" she asked tonelessly.

"Dead, too." There was no mistaking the finality in his voice.

"Oh." She hesitated for a second, then let the words rush out. "Will you tell me about it?"

He sank down on the chair. "Some time. Not now. You've got enough to deal with."

So have you, she thought, compassion welling up in her. He'd lost a child and a lover or wife. Most likely wife, she figured. He'd marry the mother of his child. Or he would have before whatever event had triggered his cynicism and made him drive her away last summer. The two deaths had probably done it, she decided. Nothing could have been more traumatic than that.

And last night she'd hit him with the news that another child of his was also dead. No wonder he had looked utterly devastated.

"I'm sorry," she said helplessly.

"So'm I."

The door opened and Alexander walked in. Tessa saw Nick stiffen. Alexander smiled at her. "How are you today, Tessa?"

"A little better, but Dr. Ivers still won't let me go home."

"All in good time." Alexander patted her shoulder, then nodded toward Nick. "Marcopoulos," he said coolly, by way of greeting.

"Roth," Nick replied in an identical tone.

Tessa glanced from one to the other. "I take it you've met."

"This morning. Outside the hospital," Alexander said.

"Briefly," Nick said.

Tessa frowned. She sensed an undercurrent of animosity between the two men. Yet why that should be, she couldn't imagine. Alexander couldn't know about Nick and her brief interlude with him. Her face cleared. Of course. One of the nurses must have talked to Alexander about Nick's visits. Alexander was very protective of her, not to mention that he must be curious.

Nick looked at his watch and pushed himself to his feet. "Look, I've got an appointment. See you, Tessa."

Before he could reach the door, Alexander cleared his throat. "Uh, Marcopoulos—Nick, I think I owe you an apology. I was out of line this morning and I'm sorry."

One of Nick's brows lifted. "No problem." He glanced at Tessa. "I'll be back later."

"What was that all about?" Tessa asked when the door had closed.

Alexander shrugged. "Just a little misunderstanding, that's all. I thought he was upsetting you but you seem to want him around. I'll accept that."

NICK DROVE through the center of town, frowning thoughtfully. Very odd. What kind of a game was Alexander Roth playing? In front of Tessa he acted as if he'd never talked to Nick before that morning outside the hospital. Yet Nick had spoken to him on the phone last fall. And again Tuesday when he'd asked for Tessa's phone number, having found that the number she'd given him last summer was disconnected. He now realized why; Tessa had moved back to her family home.

Still, it was possible that Alexander hadn't made the connection between Tessa's baby and Nick.

Nick's frown cleared. Roth had apologized for his comments this morning. Must have realized he'd overplayed the father role and that Tessa was capable of choosing her own friends.

At least it eliminated Roth as the author of that note. Nick didn't feel like being responsible for a breach between Tessa and her "uncle."

Nick glanced in the rearview mirror. Was that black Mazda following him? For a small town. the traffic was fairly heavy, moving slowly, stopping whenever anyone had to pull out of a parking space. Nick had made several turns and the Mazda had tracked him, once changing lanes abruptly enough to earn an irritated blast from a car horn.

Nick turned into the parking lot of Brownsville's biggest

supermarket, driving down a couple of rows before he pulled into a parking space beside a large utility van.

Nick got out of his car and started toward the store entrance, keeping an eye out for the Mazda. He spotted it, one row over from where he'd parked, slowly cruising down the line of parked cars. Nick deliberately stepped out into the open. The Mazda made two quick left turns and cut down the next row, heading for the exit of the lot. A moment later it merged into traffic on the street, disappearing from view.

Swearing under his breath, Nick went into the store. The car had turned too quickly for him to get the license number, and tinted windows prevented him from seeing the driver. Well, he'd keep an eye out.

He picked up one of the free real estate papers displayed by the door of the store, and used the pay phone to confirm his afternoon appointment with the agent he'd called yesterday.

HE RETURNED to his hotel room in the late afternoon, blearily rubbing his eyes. His restless night, minor jet lag, and brain overload combined to give him a dull headache even aspirin couldn't dislodge. He'd looked at five houses for sale, three townhouses, and one condominium apartment, all of them completely unappealing, either because of location or condition.

The agent had seemed particularly eager to unload the apartment, even emphasizing that the owner would consider any offer. If it had been remotely suitable, which it was not, since it was on a ground floor and faced north, with nothing to recommend it architecturally, he might have been tempted to make some ridiculous offer.

He'd resisted the temptation, coming to the conclusion he'd be better off to rent for the time being. Tomorrow he'd look at apartments advertised for rent, using the listings in the newspaper he'd bought earlier.

He took a shower, shaved, and got dressed again, strapping on his watch. Almost seven o'clock. He'd go see Tessa.

SHE WASN'T ALONE. A dark-haired woman sat beside her bed, holding her hand. A longtime friend, he assumed. They were about the same age and the censorious look the woman cast him reinforced his thought. She knew exactly who he was, and she wasn't about to welcome him with open arms.

"Nick," Tessa said. "I didn't think you'd be back."

For once her mobile face gave nothing away; he couldn't tell whether she was happy to see him or not. "I'm still around," he said coolly.

Tessa gestured toward her friend. "This is my best friend, Sophie Marsden."

"And you're Nick," Sophie said before Tessa could go on. She rose to her feet. "Nice of you to show up at this late date."

Inwardly he groaned. As he'd figured, no ally here. "I'm sorry," he said, feeling like a heartless bastard. He guessed he'd apologized more in the past two days than in his whole life before.

"And so you should be," Sophie said acerbically. "What are you planning to do now?"

"Sophie!" Tessa hissed.

"Hush, Tessa. It's about time someone told these 'love-them-and-leave-them' types a thing or two."

"I'm sorry," Nick said forcefully. "What can I say?"

"You can grovel," Sophie said.

"Would it help?"

Sophie pretended to consider. To his relief, her face softened and she almost smiled. "No, I suppose not." She sobered and her eyes grew glossy with tears. "You would have enjoyed your son."

She couldn't have hurt him more if she'd stabbed a carving knife into his chest. His throat closed. "I know," he whispered. "If I could do things over—"

But he couldn't, so it was pointless to flail himself with regrets. At the time, family obligations had of necessity come before any personal consideration. Although if he'd known about his son, he might have found some way to cut those obligations short.

But he hadn't known. And now he would never have the joy of holding this child of his in his arms.

Tessa watched the play of emotions over his face and marveled at how much he'd changed. They were deep, real feelings he couldn't hide. Last summer she'd sensed the turmoil within him but he had kept his guard up. They'd laughed and talked but he'd kept it light and superficial. She asked herself now whether she had fallen in love with the lighthearted summer lover or with the intensely emotional man she'd sensed beneath the carefree exterior.

The man who stood before her now.

If this was the man she'd loved, she was in big trouble. If he hung around, it might be all too easy to fall for him again. She consoled herself with the thought that he'd be gone soon, back to Montreal or wherever he lived now.

He squirmed uncomfortably beneath Sophie's thinly veiled sarcasm. Tessa took pity on him. "Enough, Sophie. As Nick said, there's no way to fix what's happened. We can't bring Andrew back." Her voice didn't even shake although she clenched her fist under the sheet against the pain that shot through her. Pain that had nothing to do with her banged-up head and bruised muscles.

Sophie's brown eyes widened. "If you've accepted that, then why are you still—"

"Never mind," Tessa interrupted.

She saw Nick cast a puzzled look at Sophie. Sophie finally favored him with a thin smile. Tessa lay back, satisfied. Sophie had decided not to be Nick's enemy. Not that it mattered much, since he wasn't likely to be around for long.

Why should he? Andrew, his reason for coming, was dead. There was nothing to keep Nick here.

Alexander entered, carrying a bouquet of red roses. Conversation became general. Her heart aching, wishing she had Andrew back, Tessa lay back against the pillows and tried to lose herself for a short time in the warmth of her friends. All too soon, she would be alone to deal with the pain again.

SHE HADN'T ACCEPTED Andrew's death, no matter what she said.

Nick stared at the ceiling of his room, watching the red neon of the old-fashioned hotel sign ebb and flow. It reflected in the mirror, and through the open window he could hear the gas hissing in the defective tubes. The *E* of HOTEL was burned out, so that the sign spelled HOT L every few seconds. Hot was right. Sweat lay in a clammy sheen on his skin, and he debated taking another shower. The air-conditioning, if this building had ever had such an amenity, also didn't work.

To take his mind off the heat and his sleeplessness, he let his thoughts wander back to Tessa. He couldn't believe how much it hurt him to see her pain. She was determinedly denying the baby's death. She still used the breast pump. He'd glimpsed it in the bathroom on his way out the door. And he was sure Sophie had been about to mention it when Tessa interrupted her.

Tessa, whose every emotion showed on her face, had turned off her feelings, insulated herself against the grief. He was willing to bet she'd never cried at all.

Last summer she'd cried brokenheartedly over a dead starling. Her emotions had been on the surface, laid bare by the callous way her fiancé had broken off their engagement when her father had demanded a pre-nuptial agreement. Scott Glidden had been after her money, nothing else.

Her grief over the baby went too deep, buried like a virulent infection festering beneath the apparently healed skin. Not even Sophie's sympathy and understanding could penetrate the defenses Tessa had erected to protect herself.

Sophie, his son's godmother. He smiled, lacing his fingers behind his head. She'd been protective of Tessa, outraged with him, but he sensed he would someday count her as a friend. He liked her, her loyalty to Tessa.

He had to do something to jolt Tessa out of that deadly lethargy. Well, they still had the funeral to get through. Maybe then she would accept. And cry. And he would be there to support her, comfort her, help her to heal.

He'd done some of the damage. He had to fix it.

In the meantime, he had a few other things to do. That threat—somebody didn't want him here. Not Sophie, though, despite her words. Sophie wasn't the sort to make anonymous threats; she was too direct. This must be something about Tessa's accident.

HE GOT UP EARLY in the morning, reaching the police station by half past seven. "I'd like to see the report on Tessa Lee's accident," he told the burly officer at the front desk.

The man looked startled for a moment. Almost at once, though, his face smoothed out. "Your name, please?"

"Nick Marcopoulos."

"Could you spell that, please?"

Nick complied. The man picked up the phone and punched in a couple of numbers. He spoke briefly, then nodded to Nick. Putting down the phone, he said, "Someone will be with you in a moment."

Not much going on in the police station, Nick noted as he waited. But this was probably the slow time of day. On the other hand, maybe it was like this all the time. Browns-

ville had struck him as a quiet town, not exactly a hotbed
of crime.

"Mr. Marcopoulos?"

"Yes."

"I'm Larry West." The cop who had emerged from a
door at the end of the room was tall, blond and muscular.
He put out a large hand and shook Nick's, his grip a bit
overenthusiastic. Power play? Nick wondered, flexing his
fingers as he followed the man down the hall.

They reached a drab office furnished with a desk and a
couple of filing cabinets. The dregs of coffee had dried into
mud inside the glass carafe of the coffee machine on one
cabinet, and smelled like burnt rubber.

West sat down behind the desk, motioning Nick toward
one of the straight wooden chairs along the wall. "Pull up
a chair." Leaning back, he steepled his fingers. "Now,
what can I do for you?"

"I'm a friend of Tessa Lee's," Nick said. There was
something about the man's attitude that bothered him. His
arrogance, perhaps? Typical small-town cop, prepared to
dislike him simply because he was a stranger? "I'd like to
see the report on her accident, if that's possible," Nick
went on evenly.

The guy knew damn well what he wanted.

West didn't move. "Yeah, that's what Bill said. Why?"

Nick tipped his chair back against the wall and stuck his
hands in his pockets. "No particular reason. Just curiosity."

"Nothing to be curious about, Mr. Marcopoulos." He
arched one eyebrow. "Greek, isn't it? We don't get many
Greeks here."

"I'm probably as Canadian as you are," Nick couldn't
stop himself from saying. "Do I get to see the report?"

West's mouth tightened. "No point. I'll tell you what
happened. I wrote it up."

"You were the first officer at the scene?"

"Yes, although an elderly couple called 911 from a pay phone at the store down the road. They saw the car in the trees. Lucky they happened by. It was a foul night. Not much traffic."

"Why were they on the road?" Nick wasn't sure why it mattered, but it was a place to start. If they'd seen another car leaving the scene—

"They've got a cabin up there, too. It was pure luck that they saw Tessa's car. Their headlights glinted off the side window and they stopped to check it out. Lucky that they did. She was unconscious and soaked to the skin. This may be July but it was pretty cold that night, with the rain. She mightn't have lasted until morning."

A chill shuddered through Nick. "That serious?"

"Yes. Hypothermia can happen even in summer."

"What about the baby?"

West shook his head although his expression didn't change. "He wasn't there. In fact, there was no sign that he'd been in the car except for the infant seat strapped to the back seat. At first I thought Tessa had gone up there alone, that she'd left the baby with her friend Sophie."

Nick's heart raced. "Then how did you find out he'd apparently died in the accident? What about the couple who were at the scene?"

"They couldn't get very close to the car because of the treacherous slope and the precarious angle of the car. But they said they saw no one else around. The first I knew that Andrew had been in the car was much later when I got back to the police station. Someone else had written the report of a phone call that Andrew had been brought to the clinic and subsequently died of head injuries."

Nick closed his eyes briefly, feeling the news like a blow to the heart. "Did you actually go up to the clinic?"

"No. After the ambulance took Tessa to the hospital, I attended a five-car pile-up at the other end of the district. It was almost morning by the time I got back to the station and received the report about Andrew. I tried to call the clinic then but it had closed. Besides, the report said the body had been transferred to the funeral home so there wasn't anything to do.''

"The funeral home at that time of night?"

Annoyance crossed West's face. "The funeral home is on call twenty-four hours a day. You see, we don't have a morgue."

"I went to the funeral home and it's closed."

"Mr. Faversham is away for a few days. He was there last weekend."

Nick pinched the bridge of his nose, feeling cold and empty. "What about an autopsy?"

"In cases where cause of death is obvious, like massive head injury, and a doctor has seen the victim, an autopsy probably wouldn't be done. And Alexander Roth would have been notified since Tessa was unconscious at the time. I can't see him letting anyone autopsy Tessa's child if it wasn't necessary."

"And you went back to the accident scene later?"

The chair creaked as West shifted his weight. "When it got light in the morning, I went back and thoroughly checked out the scene. Then I called a tow truck to take away the car."

"Where is the car now?" Nick asked.

"In the impound yard. It'll go to the wrecker as soon as the insurance adjuster finishes his estimate and gives us the okay."

"Can I see it?"

West shook his head. "Sorry, that's against regulations. The insurance, you know. They don't want anyone tampering with the car, making the damage greater."

"Didn't you just say the car's a write-off?"

"Yeah, it looked like it, but that's up to the estimator. Makes no difference. We can't let civilians into the impound yard."

Nick stood up. "All right, then. Would you mind giving me the name of the couple who called in the accident? I'm sure Tessa will want to thank them once she's released from hospital."

West rummaged through a stack of papers on the corner of the desk. He scribbled a name on a sheet of paper and handed it to Nick. "John and Emma Crossley."

"Address?"

"Sorry, I didn't need it for my report. The accident was straightforward. Car skidding on the wet road. No big mystery." He checked the report again. "I've got the phone number." Snatching the paper back from Nick's hand, he scrawled a number. "Will that do?"

"Fine." Nick hid a grin. "Thanks. I'm sure Tessa appreciates everything you did."

The man's eyes softened. "Tell her I'll be in to see her. I've got a couple more questions for her but it can wait until she's feeling better."

"I'll let her know." He glanced down at the paper in his hand. "If the baby wasn't in the car when the Crossleys saw it, who brought him to the clinic?"

Larry frowned. "I don't know. That wasn't in the report. Just the doctor's statement that he died of his injuries."

Strange, Nick thought, but on the other hand, some people didn't want to get involved. Maybe he should be grateful for the actions of the anonymous Good Samaritan, as far as they went.

"And this person just left Tessa in the wreck and didn't call 911?" he asked.

"He or she might have. There were several calls to 911 about accidents in the area that night. I'm sorry I can't help you more." For the first time, West sounded sincerely regretful. Nick bit back his frustration and thanked him.

He'd reached the door when West spoke again. "Before you go, d'you mind answering a question."

"What is it?"

"Why are you so interested in this? Tessa's never mentioned your name. It's not exactly a forgettable one."

"As I said, I'm just a friend." Nick held up the sheet of paper. "Thanks again."

He walked out to his car, pausing before he opened the door. Behind the police station, a chain-link fence topped by rows of barbed wire encircled a compound in which stood a number of smashed cars. He walked over to the gate. As he had expected, it was locked. Some of the cars looked as if they'd been there forever, those at the back of the lot shrouded in blackberry vines.

Nick hooked his hands in the fence mesh, leaning as close as he could. The nearest car was a red Volvo covered with mud, the roof and body panels crumpled beyond repair. Both front and back windshields were missing. Only the back seat window on the driver's side remained in its twisted frame, crazed into a myriad cracks.

"Hey, you're not allowed over there."

Nick stiffened, recognizing the nasal tones of Bill, the burly cop who manned the front desk. He must have followed him out, likely on West's orders.

Nick turned slowly. "Just looking," he said mildly. "Is that the car Tessa Lee was driving?"

"Sure is. And a crying shame, too. Car was almost new."

Still only a car, Nick thought. What about Andrew's life?

"You can't hang around here," Bill said belligerently.

"I'm leaving."

Nick got into his car and started the engine. The starter whined as it turned over. Rental car abuse. He wouldn't put up with that for much longer. Now that he'd decided to stay for a while, he'd have to see about getting a car of his own.

He had just turned onto the road when he saw a tow truck coming down the street. On a hunch he pulled over to the curb and waited. Sure enough, it turned in at the police station.

He drove a little farther up the street and parked between a van and a pickup truck. Ten minutes later the tow truck came by, the red Volvo rolling behind it.

He almost laughed aloud as he pulled out to follow it. He'd have his look at the car and no cop would stop him. Wrecking yards were public property. He hoped this was one of those that let customers go in and salvage parts on their own.

Car Crunchers was located a couple of kilometers out of town, near the landfill, judging by the flocks of gulls swooping over the trees surrounding it. A number of people wandered among the cars, carrying an assortment of tools and greasy car parts.

His kind of place, Nick thought in satisfaction, fondly recalling an old Jaguar he'd helped a friend restore years ago. He parked in the front lot and walked into the office. "All right if I look around?"

The blue-jeaned young woman behind the counter gestured toward the back. "Help yourself. Just don't get near the crusher."

The crusher. A dark premonition rushed through him and he broke into a run. The tow truck had released the Volvo at the end of a line of cars waiting to be hoisted onto a conveyer. A machine that looked like a cross between an overgrown Dumpster and a car wash engulfed a small Honda. The gates at the ends folded inward.

Nick shuddered at the horrible gnashing sounds as the machine crunched up the car. The noise stopped momentarily and a neat pancake of crushed metal popped out the far end and trundled up another conveyer onto a waiting flatbed truck.

"Hey, you, get away from there."

A kid, probably in his teens, leaned down from the crane he operated, and waved his arm at Nick. Nick put his hand to his ear as if he hadn't heard. The kid pushed a lever. The engine dropped to idle. "You're not allowed in this area," the kid said.

"I want to have a look at the Volvo that just came in."

"Well, make it quick. It's going to the crusher."

Just as he'd figured, fresh suspicions rising. Late-model cars never went to the crusher this quickly. Even if there were no salvageable body panels, the interior could be re-used and perhaps the dash and other parts as well. Wreck-ing yards made their profits from cars like this. "Why so soon? It just got here."

The kid shrugged. "Orders, probably. Some people don't want to see their car again when they've had an accident."

Tessa probably did feel that way, if she'd considered it, but Nick would lay odds that, her mind filled with Andrew, she hadn't given the car a thought. "Let me have a look," he said. "A friend of mine might want the seats. They're leather, aren't they?"

For answer, the kid revved up the engine. Nick picked his way through the mud to the car. The driver's door had been torn off, by the fire department when they'd gotten her out, no doubt. It lay on the front seat. Deflated airbags hung from the steering wheel and from the dash on the passenger side. Probably they'd saved her life. She had a superficial abrasion on her cheek but he had no doubt she'd have been more seriously injured wearing only the seat belt.

The rear door on the driver's side showed little damage. He pulled at the handle. It didn't open.

He studied it, running his hand over the once shiny paint. The frame was slightly buckled. Bracing his foot against the fender, he pulled, using his weight as leverage. The door suddenly popped open. His fingers slipped off the han-dle and he landed on his butt in the mud.

Scrambling to his feet, he leaned inside the car. The in-fant seat sat in the middle of the back seat. Cartoon cats scampered over the padded liner. He pulled on the sturdy plastic shell. It was firmly attached to the seat belt, a shoulder harness even in the center position, a new innovation to safeguard seated passengers and facilitate holding an infant seat. A tether belt at the back further secured it. The network of straps meant to hold the child in position lay open along the edges of the seat.

The buckle was undone. He lifted it and examined it, the metal cool against his fingers. Not a scratch. The entire passenger side of the car resembled a stepped-on tin can and not a sliver of glass remained in the windows. But for the baby to have been thrown out of the car, there should have been damage to the seat or the straps, and he couldn't see any.

He glanced at the cars waiting for the conveyer. The crane was picking up a rusty relic five cars down the line from where he stood. He had a little time.

Crawling inside the car, Nick minutely examined the straps on the seat. No sign of damage or severe stress. He pulled again at the straps holding it in place. Tight, and properly positioned. He clicked open the safety belt, and lifted the baby seat out. Backing out of the car, he set the seat on the ground.

The crane was lifting the third car in the line. Not much time. Nick had another quick look inside the Volvo while he waited for the machine to turn back toward him. Nothing. No diaper bag or any of the other paraphernalia people always carried when they traveled with babies.

He was about to withdraw when he spotted something on the floor, against the far door. He crawled farther in and picked it up, a furry yellow duck whose orange beak was locked in a perpetual smile. His nose prickled with unshed tears as he clenched the soft toy in his hand.

He backed out of the car and turned to pick up the infant seat. The kid had cut the crane to idle again. "Okay, mister?" he yelled.

Nick waved. "I'm leaving. Thanks."

In the office, the girl waved him through with the warning that it wasn't a good idea to reuse infant seats after they'd been in a crash.

Nick sat in his car, staring at the little duck in his hand. The tip of the saucy tail was threadbare. A lump sat painfully in his chest; it hurt to breathe. His child, his son, had chewed on this toy. And never would again.

Anger at the injustice of it stirred him to examine the car seat again. All the straps looked perfect. He fastened the central buckle and tugged as hard as he could. Solid.

Setting it on the back seat, he shoved the key into the ignition, the question burning in his mind. How had the baby been thrown out of the overturned car without any visible damage to the seat or the straps?

Chapter Four

Unless the harness hadn't been fastened?

His whole being recoiled at the idea that Tessa could have been careless with a child's safety. There had to be some other explanation.

And what about the baby's things? Had they been removed at the accident scene? If so, by whom, and where were they now?

The questions rolled around in his mind like hamsters in a wheel as he drove back to the center of town. He stopped at the hotel to change out of his muddy clothes, taking a quick shower before putting on fresh jeans and a shirt. He smiled sadly as he looked at the little duck he'd set on the bedside stand. When he left the room, he took it with him.

Downstairs, the desk clerk called out to him. "Will you be checking out soon, Mr. Marcopoulos?" he asked.

Nick paused. "I thought you weren't full."

The man's bony face colored and he fumbled with a pen. "Well, uh, some of the rooms are being painted, and are unusable. We have a tentative booking for your room for tomorrow night."

"If it's not confirmed, they may not show up," Nick said, temper rising. First a note, now a subtle hint to reinforce it?

"Uh, I'm sure they'll be here," the desk clerk said. "They're regular clients."

"I'll let you know," Nick said tightly.

"By tonight, if possible. I'm sorry, Mr. Marcopoulos."

Yeah, right, Nick thought as he went out into the sunlight, gulping in fresh air. He started the car and slammed it into drive. He drove through town. Fists clenched on the steering wheel, he braked in front of the hospital.

Abruptly he made a U-turn, cutting off a van about to enter the parking lot. He couldn't let Tessa see him like this, especially when he had to question her about the infant seat. The last thing he wanted was to upset her, but in his present frame of mind he doubted he would be diplomatic.

He cruised the streets until he found the apartment building he'd passed the day before in his search for housing. Good, the Suite for Rent sign still stood on the lawn. He rang the manager's apartment.

A dour, middle-aged woman answered the door. A cigarette dangled from her lower lip. "Yeah, I'll show you the suite."

He followed her up to the second floor. She wheezed asthmatically as she unlocked the door. "Two bedrooms, a large kitchen and living room, bathroom. All recently upgraded." She waded through the place, showing him the suite.

To his surprise it was spotlessly clean, with glossy hardwood floors and built-in bookcases. Large windows overlooked the street. "First and last month's rent in advance," the woman said, dropping her cigarette butt in the sink and turning on the garbage disposal to get rid of it. "You can pay with a certified check or a credit card."

"Fine," Nick said. "I'll take it."

"You'll have to give me references but you can bring them by later."

Fifteen minutes later he stood on the street again, looking

up at the windows of his new home. Not much, but it would do for now, and he'd be out of the hotel.

He opened the car door, realizing belatedly he hadn't locked it. He smiled wryly. Who would steal a nondescript rental car anyway, especially in broad daylight?

He had started the engine before he noticed it. With a wrench, he jerked the key out again. The infant seat, which he'd laid on the back seat of the car, was gone. In its place was a computer-printed note: *You've been warned. Get out of town.*

He crumpled the paper in his hand. Like hell he would.

He restarted the car. Within an hour he had returned it to the rental office, and he was driving a Peugeot he'd picked up cheap in a used car lot.

His own place. His own wheels. And now to talk to Tessa.

HE FOUND HER ALONE, sitting impatiently up in bed. "The doctor's late," she grumbled. "They say he might release me today."

He eyed her closely. Yesterday she'd been pale. Today hectic color spotted her cheekbones and her eyes were too bright. He wisely kept any comment on her appearance to himself. "No more headache?" he asked.

Two little creases materialized above her nose. "Not as long as I take it easy." She smiled. "I even had a shower."

She pushed her fingers through her damp hair, taking pleasure in its clean silkiness. Nick had his hands deep in the front pockets of his jeans and he rocked his weight from his toes to his heels and back again. She didn't have to be a mind reader to know that something had upset him. He was trying to hide it from her, but the kinetic energy he gave off electrified the room.

"Well, spit it out, whatever it is," she said. "And sit down. You're making me nervous."

He arched one eyebrow. "I'm not even moving."

"No, but you look as if you are. Every muscle in your body is tense, as if you're expecting a hungry grizzly to pop out of the cupboard."

He laughed, although there was little humor in the sound. He came to stand next to the bed, still restlessly rocking, as if his body were full of emotions too volatile to contain. She suddenly realized what it was, a hard-edged anger.

"Bad morning?" she asked mildly.

He clenched his teeth. "You might say that."

"Want to talk about it?"

"No," he said at once, not that she'd expected anything different. Last summer it had been the same. He never talked about his feelings.

But then he surprised her by pulling a chair close and sitting down. "No, but there's something else we need to talk about."

Andrew's death. The accident. But what more could they say about it? She waited, hardly breathing. Maybe he wanted to talk about their relationship and abrupt parting. How would she react if he showed the slightest regret? She should send him packing, and consider herself well rid of him, as Sophie had told her often enough. Who needed a man who couldn't commit?

But what if he'd really changed? Sick as she'd been, devastated over Andrew, she still felt the faint tug of attraction. Felt the memory of passion warm the feminine regions of her mind and body.

She steeled herself against the feeling. She'd gotten over him, found contentment with her child and her work. She bit back an anguished cry. Andrew was gone. Maybe that was why she and Nick had this tenuous rapport. He had lost his child, too.

Common sense asserted itself. She'd be a fool to let a few pretty words, if that was what he had in mind, seduce her again.

"What do you remember about your accident?"

She wrinkled her brow. That wasn't the question she'd expected. "I remember being cold and wet," she said hesitantly. "I remember pain. I could only move my left arm a short distance. My right arm was stuck between the seats."

"No, I mean before the car crashed. Do you remember what happened to make you go off the road?"

Hadn't she searched her mind for the answer to that for hours last night? And found nothing but a black void? She shook her head. The cut on her temple ached dully, and her stomach shifted a little queasily, reminding her she wasn't supposed to exert herself. "No, I only remember it was raining. The road was slippery but I wasn't having any problems controlling the car. Andrew was sleeping in his seat."

"Which was fixed in the back seat of the car. Is that right?"

"Why, yes," she said, surprised that he would ask. "That's considered the safest place. Why? Did the seat work its way loose? Is that how he was thrown out of the car?"

He closed his eyes as if he were in pain. "No, the seat was still in the car. It was fastened properly. The straps that hold the baby were unbuckled."

Waves of heat and cold washed through her, her bland lunch threatening a return appearance. "That's impossible. I double-checked that he was securely strapped in. With that road and the threatening weather, I wasn't taking any chances." She gave a little whimper. "I shouldn't have gone but I thought it would be only a shower. It doesn't often storm like that in July."

"Not your fault, if you secured the seat. Must have been a defect I couldn't see." Leaning forward, he took her hands in his. She could hardly think straight through the renewed pounding in her head but she felt the heat of his hands against her cold skin and hung on as if she were in danger of falling over a cliff. "Tessa, think. Did you hear the baby crying after the accident?"

She bit her lip, her eyes dark as storm clouds. "I'm not sure. I might have, but Alexander said he died almost instantly, so I must have dreamed it. I've had some pretty weird dreams since the accident. They say it's because of the medication they gave me for my concussion." She shook her head, wincing. "I just don't know."

She fell silent, straining to remember. Nothing, except— "Even now, sometimes I think I hear him crying. But then I wake up and I know it's only a dream."

He stood up, picking up his jacket from the back of the chair. "Do you have to leave?" she asked tremulously. Talking about the accident had worn her out, made her feel fragile when earlier she'd felt she could walk home if necessary. She didn't want to be alone yet.

"No, I'm not leaving." He reached into the pocket and pulled out a fuzzy yellow duck. "I thought you'd like to have this."

The tears trembled on her lashes but again refused to overflow. She could feel them clogging her chest, making it hard to breathe. She hugged the little toy against her sore breasts. "Was that all that was in the car? Where's the car now?"

"On the way to the smelter, probably. That's all I found inside. Wouldn't you have had a diaper bag or something?"

"Yes, but Larry told me—"

"Larry West?" he cut in.

She blinked at him. "Yes. He wrote the accident report. How did you know his name?"

"I talked to him this morning." He rubbed his hand over his face. "I wanted to find out what happened. But no one really knows, do they?"

She picked at the edge of the blanket. "No, and I don't remember. Larry said the diaper bag was missing. He figured it fell out of the car and rolled down the embankment and got lost in the bushes.''

''Did he look for it?''

She stared at the duck in her hands, pain holding her skull in a vise. ''Yes. He couldn't find it.''

''Did he say whether anyone checked the car for a cause of the accident?''

''Of course he did.'' Indignation sharpened her voice. Why was Nick asking all these questions? Did he think the police were incompetent just because Brownsville wasn't the big city? ''No sign of defects. He says it's most likely the car just skidded on the wet road.''

Nick nodded distractedly, glancing at his watch. ''The doctor should be here soon,'' Tessa said. ''If you've got something to do, go ahead.''

''How will you get home if he lets you go?''

''The nurse will call Alexander or Sophie. What time is it?''

''Half past eleven.'' He gazed down at her, his expression somber. ''If you ask me, you could use another day in here. You looked wiped out.''

''Thanks,'' she said wryly. ''And I didn't ask you.''

''Okay. I'll check on you later.''

Tessa settled down in the bed after he was gone. He was right, of course, blast him. Taking a shower and washing her hair, followed by the ordeal of reliving the accident had exhausted her.

She fell asleep and dreamed she was a bride, dressed in a flowing white satin gown and veil. The priest before her was wearing a golden robe and some kind of hood over his head. ''Do you, Tessa—''

He broke off and she saw that she stood alone. No sign of a groom or a church. She was in a cemetery.

Urgency seized her. Andrew. She had to find Andrew. She began to run, stumbling against the nearest gravestone. Andrew Joseph Nicholas Lee. The engraved name jumped out at her. Crying out in pain and grief, she scrambled to her feet, tearing at the clinging folds of the veil. She fell back against another stone, recoiled and ran up a little hill where a dead tree loomed over her, brittle twigs clacking in the wind.

On her knees in the wet grass she saw the stones around her. All of them bore his name. Andrew Joseph Nicholas Lee.

Andrew. Andrew. Come back. Aaandreeewww. The long cry wailed on the wind, echoing across eternity.

She woke with a start, dragging the sheet away from her face. Wendy grasped her shoulder. "Ms. Lee, Tessa, wake up. You're having a bad dream."

Worse than bad. She gulped for breath, her heart hammering against her ribs. Would the pain never end?

NICK PACKED HIS SUITCASE, his hands working mechanically as his brain puzzled over the events of the past couple of days. For a quiet, nothing town, Brownsville certainly seemed to have unrest seething beneath its placid surface. Or was it just him?

First he'd received the phone call that had summoned him here. Since his arrival, he'd had warnings to get out of town, messages that he wasn't welcome. Why?

Was it something about the baby? Or was it Tessa's accident?

Wait a minute. When had the accident happened? Friday night, wasn't it?

He dropped the shirt he was folding and rummaged through his open briefcase. Calendar. He'd received the phone call Monday night. That was after the accident. What exactly had the caller said? *You've had a son. Tessa needs you urgently.*

Without hesitating, he'd rushed to the airport the next morning and taken the first available plane to Vancouver. There he'd rented a car and driven to Brownsville. He'd checked into the hotel and found out where she lived. Her phone was unlisted. He'd gone to the house but no one was home. After waiting several hours, he'd called Alexander Roth, at his house since by then it was well after office hours. Roth hadn't questioned him, merely saying that Tessa was in the hospital.

The news had thrown him. Tessa hurt? He'd been astonished at the cold dread that swept through him. He'd only known her for one month; he couldn't be feeling this powerful emotion. He'd driven to the hospital and stormed her room. Not very polite of him but he couldn't wait until morning to reassure himself.

You've had a son. The caller had been too late. He had no son now. But maybe Tessa needed him. She'd asked him to stay this morning. He made a derisive sound. Maybe he was just kidding himself. Maybe anybody would have done. He was probably causing more harm than good. It would be better if he left; she couldn't help but be painfully reminded of her dead baby every time she saw him.

No, she didn't really need him. She had Alexander and Sophie and her other friends. He would only hurt her again.

Doubts assailed him. Why had he rented the apartment? She was indulging him now because she was too sick to fight, but once she was well again, he was the last person she would want around.

He shoved the doubts ruthlessly into a corner of his mind and slammed the door on them. He would stay and no one would drive him away.

Not until he was good and ready to go.

He resumed packing, stuffing his clothes every which way into the suitcase. There was something very odd about this whole situation. And about the accident. The baby killed but the seat intact. The missing diaper bag. He had to find answers.

He'd received the call Monday. The caller had not hinted that the baby was dead. *You've had a son.* Granted, it could be taken either way. But what if the caller had meant that his child was alive? After the accident. What if the caller knew something no one else did?

The bed sagged under his weight as he sank down on it. He buried his face in his hands. It was too crazy. The scenario that had just emblazoned itself on his brain couldn't be possible.

"What if he's alive?" He said it aloud to the empty room.

Lifting his head, he stared at the opposite wall, again thinking how the crack in the plaster looked like a streak of lightning. Lack of sleep and the upsets of the past days must have addled his brain. Andrew was dead. Hadn't he seen his obituary?

The alternative was just too bizarre. Yet it made a crazy kind of sense. Larry West hadn't found Andrew at the scene. There was no blood or other indication of anyone being injured in the back seat. Therefore it followed that Andrew must have survived the accident. Someone had taken him from the car. *Unstrapped* the little harness that held him in his seat.

Someone. The unknown Good Samaritan? What if the clinic had made a mistake? What if another baby had died? And Andrew was alive?

But where was he now?

If he'd been kidnapped, there should have been a ransom demand by now. Tessa was rich. They would ask for money.

But what if he had simply been taken by someone who wanted a baby? And the obituary notice was a fake. Usually it was the funeral home who made up the obits and sent them to the newspaper, but what if someone else had?

He must be going crazy.

He set his jaw. He'd check it out anyway.

He packed the rest of his clothes and zipped the case

shut. After checking the bathroom to make sure he hadn'
forgotten anything, he went downstairs and paid his bill.

"Leaving town, are you?" the desk clerk asked as he
signed the credit slip.

"No, I thought I'd stick around a while longer." He
paused, then decided he might as well issue his own chal-
lenge. "I've rented an apartment." There, that should dis-
comfit whoever wanted him out of town, show them he
wasn't easily intimidated.

He tucked the credit slip into his wallet, picked up his
suitcase and briefcase, and walked out the door. He paused
on the sidewalk outside and glanced back. Sure enough, the
clerk was holding the phone to his ear and he didn't look
happy.

NICK SPENT THE AFTERNOON buying a minimum of furniture for the apartment and waiting for it to be delivered.
Using the new pots he'd also bought, he cooked his dinner.
Then he sat down on his new sofa with a book he didn't
read.

He waited until visiting hours were over before he went
to the hospital. Only one nurse, the same one who'd been
on duty the night he first arrived, sat at the desk. He debated
whether to prevail on her good nature, if she had one, to
let him see Tessa. The decision was taken from his hands
when the phone rang and she swiveled her chair to reach
for a file in the cabinet behind her.

Silently he tiptoed past, looking back only when he
reached Tessa's door. The nurse still spoke into the phone,
head bent over the file. She hadn't seen him.

No light shone in the room and for a moment he wondered if she had been discharged. He moved closer to the
bed. The sweet vanilla scent of her drifted to his nostrils,
overriding the smell of hospital disinfectant. Disturbingly
familiar. He would have known her in a crowd.

"Who is it?" Her voice was quiet, a little uncertain.

"It's me, Nick."

He snapped on the lamp by her bed, turning it toward the wall so the light didn't hit her eyes. He sat down, putting on a relaxed pose by letting his hands dangle loosely between his knees. Inside, tension knotted his stomach, and a headache nibbled at his temples.

"Tessa, I've got something to tell you. And it's going to be a shock."

"Oh?" Her eyes were dark and wounded but no longer glazed with exhaustion or medication. Yes, he'd been right to come now, before she left the hospital. She had to know, and if the news had adverse effects, at least here the trained staff would take care of her.

"Are you feeling better?" he asked, calling himself a coward but recalling some old proverb about shooting the messenger for delivering bad news.

Her mouth turned down. "They didn't let me go home."

"I see that."

"Dr. Ivers is a worrywart. He doesn't want me to be alone yet. As if I would be. My dad's housekeeper, Mrs. McPherson, is still looking after the house. She'll be only too happy to look after me as well."

He frowned. "Where was she on Tuesday afternoon?"

Tessa's brow wrinkled. "Tuesday? Oh, she must not have been back. I told her to take a few days off before I went up to the cottage on Friday. But she's back now. She came to see me this afternoon." Her frown deepened. "How do you know no one was at the house on Tuesday?"

"I went up there to see you. I knocked but no one answered. I only found out later, when I phoned Alexander, that you were in the hospital."

"Oh." She lay propped against the pillows, the frown remaining. He couldn't tell what she was thinking. "How did you find my house?"

"I asked in the coffee shop. They said it was your dad's

house but you were living there, and that's why your old phone number didn't work.''

She closed her eyes for a moment. "Yes, I decided to stay on after he died, at least until his affairs were settled." Opening her eyes, she looked straight at him. "What is it you came to tell me?"

Now that the moment had arrived, he wasn't sure he could go through with it. Maybe he should wait until after he checked the funeral home. No, better get it over with. Drawing a long breath, he just blurted it out. "I think— I've got no proof, just a gut feeling based on what I've discovered so far—I think that Andrew may still be alive."

She turned as white as new snow. Whiter, as if all the blood had drained out of her. Her mouth opened and closed, opened and closed, but only a tiny sound came out. He twisted his hands together, wishing he hadn't said anything, wishing he had proof. Wishing he could be sure.

She finally forced the words out of her mouth, her eyes sparkling with angry tears. "If this is a joke, it's not very funny. Just get out, Nick. I don't want to see you again."

He swallowed down the nausea in his throat. "No, Tessa, listen," he said desperately. "I'm serious. Look at the facts. His stuff disappeared, the seat was intact but the belts undone, as if someone had unfastened them."

She let her head fall back onto the pillow and sighed wearily. "Then why has everybody been telling me he was killed in the accident?"

"Maybe it wasn't Andrew. Maybe they made a mistake."

"We would have heard if another child had died in an accident. This is a small town, remember?"

"I don't know what happened," Nick said. "But I'm going to find out."

"The obituary notice was in the paper." The words left her mouth as carefully as if she'd had to pick them out of a bucket of crushed glass.

Nick's skin crawled. "You mean someone brought you a paper?" he asked incredulously.

"A day late, of course. It was my own fault. I asked for one. I didn't know that would be in there."

Damn it. Why hadn't he thought to make sure she didn't see the paper. "Where is it now?"

"There." She pointed to the floor. The paper, crumpled by an angry fist, lay under the bed.

Nick picked it up. The page with the obituary notice was torn in half. "I saw it too, but I can't get hold of anyone at the funeral home."

"Why would they schedule a funeral if he wasn't dead?" Tessa asked dully.

"A cover-up?" Even to his own ears, it sounded lame. Not to mention insane.

"Of what?"

"I don't know." He shifted his shoulders, frustrated. Now that it was out in the open, the whole thing sounded stupid.

Silence stretched between them. Then Tessa said in a barely audible voice, "He keeps crying."

He jumped to attention. "When?"

"In my dreams," she whispered. "He needs me and I can't get to him. Do you think the angels are taking good care of him?"

He patted her hand. "I'm sure they would, but I think he's alive." He didn't know why he persisted when he knew it would hurt her more if he found out he was wrong. But if there was the slightest hope, he had to give it to her.

He clasped her hand firmly. "I have to check out a few more things, Tessa, but if he's alive, I'll find him. I'll find our child and get him back to you."

Chapter Five

Midnight. He'd thought he would have to wait until it was later before he went to the funeral home, but it seemed that Brownsville residents went to bed early, even on Friday night. A few diehards lingered in the local pubs, but the streets were virtually deserted.

He'd parked his car on a dark, tree-lined street a couple of blocks away. He wore black jeans and his leather jacket, and runners on his feet in case he had to make a fast getaway.

The two limousines were still parked out front. As Nick approached the building, a security light came on. He ducked between the big cars, waiting until it clicked off, timing the interval. Five minutes.

He glanced around. No houses were visible from the parking lot. Across the street a compound of mini-warehouses stood in a double row, each lit by a single fixture above the roll-up doors. The light didn't reach this far, nor did the orange glow of the street lamp.

Keeping his head low, he backed out from between the limousines. The motion-activated light did not go back on. Good, now he knew its range.

He walked around the periphery of the lot, a juniper hedge along one side providing cover. There had to be a door at the back of the building. Hearing a car engine, he crouched down at the corner, ducking behind an overgrown rhododendron. A police car cruised by.

Nick's heart rapped against his ribs, then subsided as the cruiser kept going without slowing. Good thing it hadn't happened by a little earlier. A blazing security light would have prompted an investigation.

Nick watched the red taillights disappear as the car turned into the next street. Keeping low, he ran around to the back of the building, pausing again to listen. He could hear the murmur of cars on the freeway two kilometers away. Crickets chirped in a honeysuckle vine that filled the air with a cloying, sweet perfume.

Normal night sounds. Involuntarily he shivered, his overactive mind conjuring up pictures of people breaking into funeral homes and being attacked by an undead corpse. He shook his head. Too many movies in his youth. His mother had been right when she warned him about brain damage.

He reached the door, pausing to run his gaze up and down the steel panel to check for alarm-service stickers. Nothing. Small-town mentality again, although he had to ask himself who in their right mind would break into a funeral home.

A silent chuckle of self-derision escaped his lips as he turned his attention to the lock. He gave a grunt of satisfaction when he noted that it was so simple a child could have opened it. He stuck a slender wire into the keyhole, and wiggled it around until he heard a soft click. Another little skill his mother didn't know about. As children, he and his brother had dared each other into minor crimes that would have shocked her. Luckily they'd never hurt anybody or been caught.

His palms were sweating inside the leather driving gloves he'd purchased that afternoon. Lifting one hand, he tried the doorknob. It turned easily. He pushed open the door and slid inside like a shadow, locking it again behind him.

So far, so good. He looked around. Not that he could see anything in the thick darkness. Reaching into his pocket for the small flashlight he carried, he slid along the wall away from the door. Soft, dust-scented cloth brushed against his face and he recoiled. His sharp gasp sounded like a shot in the silence.

Turning on the flashlight, he kept his fingers over the light to dim it. He shone the shaded beam over the wall next to him. Velvet curtains covered tall windows, the cloth that had startled him. He briefly debated whether they were thick enough to screen out the room light. Better not risk it.

Now, where would they keep a body prepared for burial? His rubber soles made no sound on the carpeted floor as he crept out of the back room into the display room at the front of the building. Open caskets were set out along the walls, labeled with discreet price tags.

Nothing here, he decided when he'd circled the room. He opened a door at the side and found himself in a tasteful chapel. At the front of the room, a stained-glass window depicted the Ascension of Christ.

Nick played the light back and forth, highlighting wooden benches and a couple of easy chairs under the window. The reading stand had been pushed to one side of the raised platform. A vase of lilies next to it scented the air.

Too sweet, like the honeysuckle. Why did funeral homes have so many flowers? Did they hope their patrons would forget the reason they existed? Nick vowed then and there that he would ban flowers from his own funeral. Flowers were better bestowed on the living, not the dead.

On that morbid thought, he closed the door quietly and walked past the elaborately fitted caskets for sale into a hall. There had to be a vault or cold storage room. He tried several doors. Two proved to be what he supposed were called viewing parlors, where people could come and look at their deceased friend or relative laid out in a casket.

Another was an office, very conventional, furnished with a desk, filing cabinets, and comfortable chairs.

When he opened the last door, a stairwell confronted him, leading to a basement. His hands began sweating again as he tiptoed down the cement stairs.

He cast the flashlight beam around the large room. Seeing that there were no windows, he hit the light switch at his side. Fluorescent fixtures sprang to life, filling the room with a flat white light. His heartbeat thumped in his ears, nearly deafening him. The room smelled of antiseptic, too clean, too sterile.

Unadorned concrete formed the walls. The only furnishings were several white enameled tables and a wall of cabinets. This must be where they prepared the bodies. He shuddered, trying not to imagine the procedure.

There was no sign of any bodies or of a storage facility to keep them. He was about to go back up the stairs when he saw a door set in an alcove.

He walked closer to it, his feet leaden. The door was heavy, with a large handle set in the middle, like the door of a walk-in cooler. He touched the handle, felt the cold metal even through his gloves. He held his breath, half praying it would be locked even as he berated himself for being a coward.

It gave under his touch. He pulled it open, knowing he'd come too far to turn back now. For Tessa, if not for himself, he had to find out the truth.

A wall of drawers faced him, resembling those he'd seen in morgues in the movies. He hesitated, hoping he wouldn't have to open each one. There had been only one obituary notice in the paper but someone might have died who hadn't rated a notice or who'd been too late to make a deadline.

Deadline. He almost laughed at the choice of words. He knew he was going crazy, snooping in a funeral home vault in the middle of the night.

Then he saw it, pushed into a corner, a little white casket on a wheeled stand. His stomach flipped coldly. He was afraid he would be sick right there and his gaze skittered around the room, searching for a sink. Finding nothing, he swallowed hard and brought the nausea under control. His throat was sore, and he could taste the bitterness at the back of it.

Forcing himself to go on, he moved across to the little coffin. A small tag attached to the stand read Andrew Joseph Nicholas Lee. He closed his eyes. Could he stand to look?

He knew he had to. He couldn't leave without being one-hundred-percent sure.

He lifted the lid. It was surprisingly heavy. Bracing himself, he opened his eyes and looked inside. An expanse of ruffled white satin met his gaze. No one lay inside.

Startled, he dropped the lid. The thump echoed around the room and reverberated in his head. He stood there, icy sweat trickling down his spine. This was Andrew's coffin. Where was Andrew?

He ran to the row of drawers, jerking each one out, not an easy feat since they were very heavy.

All of them were empty. Baffled, he remained standing in the middle of the room. Where was Andrew?

Renewed conviction that his original hunch was right soared through him. Andrew wasn't here because he wasn't dead.

A smile broke over his face. His son was alive. He had to be.

As he closed the vault door, the floor above creaked. He jerked his head up, the smile slipping. Another creak. The building settling, or someone upstairs? The sound seemed stealthy somehow.

He ran silently to the stairs and flattened himself along the wall. If there was someone up there, they'd soon come down and investigate. If they didn't see him, he might have a chance to sneak upstairs and get out without getting caught.

No such luck. The door at the top of the stairs opened. Heavy footsteps descended and a loud voice said, "Stand right there. I've got you covered."

Nick groaned. He knew that voice.

He stepped away from the wall, relieved to note that Larry West hadn't drawn his gun, although he carried a short nightstick in his hand.

"Oh, it's you, Marcopoulos. Unless you have a very good explanation, I'm going to have to arrest you for breaking and entering."

Nick spread his hands, arranging his face into what he hoped was a reassuring and innocent expression. "I haven't broken anything."

West's brown eyes were as hard as pebbles. "You came in through a closed door."

"Would you believe it wasn't locked?"

"No."

Nick smiled weakly. "I was afraid of that. Still, I'd suggest they get a better lock. Any self-respecting burglar would find that one child's play."

West didn't even crack a smile. "Are you?"

"Am I what?"

"A burglar."

"No, of course not," Nick said forcefully. "I had to see Tessa's baby. I tried to phone the number outside but I didn't get very far. No one seems to be around so I thought I'd just come in and have a look."

"And what did you find?" West asked ominously.

"Nothing. And I was about to call you."

West's expression said, Yeah, fat chance. Then his eyes sharpened. "What do you mean, you found nothing?"

"Just what I said. The casket's ready but there's no body. Go look for yourself."

"Okay, but I'm taking you with me. Don't try any funny

stuff.'' He slipped the nightstick into its holder at his belt and gripped Nick's elbow. Steering him across the room, he opened the vault door. Cold air surged out, swirling around their feet.

Nick belatedly remembered he hadn't closed any of the drawers. ''Stand right there,'' West ordered.

Nick remained next to the door as West pushed the drawers shut and peered inside the little coffin. ''You're right, Marcopoulos,'' he said as he turned around and led the way out of the vault and up the stairs. At the door, he paused. ''I'm going to let you go. It's not a crime to want to see your child.''

His rugged face softened. ''I've never lost a child but I've dealt with plenty of people who have. I have an idea how you feel. You're free to go.''

Relief rushed through Nick, almost making him dizzy. Hard on its heels followed irritation. ''Just like that? You're not going to look for the baby? It's obvious a crime has been committed—'' He broke off, realizing he was babbling when he should be weighing his words carefully. Hadn't he already considered Larry a suspect in the child's disappearance?

West regarded him steadily. ''What crime? The clinic called the police station late that night, saying he'd been transferred here, as per procedure. It's obvious something's gone wrong. Don't worry. I'll get to the bottom of it, first thing in the morning.''

He and Nick stepped out into the honeysuckle-scented night. Again Nick's stomach heaved. But he forgot its antics as he saw West lock the door with a key from a ring he carried.

''Can you get to wherever you're staying okay, or do you want a lift?'' West asked.

''Don't you need me to make a report or something?'' Nick asked the question mechanically while his mind whirled over new possibilities. Larry West had a key to the funeral home. He could have made the phony funeral arrangements all on his own.

The only problem with that was that Nick could not think of a single logical motive for such a scheme. And, on the other hand, there might be any number of other people who also had a key.

"No, I don't think it's worth the paperwork. Good night, Mr. Marcopoulos." He opened the door of his cruiser which he'd parked at the back of the building. "Oh, by the way, I'd better not find you breaking any more laws or I will have to take you in."

"THE COFFIN WAS EMPTY."

Nick's words fell into the elegantly furnished living room like a rock into a pond. Millie McPherson, the housekeeper, turned as white as paper and gasped in disbelief.

Tessa felt all the blood drain from her face, leaving her shaking and cold. "What did you say?" The words emerged as an inaudible strangled croak. The room turned dark, the sunlight changing from butter yellow to bloodred. Her legs collapsed and she sank down on the sofa behind her.

"You don't suppose somebody stole his body for some kind of satanic ritual," Millie said, her voice trembling. "You hear about that kind of thing all the time."

Nick shook his head. "I doubt it very much. I don't think there ever was a body."

"No body?" Tessa's voice rose to an anguished cry. "You mean he's been kidnapped? Then why haven't there been ransom demands, or was that another thing no one told me about because they wanted to protect me?"

"No ransom demands," Nick said flatly. "The missing body is as much a surprise to the police as it was to me."

Millie's eyes widened. "Maybe it was a black-market-baby gang." She sat down at Tessa's side.

Tessa clenched her fingers together to stop their trembling. "Millie, I'm sure there's some simple explanation." Even as she said the words, she knew they were more for her own benefit than for Millie's. She pressed her hand against her churning stomach and looked up at Nick. "How did you find out that there is no body?" Her voice only broke slightly on the last word.

"I checked the funeral home."

"You mean Mr. Faversham is back? What did he say?"

"He's not back." Nick shoved his hands into his pockets and paced to the windows. They stood open, letting in the scent of roses. The weather had turned hot and bees buzzed in a large planter of petunias on the patio outside. "I picked the lock of the funeral home."

"When?"

"Last night. Your friend Larry West caught me."

Tessa let out a long breath. Sweat trickled down her sides under her shirt. "Then he's checking it out." She grasped the arm of the sofa, fighting dizziness. "I have to see him."

"We'll go down in a while." Nick laid his hand on Tessa's forehead. "Are you sure you shouldn't rest? You're a bit warm."

She closed her eyes, gathering her strength. The temptation to lean on him was nearly overwhelming, but she knew if she gave in to it, she would break down totally. She had to function; she had to think logically.

Stiffening her rubbery knees, she braced herself to get up, but subsided once again when the room swirled sickeningly. "We have to go now," she said desperately. "We have to find Andrew."

"Maybe poor little Andrew isn't missing at all," Millie said. "Maybe someone took him away where he would be safe."

A mistake? It was possible. Tessa felt a faint stir of renewed hope and threw herself into Millie's arms, taking refuge in the peppermint-scented haven of her childhood. She could lose herself in Millie's embrace as she didn't dare to with Nick. If she touched him, it would never be just comfort. She had to find Andrew first; then she would find the strength to deal with Nick.

"Yes, that's probably it," she murmured. "And maybe they don't know who he is so that's why they haven't contacted me."

"Somebody identified him, according to the police report," Nick reminded them.

The fragile bubble of hope burst. Tessa burrowed closer to Millie's ample chest. A black void yawned in her mind and for a moment she was tempted to fling herself into it, to bury the pain in dark oblivion.

She fought the darkness, pulling back from the abyss, grasping the thin thread of hope that Nick had untangled. If Andrew was alive, she had to get him back. She had to be strong.

Slowly, her arms as heavy as if she were swimming through syrup, Tessa disengaged herself from Millie's embrace. "Millie," she said gently, "maybe you could make us some tea. I think, after all, we need to talk about this before we do anything. If Andrew has been kidnapped, he could be in danger."

Millie clasped her hands together in front of her chest. "Oh, I'm sure no one would harm the sweet laddie." She turned and went into the kitchen.

Tessa stopped trying to get up, concentrating on clearing her brain. "Nick, all we've got here is the fact that Andrew was not in that coffin. Nothing else."

Nick paced back and forth across the spacious room, restless as a caged cougar. "I know."

"Larry did his job. We went to school together. I know he's doing the best he can. But there must be something else going on here that we're not thinking of. Nick, will you sit down? That pacing is driving me crazy."

He sat, although he looked like a coiled spring under pressure. "Either it's a major breakdown in communications or someone deliberately called the obit to the paper and arranged the funeral, likely to throw us off the track. But there should have been a ransom demand by now.''

''Unless the kidnappers did it because they want a baby,'' Tessa said, fighting the urge to scream. ''Maybe Millie is right about a black-market-baby gang.''

''At this point, anything is possible.'' Nick stood up again, jingling his car keys in his hand. He regarded her critically. ''Your color is coming back. We'll go down to the police station as soon as we've had some tea.''

Tessa opened her mouth to argue with him but icy tremors still quaked through her body. She needed a few more minutes before she could get up.

She twisted her fingers together so tightly the tendons stood out on the backs of her hands. ''Andrew can't have disappeared off the face of the earth. Someone must have seen something.''

''Starting with Larry West.''

''Larry?''

''Yes, Larry. I think he knows something he's not telling us.'' Nick stepped forward and took the tray Millie brought in, setting it on the coffee table. ''Join us, won't you, Millie?'' he said, as if he were the host.

''Yes, please do,'' Tessa said, her voice cracked as she fought for normalcy in a world that had tilted sharply. ''I wouldn't mind some support here. This man is so stubborn he can't understand the way it is in small towns. Nick, I've known Larry all my life. He wouldn't lie to me.''

''I think Tessa's right, Mr. Marcopoulos,'' Millie said quietly. ''Larry is an honest person.'' She smiled reminiscently as she poured tea for all of them. ''I've known him since he was a child. He was such a good boy.''

''That's what they always say about serial killers,'' Nick muttered darkly.

Tessa set her cup into the saucer with a click. ''Larry's not a serial killer. Or a baby snatcher. And he told me he checked the accident scene thoroughly but by the time the storm was over he couldn't tell if anyone else had been there.''

She reached for a cookie, her favorite raspberry chocolate chip, then drew her hand back, knowing she wouldn't be able to eat it. She gulped her tea, scalding her tongue.

"Okay, let's go see Larry," Nick said. "At the very least make sure he's already mobilized a search and issued a missing child bulletin.''

A missing child bulletin. Tessa nearly choked on her tea as she pictured Andrew as one of those sad photos of children on milk cartons. No, he couldn't be gone. It had to be a mistake.

She looked up to find Nick gazing at her intently. "Are you sure you feel up to going out?" he inquired gently. "I can go by myself. Maybe you should rest.''

How could she rest until she made sure the police were searching for Andrew? Her head ached, not severely but just enough to remind her of the accident. She had to be careful not to stand up too fast or she would black out. Her body was still stiff and sore and the ribs on her right side hurt if she moved too quickly. But other than that, she was just fine.

"I can make it," she said sturdily. She patted Millie's hand. "And don't you start, too. It won't take long and when we get back, I'll go straight to bed, I promise.''

"Well, as long as Mr. Marcopoulos drives. You know what the doctor said about taking it slow.''

"Call me Nick, please," he said, aiming a grin at Millie. She reminded him of his own mother, thin and energetic, her gray hair pulled back into a knot at the back of her head. "Don't worry, I'll take good care of Tessa. Tie her down if I have to.''

"You and whose army?" Tessa retorted.

He lifted one brow. "Don't tempt me.''

"How long have you known each other?" Millie asked.

"Forever," he said without thinking.

"One month," Tessa said at the same time. "Nick hear I was hurt and came to see me." That was the story she' decided on. She wasn't ready yet to tell the whole worl that Nick was Andrew's father.

Millie wore a bemused expression as she looked from one to the other. "Will you be staying in Brownsville long Mr. uh, Nick?"

Nick's gaze rested on Tessa's downcast head. "That de pends."

Tessa struggled to her feet, bracing her hand on the sof back until the room stopped swaying and her queasy stom ach settled. "Shall we go?"

The phone rang on the table beside her. Tessa's hear lurched in her chest. Could it be news about Andrew? Sink ing back down on the sofa, she picked up the receiver aware of Nick and Millie frozen halfway across the room "Hello?"

"Tessa, you're home."

She let out her breath in a whoosh. "Yes, I'm home Sophie. Where've you been the last few days?"

"On a job, out of town." Sophie worked for a temp agency—flexible hours, good pay, and varied work, she always said when Tessa asked her if she didn't want the security of a steady job. "I'm sorry I've been away, no there for you. How are you?"

"Not bad," Tessa said.

"Well, I'll be back Monday," Sophie said. "In time fo the funeral."

Tessa closed her eyes. The funeral. "There's not going to be a funeral."

"What?" Tessa jerked the phone away as Sophie's shriek pierced her eardrum. "What do you mean?"

Tessa breathed quickly in and out. How could she say this? *Should* she say it, perhaps buoying up Sophie's hopes only to shatter them later? Sophie had doted on Andrew.

"We have reason to believe that Andrew may not have died in the accident. I'll let you know as soon as we learn something new."

A faint hum on the line emphasized the silence as Sophie didn't respond.

"Sophie, are you there?" Tessa said.

"Yes, I'm here." She sounded stunned, as well she might, Tessa thought. "Are you sure about this?"

"No. No, we're not. But we're checking it out."

"Good," Sophie said. "I'll call you later, okay?"

Thoughtfully, Tessa hung up the phone. She shook her head. It was just the shock; that was why Sophie had sounded so strange.

LARRY DIDN'T LOOK overjoyed to see them walk into his office. "When did you get out of the hospital, Tessa?" he asked. "You still look pale."

"Yesterday. Millie is taking good care of me, and her cooking is better than the hospital's." She set her mouth grimly. "I'd be a lot better if I knew what happened to Andrew."

"I followed procedure," Larry insisted. "It was a wild night, power out, trees down, and accidents all over the place." He spread his hands, palms up. "I'm sorry, but I did the best I could."

"Then what happened to him?" Nick asked.

"I don't know," Larry said vehemently. "I just don't know. Tessa, do you think I'd put you through this on purpose? If there was some sort of mix-up at the clinic, I had nothing to do with it. As far as I can determine, a death certificate was issued, the funeral home picked up his body, contacted Mr. Roth, and set the funeral date. That's all I know."

Each word reverberated in Tessa's head like blows from a hammer. This had to be another nightmare. It couldn't be Andrew Larry referred to as a body, a non-person. If she closed her eyes, she could see his sunny smile, the dimple in his round baby cheeks.

The details of the drab office swam before her vision, taking on an odd surreal underwater aspect. The fluorescent lights were too bright, stabbing into her brain. One of them buzzed like a wasp in a jar. She blinked but the scene before her didn't clear. Her stomach felt hollow, her feet and hands cold and numb, as if they didn't belong to her body.

"Tessa, are you all right?"

She realized that Nick was pushing her head down between her knees. It made her neck hurt. "Breathe deeply," he ordered.

Did he have to be so bossy? Why didn't he just let her sink to the floor and sleep? When she woke up, Andrew would be back and she would know this was all a nightmare. She dragged in a long breath, then another. The pressure on her neck eased.

"That's it, Tessa. Keep breathing." His deep voice played over her. The blackness receded, taking some of the pain with it. "You shouldn't be here at all. You should be resting in bed." Although the words scolded her, his tone remained even, calm, comforting.

"I'm okay." She lifted her head, wincing at the steady throbbing behind her eyes. Her limbs felt like overcooked spaghetti. She hoped they wouldn't have to leave yet. If she got up from her chair, she was afraid she would fall to the floor in an ignominious heap.

"No, you're not," Nick said. "But just hang on a little longer. I knew I shouldn't have brought you."

"You couldn't stop me," she said with as much spirit as she could muster.

"I should have tied you down, locked you in your room with Millie on guard." Keeping his arm around her shoulders, Nick turned his attention back to Larry. "The fact is, I don't think Andrew died. I think he might have been taken from the clinic, and whoever did it arranged the funeral, to cover up a kidnapping or whatever. I mean, who else would have done it?''

"I'll check it out," Larry said stiffly, putting up that stone wall cops do when they want civilians to butt out of their case.

"What have you done so far to find Andrew?" Nick persisted.

"I've sent out a missing persons bulletin. Did it first thing this morning. And I've had flyers printed, which will be posted around town. So far there's been no response, but give it a few days, Tessa. If we don't hear anything, you might go to the media. Put his picture in the papers and on TV."

The idea of Andrew's picture splashed all over the news made Tessa feel ill. On the other hand, if they heard no news in the next twenty-four hours, she was willing to do anything that might help find him.

"What about the clinic? Can they tell you anything?" she asked. Her head pounded in earnest now, a steady throbbing behind her eyes.

"I've tried to call them," Larry said. "But they're closed today and Sunday. Summer hours."

"You mean you're going to wait until Monday?" Nick demanded, jumping up from his chair. "Can't you track down any of the people who work there?"

"I'm sorry." Larry's gaze met Nick's with all the authority he'd learned to exert as a policeman. "I'm compiling a list of the people working there. I'll contact them, today if possible. Maybe the body never got transferred to the funeral home."

"You said yourself that's not likely since there's no other place to keep it."

"There's always the possibility that they shipped it to the wrong funeral home."

"No," Tessa cried. "No, he can't be dead."

Nick sat down next to her and wrapped his arm around her shoulders. "Don't worry, Tessa. I'm convinced he's alive. And I'll find him." He directed a hard stare at Larry, who glared back. "Have you checked other funeral homes?"

"Yes," Larry admitted. "No unidentified bodies. And no babies at all."

Nick suppressed a shudder, hoping he wasn't just letting his hopes blind him to the truth. He stood up, holding Tessa close to his side. He wasn't happy about waiting another day, but what could they do? Then a thought struck him. "You said something about a death certificate."

"Yes, the funeral home has to have one before they can proceed. I went back to look in the office. It was in the desk." He rummaged through the papers on his desk and came up with an envelope which he handed to Nick.

Nick withdrew the sheet inside and scanned it. "It's signed by a Dr. Benjamin Forbes. Do you know who he is?"

Larry shrugged. "I suppose he works at the clinic but no, I've never heard of him. You can't expect me to know everyone in the area."

"Is it possible this is a forgery?"

Larry shook his head. "I don't know about the signature, but the document looks authentic. Like I said, we'll check it out."

"IT'S HOPELESS," Tessa moaned as Nick drove them toward her house. "I want to believe he's still alive but it's more logical to assume they've just shipped his body to the wrong funeral home. Maybe even to Vancouver."

She felt as if she were riding an out-of-control roller coaster. Four days ago she had been sure her baby was dead. Then Nick had raised the possibility that he might be alive.

Not that she entirely accepted his suspicions. Still, she

would rather go with the theory that the baby had been
snatched from the clinic by persons unknown, and that
someone, either the kidnappers or someone at the clinic,
had made up the rest of the details, including the funeral,
to cover up the crime. The alternative, that he was dead,
was unthinkable.

"Maybe it's all a mistake," she said, grasping at her
shredding hopes. "Maybe he was mixed up with another
child and they haven't noticed. They'll come forward once
they hear we're looking for him."

"I certainly hope so," Nick said fervently. But his heart
lay like a lead weight in his chest. He wished he'd just
quietly investigated on his own until he found out the truth.
He wasn't sure Tessa could bear all this strain.

And what if Andrew was dead? Then what?

Chapter Six

Tessa awoke and found, to her surprise, that she had slept soundly for two hours. She got up, groggily padding into the adjoining bath. She hated sleeping in the daytime. She grimaced at her reflection in the mirror; her hair looked as if she'd walked through a wind tunnel.

She splashed cold water on her face and grabbed a towel to wipe it dry. Her headache was almost gone, leaving only a dull pain in her temple to remind her not to overdo. She managed a smile, despite the heaviness of her heart, as she brushed her hair back into order and clipped it into a low ponytail.

The smell of chicken soup greeted her as she entered the kitchen. Millie's cure for all ailments. Nick sat at the table spooning soup into his mouth, as if he lived there.

"I thought you would be gone by now," Tessa said.

Millie brought the toast she'd buttered to the table. "I invited him to stay for lunch."

"An excellent lunch, too," Nick said. "Sit down, Tessa. This has to be the best soup I've ever eaten."

Realizing she was hungry, she sat. Opposing emotions regarding Nick warred within her. On the one hand, she was glad he had given her hope about Andrew's fate. But she also knew, despite her worry and grief, he was far too attractive for her peace of mind, and the past tugged at her.

Funny how she remembered the good parts more than their final quarrel, the walks, the talks, the meeting of minds she'd had with him. If she wasn't careful—

But she would be careful, she told herself, stiffening her spine as she picked up her spoon.

"We're going to see Mr. and Mrs. Crossley this afternoon," Nick said.

"Crossley?" Tessa frowned. The name seemed familiar but she couldn't place it.

"Maybe nobody told you. They're the couple who saw your accident and called 911."

"There was a witness to the accident?" Anger ignited inside her. "Why wasn't I told this before?"

"Calm down, Tessa," Nick said firmly. "No one kept it from you. They didn't actually see the accident happen. They saw your car off the road. They called 911 and stayed until the emergency crews arrived."

"Oh." She felt like a fool for her knee-jerk reaction. She never used to be like this. Must have been the knock on the head that made her emotions more volatile than a rumbling volcano. "I'm sorry. I suppose I should be grateful. They may have saved my life."

"You've been through a lot, Tessa." Nick smiled gently. "I don't blame you."

The walls she'd erected against him swayed. She smiled, her lips stiff. "How soon can we leave?"

"When you're finished eating your lunch. All of it."

"By the way," Nick added, "I called the clinic and no one answered the phone, except for the recording on their answering machine. Closed until Monday. We'll go there then."

With that, she had to be satisfied. For now.

THE CROSSLEYS LIVED in a small lakeside community a half-hour drive from Brownsville. Nick handed Tessa a map he'd drawn from directions he'd received over the phone. Tessa's hands began to shake as she looked at it.

"What is it?" Nick asked. "You look like you've seen a ghost."

She stared at him, dry eyes burning. "You might say that. We have to go past the place where I had the accident."

"You mean these people could be neighbors of yours up there?"

"Not neighbors, and I don't know them. Our cottage is near the ski resort. The lake where they live is closer in." She pointed to a spot on the map. "The turnoff is right here."

"Where did you have the accident?"

"Just before the turnoff. There's a switchback curve which is very treacherous in bad weather. Everybody knows about it, though, so there really haven't been all that many accidents."

Nick frowned thoughtfully. "You know, I wouldn't mind having a look at the place it happened."

"Why? Morbid curiosity?" Her mouth felt frozen, barely able to form the words.

He shrugged, starting the car. "No, just regular curiosity. Skid marks and such."

She licked her lips to moisten them, her chest tight. She set her jaw, ignoring the fluttering in her stomach. They had to go up the road. She told herself that by this time there wouldn't be any sign of the crash. "Larry gave you these people's phone number, I suppose," she asked, to silence her thoughts.

"Yes. I called them this morning, asked if we could come." He turned his car around the circular driveway, splashing through a puddle formed by a running hose. A young man wearing a baseball cap backward on his head washed a glossy black Saab in front of the triple garage.

"Is that your dad's car?" Nick asked.

Tessa shook her head. "No, it's mine. I sold my dad's Jaguar after he died. To Alexander."

"That's yours?" Nick's voice rose in surprise. "Then whose car was the Volvo you crashed?"

"That was also Alexander's. He lent it to me because my car was at the dealer's for a minor electrical problem."

"He couldn't have been too happy about his car ending up a write-off."

Tessa shrugged. "He said as long as I was okay the car didn't matter. That's why there's insurance. He mostly uses the Jaguar these days anyway."

They fell into silence as the road grew narrow and steep, climbing into the mountains. Nick concentrated on driving, his eyes narrowed behind his sunglasses. Tessa cast him a sidelong glance, wondering what he was thinking.

"Where did you get this car?" she asked, patting the leather seat. "It doesn't look like a rental," she added, more for something to say than because she needed to know. The closer they got to the accident site the more her nerves jangled. Her head was beginning to ache again, although that might have been due to the higher altitude.

"It's not. I bought it."

That threw her. "You bought it? I thought you were only planning to stay a little while. Hardly worth the bother of buying a car."

"I wanted my own car, and it was cheap," he said. "The dealer was glad to get rid of it. Everyone here seems to favor pickup trucks." He studied the curving road ahead. "We must be getting close. Do you remember exactly where it happened?"

In truth, she wasn't certain, but her familiarity with the road told her it could only be one place. "Just up ahead, I think." She wrinkled her brow. The crash and the time just before it were still a blank. Probably would remain so, Dr. Ivers said. If the memory didn't return within a couple of days of the trauma, it was likely lost forever.

Suddenly her heart sped up, hammering in her throat. She put out her hand to brace herself. "Be careful on that curve." She almost screamed the warning.

Nick reached over and clasped her hand, wrapping it in comforting heat. "Somewhere in your subconscious you remember. But don't worry. It's dry today and the road's plenty wide enough." He slowed as he entered the switchback. A wide gravel shoulder had been graded to allow a margin of error if the curve was taken too fast.

He pulled to a stop at the side of the road, leaving plenty of room for any other cars to pass. "Let's have a look." Frowning, he eyed her pale face. Despite the heat of the sun pouring into the open car window, she shivered. "Stay here if you want. You don't have to come out."

She gathered her unraveling courage, gritting her teeth as bile rose in her throat. "I have to see."

"That's odd," Nick muttered moments later. "I would have thought you'd gone off the far side, in other words straight ahead when you should have steered to the right. There are no tracks."

"The rain washed them away." Tessa stared down the thickly treed slope. She touched her fingers to the tender spot on her forehead. Dr. Ivers had removed the stitches before discharging her yesterday. All that remained was a small bandage covering an uneven scar he assured her would fade with time. "I bumped the right side of my head. I'm not sure how."

"On the steering wheel, probably," Nick said. "Or the dash. You were wearing a seat belt, weren't you?"

"Of course. Dr. Ivers said I would have been killed otherwise. And the airbag also cushioned the crash. I sort of remember the firemen working on the car to get me out. It was tilted to the right."

"Which means that unless it spun around—unlikely, since you wouldn't have been going that fast in the rain—it .

must have gone off the right side of the road.'' He grasped her arm. "Let's have a look past the curve.''

Half way up the short straight stretch beyond the curve, heavy tires had churned up the gravel at the edge of the road. Probably left by the emergency vehicles, although after the heavy storm they were blurred and faint.

Nick pointed down the embankment that sloped steeply from the road. "There. That must be where the car landed.'' A white scar marked a tree trunk where the bark had been scraped off. "I'm going down.''

"I'm going with you.''

"Are you sure you can make it?''

She glared at him "I told you I'm fine. Don't make me into an invalid.''

"I'm not. I was thinking that those shoes are hardly meant for hiking.''

"I can manage," she said stubbornly. Faced with the scene, she felt numb, as if the crash had happened to someone else. No latent memories surfaced.

Without waiting for his help, she scrambled down, using the low bushes to brace herself. She had no desire to go tumbling head over heels into the ravine below.

At the bottom of the slope she paused and ran her hand over the smooth area on the tree trunk. Bits of bark, dried now, lay on the ground. Just ahead of her another tree had been similarly damaged. Between them lay a large boulder.

"That's what the car must have been resting against, why it was tilted.'' The sound of Nick's voice at her side made her jump. He stooped and touched the rock, showing her his fingers. "That's oil. The oil pan likely split open when it hit.''

Eyes narrowed, he gazed at the second scraped tree. "You know, you were incredibly lucky. The car wedged itself between those two trees, tilted nearly on its side. If it hadn't, hitting the rock at that angle would have flipped it, and you would have rolled over and over until you hit bottom.''

Bottom was nearly a hundred feet straight down, a ravine full of jagged rocks amid scattered trees. Tessa shuddered as she stared down into the green abyss below her. ''It could have caught on fire. We would have burned to death.'' Andrew! Her poor defenseless baby, flames licking at him, and she would have been helpless to save him.

The numbness dissolved under the onslaught of horror. She gave a strangled cry and turned to run up the slope.

Nick caught her, pulled her against his chest. ''That's what always happens in the movies. In real life, it's very rare for a car to burn on impact. Gas tanks are pretty sturdy. Flexible, too, since they started making them out of fiber-glass. They can stand a great deal of punishment.''

''I smelled gas.'' Now where had that come from? Something she hadn't remembered until now. And the firemen had used a flame retardant chemical to eliminate any danger of fire while they worked to cut her free.

Nick tensed. ''When?''

She shook her head, rubbing against the fine cotton of his shirt. Feeling the heat of hard muscle, the crinkle of dark curling hair that covered his chest. ''I don't know. After the crash, I suppose.''

''Probably a bit of leakage from the engine or the fuel filter. In the rain, it wasn't likely to cause a fire.''

''Nick, I couldn't reach him. I was trapped.'' She clenched her fists, pounding against his chest. He grunted in pain, then pulled her closer, catching her hands between them.

She struggled for an instant, then let her face fall against him. Breathing deeply, she stood in his arms, letting the horror seep away. He smelled faintly of spicy aftershave. Comforting. Familiar. It hit her suddenly. He'd smelled the same last summer but then she'd been so enthralled she'd hardly noticed details like that.

Last summer when she'd thought she was in love, and that Nick returned her love. Last summer when he had disappeared after their quarrel.

He was back. He was here. He shifted his weight and she felt his thighs lined up with hers, just as they'd stood so many times, in shadowed corners, dark doorways, as they'd explored the city. Touching. Kissing. Wild about each other. It would be so easy to let the present drain away and just lose herself in that dreamlike past.

A magpie squawked near them, and reality jolted her. Andrew. They had to find her baby.

She pulled away and hauled herself back up to the road, using the bushes as handholds. At the top, she brushed off her denim skirt. Just dust, fortunately. She slipped off her shoes and clapped them together to empty out the dried leaves. Bracing her hand on the car fender, she put them back on.

"You look fine," Nick said, watching her take out the clip and comb her fingers through her tangled hair. She glanced at him. His face gave away nothing but his eyes glowed with lambent blue fire. A fire she recognized, as heat rushed through her. Passion. Desire.

No time for that now, she thought, desperately trying to smooth her hair. "Look in the glove box," Nick said. "You'll find a hairbrush."

She used it, checking the results in the vanity mirror behind the sun visor. To her relief, she didn't look as drawn and pale as she felt. The climb up and down the slope had brought out pink color in her cheeks. She tossed the brush back into the glove box and slammed it shut.

"Okay?" Nick asked.

She crossed her fingers, hiding them from him. "Okay."

THE CROSSLEYS LIVED in an A-frame, which had been remodeled and enlarged from a standard vacation cottage into a substantial house. A wall of windows overlooked the small, picturesque lake. As they turned into the driveway, a battered van rattled by, its exhaust belching blue smoke.

Nick and Tessa walked up to the front door. She grasped the dragon's-head door knocker and rapped it against its backplate.

She turned and gazed out over the lake as they waited for someone to answer the door. Years ago her father had brought her here to swim off the fine sand beach. There hadn't been as many houses then, or as many boats. Today the beach was crowded. Children screamed as they splashed one another in the shallows. Farther out, a water skier tacked back and forth across the lake, the tow boat roaring as it banked to avoid the jetty.

A plump, sixtyish woman opened the door. Her inquiring expression changed to a smile as she saw Tessa. "I'm so happy you're all right, Miss Lee, isn't it?" she said, her accent as British as Devonshire cream. "I'm Emma Crossley,"

Tessa shook her hand. "Please call me Tessa. I can't tell you how pleased I am to meet you. This is my friend, Nick."

"How do you do?" Mrs. Crossley shook Nick's hand. "Please come in. My husband is making tea. You'll join us, won't you?"

"Of course. Thank you." Tessa followed their hostess into the living room, acutely aware of Nick's hand on the small of her back. His touch burned through her thin summer clothes. She pulled away from him and sat down on a sofa upholstered in flowered chintz. He lifted an eyebrow, his eyes amused as he sat down beside her, leaving a discreet space between them.

John Crossley, a stocky man with a short gray ponytail, came in carrying the tea tray. Mrs. Crossley poured their tea and offered them a plate of flaky biscuits spread with butter and strawberry jam. A fat spaniel wandered in from the kitchen to sniff at their ankles before flopping down in front of the empty fireplace.

Tessa set down her teacup after she had taken a sip. "I want to thank you for what you did the night of the accident. I was lucky that you came along."

Mrs. Crossley blushed. "It was nothing. Anyone would have done the same."

Mr. Crossley leaned forward in his chair. "Actually it was pure chance that we were on the road that night. It got dark so quickly after sunset and the storm was so bad we'd almost decided to stay the night in Brownsville. But luckily we went on and saw your car off the road." He frowned. "We saw you pinned inside and knew we had to get help."

Mrs. Crossley clasped her hands in front of her ample bosom.

"We drove as quickly as we could to the corner store and used the pay phone to call 911. We went back to your car to see if there was anything more we could do but Larry West was already there and the fire truck had just arrived. He took our name and number and said he'd contact us if he needed more information. He said there was no use all of us standing around in the rain."

"I'm very grateful to you."

"Anyone would have done the same," Mrs. Crossley repeated. She turned to Nick. "You must be new to Brownsville, Nick. I don't believe I've ever seen you around. What do you do for a living?"

"I'm an architect, from Montreal. Tessa and I met last year on holidays. I came to see her when I heard she'd been in an accident."

Mrs. Crossley smiled. "I'm sure you've been a comfort to her."

"I hope so," Nick said, his eyes on Tessa's profile.

Tessa bit her lip, thinking of how she could phrase the questions she had to ask.

Nick saved her the trouble. "Were you the first at the scene?" he asked.

Mrs. Crossley looked at her husband. "I believe so. We

didn't see any other cars. It was very dark and raining heavily. We knew Miss Lee might be seriously hurt but we didn't dare get too close. The car looked as if it would slide into the ravine at any moment. It was terrible, just terrible.''

"I'd say you were a very lucky young woman," John said gruffly. "The way the car was wedged between the trees—a little to the right or left and you would have gone down the ravine. No one would have seen the car until morning and maybe not then, with the rain washing away tire tracks.''

Tessa touched the small bandage on her head. "I'm afraid I don't remember much of it. That's the other reason we've come. Did you see my baby in or near the car?''

Mrs. Crossley gasped. "You don't mean to tell me you had a baby with you in the car?''

Tessa swallowed, unable to speak for a moment. She clutched the hand Nick extended to her, with no thought of motives or consequences. "Yes," she said at last. "And he seems to be missing.''

"Missing?" Emma exclaimed. "Was he hurt in the accident?''

Tears gathered in Tessa's throat again. "We don't know. We can only pray he wasn't.''

"We didn't see or hear anything, did we, Emma?" John said.

"You didn't walk around the car?" Nick said.

"No. The bank was too steep, and there was too much undergrowth. And we thought it was more important to call for help as quickly as possible." John's brow creased. "I'm dreadfully sorry. If we'd known, we would have checked more carefully.''

"I'm sure you did the best you could," Nick said, keeping a tight hold on his frustration.

Emma's pale blue eyes were wide with shock. "And your baby is still missing? My dear, how worried you must be.''

"We'll find him," Nick said grimly.

"I suppose the police are working on it?"

"Yes, they've put out bulletins."

Emma smiled again. "You'll find him. Larry West is very good at his job. He was right there pitching in with the firemen."

Tessa sat up at attention. "Oh, do you know Larry?"

"Of course I do. I was his Sunday school teacher years ago. I'm sure he will give this top priority."

They drank their tea. Tessa forced down one of the biscuits to be polite. They were delicious, but worry had closed her throat. She wondered if Nick was having the same problem. He surreptitiously fed half of his biscuit to the spaniel, who had sidled up with longing in his soulful eyes as soon as they began eating.

"Again, I want to thank you," Tessa said sincerely as they were going out the door.

"Glad we could help," John said.

"And it was so nice of you to drop by," Emma said. "Do come and see us again. With the baby, when you find him." She hugged Tessa impulsively. "Don't worry, Tessa. Just leave it up to Larry."

"HE WAS SUCH a good boy," Nick muttered sarcastically once they were in the car heading down the mountain toward Brownsville. "If I hear that one more time, I'm going to throw up."

"He was, though," Tessa said seriously. "And he's a good cop. He keeps up with the latest technology, which is unusual for a small-town policeman. He's always taking night courses."

"Maybe so, but there's something about him that rubs me the wrong way."

"I'm sure he's doing the best he can. We'll call him again when we get to town. By this time he should have the list of clinic employees."

She glanced at him. His jaw tightened as he clenched his teeth. ''You're just frustrated that this isn't progressing faster.'' The sunshine streaming into the car mocked her. Thoughts of Andrew hung like an ominous black cloud over her. Where was he? Was he tired or hungry? Were they taking care of him, whoever had him?

Damn it, it was her job to be his mother, not some stranger's. She clenched her fist around the armrest, willing the car to go faster, to get down there and do something.

Nick downshifted to negotiate the switchback. ''Damn it, what's that guy doing?'' He jerked the steering wheel to the right. The car skidded, started to fishtail but he brought it expertly under control.

A white van overtook them, spraying gravel as the off-side wheels hit the shoulder. Leaving behind a plume of dust, it rocketed down the hill, disappearing around the next curve.

Nick pulled the car to the side and braked. Tessa sat with her hands clenched in her lap, her eyes enormous in her dead white face. ''Are you all right?'' Nick asked. Her hands were cold, trembling in his as he grasped them. ''You didn't bump your head when I swerved, did you?''

''No,'' she said faintly. ''I'm okay. Who was that? Did you get the license number?''

''Too dusty. But I'm almost positive it was the same van we saw going past the Crossleys.''

Chapter Seven

"What?" Tessa gaped at him. "Are you sure?"

"Pretty sure. Because I think he's been following me. The other day I thought a black Mazda was following me but I might have been mistaken. But I know I've seen that van before."

"Why would anyone follow you?"

"Don't ask me." Nick shrugged. "Your guess is as good as mine."

"Well, since he passed us, he's not following us anymore," Tessa said, shudders racking her body.

"That's true, but he doesn't need to now. The only place this road goes is back to Brownsville. He can always wait around and pick us up again later."

Tessa leaned back against the headrest, closing her eyes. Her head ached faintly, not a big problem. If only she didn't feel so wiped out. The slightest exertion and she felt as if she'd run a marathon. Uphill.

"You need to rest," Nick said. "I'm taking you home."

Her eyes popped open. "We need to check with Larry."

"I'll do it while you take a nap. I'll keep after him."

Tessa struggled to keep her head up, but the adrenaline rush had died, leaving her as limp as a dishrag. "I need to help."

"I'll do it," Nick repeated. Nick glanced into the rearview mirror. The van hadn't reappeared, nor did anyone else seem to be shadowing them.

Nick turned into the driveway. Tessa straightened in the seat, pressing her hand to her forehead as the vise of pain tightened.

Nick kept an arm around her as they left the car, holding her up. She was too exhausted to protest. Millie opened the front door, immediately tut-tutting over Tessa's pallor. "I'll take care of her, Millie," Nick said.

He laid his palm on Tessa's cheek, his eyes tender. "Rest, Tessa. I'll get back to you after I check a few more things."

"I want to go with you." Her voice slurred, and she leaned heavily against him.

Nick gathered her closer. His chest tightened as he realized how thin she'd become, mere skin and bones. She must have lost even more weight in the past two days.

He set his teeth. They had to find Andrew. They had to. "You're in no condition to go anywhere right now," he said gently. He scooped her up into his arms and carried her toward the stairs. She settled bonelessly against him. He inhaled the soft vanilla scent of her, remembering the passion of last summer, Tessa's laughter. Once they found Andrew, she would laugh again.

"Show me her room, Millie, please."

She walked up the stairs ahead of him and opened a door. Nick barely noticed her leaving them. Tessa's head lolled over his arm, despite her determined efforts to stay awake. Good, he thought. She would sleep. Forget this for a while. Maybe by the time she woke up, he would have news for her. Not that it was likely, he realized bleakly. So far any leads he'd picked up were as thin and ephemeral as spiderwebs.

Still, he had to keep trying.

Nudging the quilt aside with his knee, he laid her on the bed. She slept, limp and boneless, her hair spread like sunshine over the rose-printed pillowcase. He slipped off her shoes and tucked the quilt around her.

Sitting down on the edge of the bed, he stared at her pale face. Too white. The dark lashes fluttered, and she sighed, frowning faintly even in deep sleep. Her fragility tugged at him, despite his efforts to cool his emotions by remembering that she'd hidden the birth of their child from him.

To his surprise, the anger he'd felt at first was gone. Now he only wanted to protect her, to help her get their child back. But was he doing any good with his digging? He'd let her hope, and now he wondered if that hope was going to be shattered. He should have just let the police, her friend Larry, handle it. Even if the body was missing, they would find it.

No. He clenched his fist. Andrew couldn't be dead.

He got up and moved around the room. Pine furniture, not new but showing the patina that came with care and age. Nothing ornate. White eyelet curtains at the windows matched the quilt that covered her.

He wandered over to the dresser on the far side of the room. A set of silver hairbrushes lay there, and a paperweight. A pang cut through him. She'd kept it, the cheap souvenir of Victoria from the day they'd gone sightseeing and indulged in afternoon tea at the Empress.

The glass ball weighed heavily in his palm as he shook it. Shimmering snow sifted down over the plastic evergreens inside. He was about to put it down when he saw what it sat on. He could hardly breathe as he picked up the folded white linen square. His handkerchief, the one he'd lent her. She'd kept that, too.

She hadn't hated him, even though he'd disappeared just when she needed him.

His heart aching, he sat down beside her again. Tessa breathed so quietly he could barely see the rise and fall of her chest. Tenderness moved in him. Leaning down, he gently kissed her forehead. Her sweet vanilla scent shot straight to his libido.

Chiding himself, he quickly stood. He had no right to think of making love with her. Not until Andrew was found, and maybe not even then.

Downstairs he found Millie wiping a cloth over the hall furniture. He hid a smile, recognizing the task as a ploy to justify her waiting for him. He'd noticed when he came in that there wasn't a speck of dust on the glossy wooden surfaces.

"Is Tessa all right?" Millie said anxiously.

"She will be once she's had a sleep. Make sure she stays in bed for the evening. I'll call later."

Millie clasped the dust cloth to her chest. "Oh, I do hope you find the little one. I don't know how Tessa will survive if he really is—" Her voice broke on a little sob. "You'll know him if you see him. His eyes are just like yours."

Nick stiffened. "You know?"

"Of course. The moment I saw you, I said to myself, that's Andrew's father."

Nick stared at her, swallowing hard. "Who else knows?"

Millie shook her head. "Only Sophie Marsden. Tessa doesn't keep anything from her best friend. No one else knows. Tessa never talked about you."

She didn't? Nick pondered this as he got into his car and drove the rest of the way into town. He parked outside his apartment building and reached into his shirt pocket for the photo he'd lifted from an album in the living room that morning. He'd seen the thick book on the coffee table and looked inside, finding pictures of Andrew from birth to what appeared to be last week staring back at him.

He couldn't have described the feelings that surged through him as he'd leafed through the album. Anger and regret, certainly, at having already missed so much of his son's life. There were no photos of Tessa pregnant but he couldn't help wondering what she'd looked like, whether she'd had that special glow expectant mothers were supposed to have. He'd never know. Unless—

He looked at the photo he held. Andrew sat in one of those little baby carriers, in the middle of a petunia patch, clad only in a diaper. Chubby pink cheeks, glossy black curls too heavy for a child his age, and those blue eyes. Millie was right. They were Nick's eyes. In fact, Andrew looked exactly like the baby pictures of himself that his mother used to trot out for visiting relatives.

Andrew's fist was full of the deep purple flowers and he had a wide toothless smile on his face as he held them up to an adult who was visible as a long shadow. Tessa, probably, holding the camera.

A hot bubble expanded in Nick's chest and he realized he wore a silly grin, almost bursting with pride that this was his child. His son.

A new child. New hope.

Sometimes he took out the photo album he'd saved after the fire in which Andrea and her mother had died, looked at the pictures of Andrea. For a year after their deaths he couldn't bear to look at them and remember. In fact, many times he'd been ready to pitch the heavy book into the trash can.

But after last summer's interlude with Tessa, he'd come to terms with his grief and his almost debilitating rage. Seeing the smiling images of his little girl still hurt, but the ache was dull, faded to a gentle nostalgia for the good times.

The grin slid off his face as he put Andrew's photo back into his shirt pocket. He had to find him. Andrew had to be alive. He had to be.

He went up to his apartment and dialed Alexander Roth's office number, almost hanging up the phone when he remembered it was Saturday. Would Roth be there?

To his surprise the phone was picked up after the third ring. "Yes? What is it?"

"Nick Marcopoulos here," Nick said, recognizing Roth's cool, precise voice at once. "I need to talk to you."

"Do you want to come to my office, or would you rather meet somewhere else?" No hesitation in his voice. No emotion either.

"Your office is fine. I'll be there in ten minutes."

"Fine." He hung up.

"IT'S GOOD OF YOU to stay around for Tessa," Roth said when he unlocked the outer door of his office complex to let Nick in. The outside door of the building hadn't been locked. Small-town complacency? Were they all that innocent, Nick wondered, or did turmoil seethe beneath the surface, as he had sensed? "I'm sure you must have business that you're neglecting."

"Nothing that can't wait," Nick said. "Nice office," he added, noting the polished hardwood floors. An Oriental rug covered the area under the receptionist's desk. Several impressionist paintings hung on the paneled walls, making bright splashes of color.

Roth's office, beyond the reception room, looked like a cross between an Englishman's den and a library. The hardwood floor here was covered with faded Persian rugs. Shelves of leather-bound books lined the walls, and heavy velvet draperies hung at the sides of the tall-paned windows.

Roth waved Nick to a leather wing chair while he sat down behind the massive desk. He set his elbows on the arms of his chair and steepled his fingers under his chin. He smiled faintly. "I appreciate your support of Tessa," he said. "Are you going to be around much longer?"

"As long as it takes," Nick said cryptically. He shifted his weight, the chair's soft leather creaking faintly, and fixed him with a level gaze. "Who arranged Andrew's funeral?"

"I did," Roth said calmly. "Tessa was in the hospital, in a coma. Someone had to make the arrangements."

"Including the obituary notice?"

"I believe the funeral home looks after that. I gave Mr. Faversham the pertinent information."

"Who identified the body?"

One of Roth's smooth eyebrows lifted. "The doctor did. Apparently he'd treated him for some minor problem several weeks ago when Dr. Ivers was on vacation, and recognized him."

"Did you talk to this doctor yourself?"

Roth shook his head. "No. I got the news from Larry West after the clinic informed the police that the child had died. It's all in the report."

Depression hit Nick. How quickly a life could be reduced to a police report. He forced himself to continue. "There's something you should know."

"Yes?"

"We think someone made a mistake. We think the baby's not dead."

Roth's jaw dropped. "What?" His voice sounded strangled. He cleared his throat. "What do you mean, he's not dead?"

"Simple. There's no body. I take it you haven't talked to Larry."

"Larry West? Why would I have talked to him?"

Nick's opinion of Larry rose marginally. Maybe the cop's fan club had pegged him correctly after all, as a good officer who did his job, competently and professionally. "No reason. It's a small town. I thought word might have gotten around that the police have launched an extensive search for Andrew."

Roth settled back although a troubled frown creased his brow. "How is Tessa taking this?"

"She's frustrated and angry, as you might expect. And

trying to do too much too soon after her concussion. That's why I'm here.''

Roth pursed his lips. "How did you find out there was no body?"

"I broke into the funeral home," Nick said flatly. "I wanted to see my—" He broke off, remembering that Roth probably didn't know he was Andrew's father. "To see for myself."

The austere lines of Roth's face gentled. Warmth came into his pale eyes. "Yes, I can understand that. You did it for Tessa."

"Yes, I did it for Tessa." Maybe Roth had more feelings than he let on, Nick thought in surprise.

"Like I took care of the car after the accident," Roth said musingly. "It was my car but her things were in it. I collected them before it went to the wrecker. The insurance company wrote it off."

Nick frowned thoughtfully. "That brings up another point I don't understand. Why did it immediately go to the crusher? The car was almost new. Parts of it could have been salvaged. Why didn't the wrecking company hold on to it?"

"Because I didn't want to take a chance on Tessa ever seeing it again and being reminded of the accident. I promised her father I'd look out for her if she needed someone. She's a strong woman but sometimes one needs help. I wanted to make things as easy as possible for her."

"Her child died," Nick said bluntly. "At least so you told her. Nothing could ever be easy for her again."

Roth looked horrified. "I didn't lie to her. As far as I knew the baby was killed in the accident." He pulled open a desk drawer. "Here's a copy of the death certificate. They always do more than one for legal purposes." He pushed the document across the desk.

Nick took it and glanced down at the signature. Dr. Benjamin Forbes. Clear handwriting. He'd assumed all doctors wrote chicken scratches. The details on the crisp paper were identical to those he'd seen in Larry's office. He handed it back. "Do you know this Dr. Forbes?"

Roth shook his head. "No, he must be new." He spread his hands. "Look, Nick, once I contacted the funeral home, I assumed it was all taken care of."

Nick shifted restlessly. "Well, obviously somebody screwed up. And I'm going to find out who, after I find Andrew."

"I thought the police were handling it."

"They've only got so much manpower." Nick stood up and stuck out his hand. "I'll let you get back to your work now."

Roth leaned across the desk and shook Nick's hand, his touch brief, dry, and cool. "What are you planning to do now?"

Nick shrugged. "Rattle some more cages and see what breaks free."

TESSA WOKE TO THE SOUND of a soft knock on her bedroom door. "Come," she mumbled sleepily, raking her fingers through her hair. She ran her parched tongue over her teeth and grimaced.

Millie came into the room. "Tessa, I didn't want to wake you but Mr. Roth is here and he insists on seeing you. You can have your supper when he's finished."

Alexander? "Tell him I'll be down in a few minutes." Her voice was hoarse but when she swung her legs to the floor, she found that she felt almost normal.

In the bathroom, she splashed cold water on her face and rinsed her mouth before brushing her teeth. Stripping off her wrinkled clothes, she dumped them into the hamper. She stared longingly at the shower, and decided to take the time for a quick one. Alexander would wait.

Ten minutes later she found him pacing the living room. "Please sit down. Has Millie offered you coffee?"

"Yes. I don't want any." He placed one hand on the mantel and faced her, his foot braced on the raised hearth. "How well do you know Nick Marcopoulos?"

He asked the question without any particular inflection but she sensed tension beneath his benign façade. "What do you mean?"

"He's Andrew's father, isn't he?"

Tessa couldn't keep the shock from her face although she tried valiantly to control the widening of her eyes. "Why do you say that?" Her voice shook.

"He's not your current boyfriend, as you implied, is he?"

"So? He's my friend."

"The friend you met last summer, who got you pregnant." Alexander's face softened. "Look, Tessa, I'm not here to give you a hard time. In fact, I think I like your friend Nick. He seems like a responsible young man. But—" He paused significantly, then rushed on, his cheekbones flushing. "Where was he all the time you were lying in bed, suffering?"

She hadn't considered it suffering, the stringent precautions she'd taken to carry the baby as near to term as possible. She'd been glad to sacrifice a few months of her life for Andrew. "I don't know. I tried to call him but the number was disconnected."

"Didn't you ever wonder why?"

"Of course I did. Uncle Alex, is there a point to this?" He was a dear man but sometimes his pomposity got to her.

"Your friend Nick was in Greece. He certainly put plenty of distance between himself and his responsibilities."

Her temper flashed. "How could he take responsibility for something he knew nothing about?"

"It's not too surprising that he left, is it? These summer romances are usually just infatuation."

"Infatuation wasn't what I felt," Tessa muttered before she could stop herself.

"No?" Alexander's eyes sharpened. "So he was the one who ended it. Just as I thought. Tessa, you have to stop falling for these men who are only after a good time and your fortune. And especially on the rebound. Your judgment was severely impaired by the breakup with Scott. Not that I ever approved of him. I saw him as a fortune hunter from the beginning."

The reminder of her engagement—broken before she'd gone on the fateful holiday when she met Nick—stung. "I don't have a fortune, do I? Or if I do, no one knows it. My father's will still hasn't turned up."

"But when it does, you'll inherit."

"Don't be too sure. You know what Dad was like. He was upset that I had Andrew."

"But not after the baby was born. Then he turned into a doting grandfather."

Tessa smiled wistfully. "No one would have been able to resist Andrew."

A faint smile curved Alexander's thin lips. "Yes, he was a sweet baby."

"Is," Tessa retorted. "He *is* a cute kid. Nick is going to find him."

"Is he?" Alexander's brow lifted. "And give him back to you, like a gift, I suppose. What if he has his own purpose in mind? He's the father. Maybe he wants to keep him."

Fear ripped through Tessa, stealing her breath. Absorbed in her grief and pain, she'd tried to deny that possibility. Nick wouldn't, would he? "Nick is not that kind of person," she said but even to her own ears she sounded unsure.

"How do you know?" Alexander said gently. "Tessa, you have to consider this. I'd have thought you'd learned not to be so naive."

"A few weeks ago you accused me of becoming a cynic, when I didn't want a date with that company rep you were doing business with." She extended a placatory hand. "Please, Uncle Alex, let's not quarrel."

"I didn't come to quarrel. I came to warn you. Don't get me wrong. It's quite possible that Nick may be only interested in your and Andrew's welfare, that he came back to face his responsibilities."

I don't want to be his responsibility, Tessa thought, her spirits sinking. I want it to be like last summer, when we loved each other. Or I thought we did. "You don't know him," she protested. But it wasn't a valid argument. How well did *she* know Nick?

"I didn't come here to upset you, Tessa. But there's something else you should know. Nick had a child who died."

"Yes, I know. He told me."

Alexander looked relieved. "Oh, then it's all right. I was afraid—"

Tessa hesitated, torn between the need to know and guilt that she couldn't wait for Nick to tell her. Curiosity won, although tension dried her mouth so that she could hardly force out the words. "What happened to her?"

One of Alexander's brows lifted.

"No, he didn't explain the circumstances." She couldn't betray him by explaining how upset he'd been just mentioning Andrea's name. Not even to Alexander.

"She was five years old," Alexander said. "She died in a hotel room fire with her mother, Nick's wife. Actually his ex-wife, I believe."

An accident. She could see why Nick hadn't wanted to talk about it. He probably blamed himself, as those close to tragic deaths often do. "When was this?" she asked quietly.

"Less than two years ago."

Comprehension dawned. It explained so much. Nick had

lost his wife and child less than a year before he met Tessa. No wonder he'd been so reticent about his feelings, and she now understood the pain that came into his eyes when they passed a park or school where children played.

She surfaced from her thoughts when she realized Alexander was still speaking. ''I don't want to worry you unnecessarily, Tessa, but you have to ask yourself this: does Nick make a habit of abandoning his moral obligations?''

Chapter Eight

Tessa gathered her scattered wits, facing the question she'd asked herself when she'd realized that Nick was gone. At times, she'd wondered if she dreamed the whole episode in Victoria. Finding she was pregnant and having Andrew made it all too real.

It was real to Nick, too. He hadn't run away once he knew the truth. She recalled the anguish with which he'd greeted the news of Andrew's death, the hope that buoyed him since he discovered that his son might be alive.

She shook her head. "No, Nick wouldn't shirk his responsibilities. He didn't leave me in Victoria. I left him."

Alexander's eyes widened and a nerve ticked at the corner of his mouth. "Why, for heaven's sake?"

"That's between Nick and me."

Alexander flushed again. "I'm sorry. I didn't mean to pry."

"Look, Uncle Alex, Nick had plenty of reason to be angry, because of the way he found out about the baby. He could hate me for not telling him."

"You didn't know where to find him," Alexander reminded her.

She lifted one shoulder, let it fall. "Maybe I should have tried harder. I don't know. All I know is that he's been nothing but kind since he came back. And he's tried harder than anyone to find Andrew.''

Alexander nodded. "Yes, that seems to be true. I'd better tell you what else I found out about him.''

"I'm sure he'll tell me once we find Andrew. We haven't exactly had time for a long talk.''

"You'll want to know this. He was in Greece for most of the past year. That's why you couldn't get hold of him. There was an earthquake in his hometown. He went to help out his family.''

An earthquake. Common enough in a country as geologically volatile as Greece. She vaguely remembered reading about it, or maybe she'd seen it on the TV news, but, sunk in her own misery at the time, she hadn't connected it with Nick.

Nick was first-generation Greek, having immigrated to Canada as a child with his parents. Of course he'd had to go back to take care of his family. She wondered if that included parents.

"You see, he does take responsibility seriously," she said.

"That would appear to be the case." Alexander got up and walked over to her as she stood by the mantel. "If there's anything I can do to help with finding Andrew, let me know.''

She closed her eyes as pain squeezed her heart. "I will, but until we get a solid lead, there's not much to do. Nick is following up on some idea he has.''

"Well, let me know what you find out." Again color stained his cheeks. He bent and gave her a kiss on her forehead, showing a physical affection he rarely demonstrated. "Take care, Tessa.''

"I will. Thank you.''

SHE SANK DOWN onto the raised hearth after he left, burying her face in her hands. Nick's child had died. Her vague doubts about his sincerity in searching for Andrew fled. He would do his best; he knew exactly how she felt, the emptiness, the self-recrimination.

But without any kind of a lead, how long would it take?

"You'll get wrinkles if you keep frowning."

She jumped at the sound of his voice, knocking over a candlestick, which landed, unscathed, on the rug. Nick picked it up and set it back on the hearth.

Tessa jumped to her feet. "Don't sneak up on me like that," she cried. "Who let you in?"

"Millie, who else? And she invited me to dinner." Nick's eyebrows rose. "What's got your knickers in a twist?"

Tessa stared at him, openmouthed. "Knickers in a twist? Where did you get that?"

"I spent a couple of years in England in my misguided youth. Quaint expressions the British have. Useful."

"Separated by a common language, as usual," Tessa muttered.

"I doubt if that's happening here."

What did it matter, anyway? "Is there any news about Andrew?" she asked.

All humor drained out of his face, making him look older than his thirty-three years, austere as a monk. "No. I'm sorry, but I'm afraid we won't even be able to check on the death certificate until Monday."

Her spirits plummeted. She turned, leaning against the mantel, her fingers gripping the thick wood. "Why?" she cried. "Why is this happening? Why doesn't anyone know anything? Didn't Larry get a list of the clinic employees?"

"Yes, he did. I've just come from his office. He's been up to the clinic, but it's closed and no one's around. He phoned as many of the staff as he could but he only got hold of two of the people on duty that night. He's going to keep trying."

More waiting. How could she bear the waiting, not knowing?

"Tessa." Nick touched her arm, his hands warm on her bare skin. She wanted to turn, to bury her face against him, breathe him in, let him take the burden. Instead she stiffened, telling herself she had to be strong, but not knowing where she could dredge new strength from. The well had almost run dry. If they didn't find Andrew soon—

Unsettled and frustrated, she took it out on the nearest target. She squarely met his gaze. "Alexander's been here."

"Oh?"

She couldn't tell what he was thinking, but she saw his eyes grow cool and alert. "Yes, and he had several interesting things to say."

"Did he?" Letting her go, Nick shifted the candlestick he'd rescued a centimeter to the right. "That's what upset you, then."

"Upset me?" Her voice rose. "Why didn't you let me know you'd gone to Greece when I thought you'd disappeared off the face of the earth?"

He stepped back a pace. "I didn't think you'd care. I did phone later, but you didn't return my call so I gave up. You made your feelings clear enough when you walked out of our hotel room. You never wanted to—"

"No, you made your feelings clear," Tessa cut in. "You didn't want to risk being hurt again by letting yourself care for anyone. I couldn't live with a man as cold as that."

His fists clenched at his sides. He quickly shoved his hands into the back pockets of his jeans. "It works both ways. You didn't want to trust another man. You told me that enough times. Scott really did a number on you, didn't he?"

"No more than your wife did on you." As soon as the words came out, she clapped her hand over her mouth, wishing she could stuff them back inside. She had no knowledge at all about his relationship with his wife, except that the marriage must have ended.

Nick's face paled, and his jaw tensed. "Who told you about my wife?" he asked in a dangerously icy tone. His hands came out of his pockets, fisted so rigidly that the knuckles shone white.

Tessa lifted her chin defiantly. "Alexander. He worries about me."

His jaw relaxed marginally. "Yeah, I guess he does. She was my ex-wife, by the way. Or as good as."

The dark blue depths of his eyes were stormy. Filled with pain? She wasn't sure, since he blinked, shielding them with dense black lashes. "Nick, I know this may not be the right time but since we can't do anything about Andrew at the moment, it's as good as any. I need to know about your wife and daughter. You said you'd tell me about Andrea sometime. I think that time has arrived."

He sank down on the big leather chair that had been her father's. Propping his elbows on his knees, he dug the heels of his hands into his eyes. She sat down on the sofa, waiting.

Time ticked by. The clock on the mantel chimed once for the half hour. Finally, he lifted his head. His eyes were bleak and red-rimmed. He dropped his hands to his thighs and spread his fingers wide. She guessed he did it to hide their trembling.

"Laura left me that spring. Oh, it wasn't the first time she'd left. And when she got tired of her friends, she always came back. But this time she took Andrea with her. I tried to find them but I couldn't. Then I received a letter from my lawyer that she'd applied to divorce me. Except for Andrea, I didn't care. I wanted custody of my daughter. But first I had to find them and the private detective I hired turned up no trace of them. It was only later that I found out she'd gone to Spain with some guy she met. By that time she was back, flat broke. She and the guy had obviously had a fight. Laura was good at that. Her relationships never lasted.''

''Why did you marry her?''

''Don't you mean why did she marry me?'' Nick laughed bitterly.

''No, I meant what I said. Anyone would be proud to marry you.'' She laughed a little uncertainly. ''At least I think so.''

He shrugged. ''Thanks. I guess.'' He cleared his throat and fixed his eyes on some point beyond her. ''Laura was the daughter of a wealthy department store family. She was spoiled and willful, as beautiful as an angel. That's how she looked to me when I met her. We married and then I found out that her appearance should have had her fined for false advertising. Marriage got her out from her family's influence. She didn't care about me. In fact, it never occurred to her to think of anyone but herself. I still can't figure out how she let herself get pregnant or why she didn't get rid of the baby, but I guess some part of her Catholic-school education must have stuck with her. I practically raised Andrea by myself and I covered up Laura's disappearances with her family.''

''Where would she go?''

''Anywhere. Bars, lounges. She still got an allowance from her father but finally he cut her off.'' His mouth turned down. ''My fault, I guess.''

''What do you mean, your fault? Was her money that important to you?''

Nick made a derisive sound. ''Important? I couldn't have cared less about her money. That's why I went to her father, told him it was senseless to give an allowance to a married woman in her late twenties, and that she was my wife and I'd support her. So he cut her off. And when her boyfriend dumped her in Europe, she made it back on her return ticket but she had no money and the guy had her credit cards. He was later arrested for fraud, theft, and a bunch of other charges.''

He dragged in a long breath. "Laura got back late one night and rented a room in a dump of a motel near the airport. I imagine she was planning to come home the next day, either to me, begging me to take her back, or to her parents. She never saw that day. She took a sleeping pill, the autopsy found, and fell asleep in bed with a lit cigarette. They both died of smoke inhalation.'' He lifted his hands and let them drop again. "That's how I lost my little girl.''

"Your wife and your little girl,'' Tessa corrected.

He looked up with angry eyes. "My wife was an adult and responsible for her own actions. But Andrea was a defenseless child, and who knows what happened to her on that trip. I'll never forgive myself for that.''

"You didn't know,'' Tessa said gently, sorry she'd hurt him with her almost accusatory tone.

"I should have tried harder. But I thought it was like the other times, that she'd be gone for a couple days, leaving Andrea at her parents' house, and come back. Andrea loved her grandparents. They were devastated when she died.''

Some lingering bitterness in his voice hit her. "I suppose they blamed you.''

"Yeah, they did, and I probably deserved some of it.''

"I doubt that,'' Tessa said firmly.

A faint smile tilted the corner of Nick's mouth. "Really? What if I told you the police questioned me?''

That shook her, but only for an instant. "Routine. The police always question the relatives in an unnatural death.''

"As it happened, I had an alibi. I was speaking at a building contractors' conference at the time of the fire.''

Tessa nodded. "No matter what your wife did, I don't think you'd kill her. And you certainly wouldn't have harmed your own child.''

He stared down at his hands. "You seem very sure of that.'' His voice sounded oddly humble.

"Yes, I'm very sure," Tessa declared, her eyes stinging. He looked up then, and met her gaze. Some unseen understanding passed between them. Trust. And something that could have been an acknowledgment of love. She felt a glow of warmth ignite in the empty space in her chest. It would be all right. They would find Andrew and they would find each other.

But Nick broke the contact, as if he were shying away from making a commitment. It occurred to her to wonder if she still felt the same way as last summer, afraid, distrustful, still deeply in pain, as she knew now. "Alexander was probably trying to warn you in case I'm another fortune hunter," he said.

Tessa shrugged. "He's always cared about me, even though he doesn't show it much. I'm no heiress. My father likely left the company to Alexander anyway."

"Likely? Your father's been gone for three months. Hasn't the will been probated yet?"

"No, it hasn't. Three months isn't that long."

"Maybe not." His black brows furrowed into a heavy line over his nose. "Could there be something in the will that would give someone a motive for kidnapping Andrew?"

Tessa chewed on her lower lip, considering this new angle. "It doesn't seem likely. If Andrew was kidnapped for ransom, there would have been a message from his abductor by now."

Nick nodded but his frown remained. He paced slowly to the opposite end of the room and back. Just as he reached the fireplace again, the door opened and Millie stuck her head in. "Dinner's ready."

Nick smiled wryly as she disappeared back into the kitchen. "I guess we'd better go eat," he said. "You look as if you could use a little nourishment. By the way," he added as he took her elbow, "what kind of a car does your friend Sophie drive?"

"A black Mazda, one of the sporty ones. Why?"

"I saw a black Mazda around town a couple of times lately. Again today. Someone waved at me as it went by but I couldn't get a good look at the driver because of the tinted windows."

"It could be Sophie." Tessa frowned. "That's odd, though. When she called, she said she'd be out of town until Monday."

Nick shrugged. "Maybe it wasn't her, then. It can't be the only Mazda in town."

"No, I think Larry drives one, too. Or maybe his is a Toyota. A black sporty thing. Something Japanese."

THEY ATE IN THE KITCHEN, cozy with its large dining area and warm golden oak cabinets. After the meal, Millie poured them coffee, stacked the dishes in the dishwasher, and went to her own room, leaving them alone.

"Okay, Nick, what's our next move?" Tessa said. "I say we badger Larry."

"We can call him again, at least so we get an update." Nick picked up his water glass. "Is there more ice water?"

"I think I poured the last of it, but there are ice cubes in the freezer." She pushed her chair back, but Nick stood up, laying his hand on her shoulder.

"Sit, Tessa. I'll get them."

He pulled open the freezer compartment of the fridge. And just stood there, as if he'd turned to stone.

Tessa could feel the chilly air even from where she sat. "What's the matter? Can't you find them?"

"Tessa." His voice sounded strangled.

Suddenly she knew what he'd seen. She jumped up so quickly her chair clattered to the tile floor. She slammed the freezer door closed, the handle narrowly missing his temple. Breathing hard, she leaned back against the fridge, the smooth enamel cool against her sweating palms and back.

Nick stared at her, emotion churning in his dark blue eyes. "Tessa, we'll get him back." His voice broke and he closed his eyes. With a muffled groan, he wrapped his arms around her, holding her so tightly she could hardly breathe.

She clung to him; he felt so good, warm and lean and strong, pressed against her. He'd held her before, comforting her, somehow now it was different. Their conversation earlier had shifted the dynamics between them. She suddenly knew how acutely she'd missed this closeness, so different from the occasional platonic hugs from her father and Millie and Sophie. And the warmth of her baby in her arms.

The baby who had been torn from her.

She submerged herself in the comfort of Nick's solid strength, and tried to ignore the hot little sizzles along her nerve endings. She had no right to remember cool sheets and hot nights with this man while her baby was missing.

But she couldn't stop herself. He was Andrew's father. If things had been different, he would have every right to comfort her, to help her, to love her.

"I thought you would have stopped saving your milk by now," he whispered, his mouth against her ear. As he lifted his head slightly, she felt cool moisture on her neck where his face had been. She drew back and stared into his face. He looked back at her, his eyes swollen and wet. "Don't worry. We won't give up until we find him."

Her own eyes remained dry, although the lump in her throat prevented her from speaking. She felt as if she were drowning in the deep blue of his gaze. She wanted to keep sinking down and down, until this nightmare was over, until Andrew lay safely in her arms.

A little longer. She breathed in the spicy scent of him, felt the dampness of sweat on his nape. She curled her fingers in his hair, savoring the familiar silky texture of it. Andrew would have hair like that soon, instead of baby-fine floss.

Andrew.

Reluctantly, she uncurled her hands, placing one palm against his chest, feeling the strong thud of his heart. After a moment, she gathered her resolve and stepped away from him. But her eyes remained locked with his, as if she made a vow. Together. Together they could do it. She had to remember that.

"You wanted ice cubes." Her voice sounded thin and weird. She cleared her throat. "If you'll move a little, I'll get them."

He stepped back, going over to the sink and yanking down a paper towel to blow his nose. Tessa opened the freezer door and retrieved the ice cube tray. The small bottles she filled every day with her own milk sat in rows, mute witness to the hope she couldn't let go.

She carried the plastic tray to the sink and twisted it, releasing the cubes, dropping three into his glass. She filled the glass with tap water and handed it to him. "Your ice water."

He reached for it. His fingers brushed hers. Electricity zipped up her arm. She let go of the glass. He hadn't grasped it properly. It fell into the sink, water and ice cubes skittering across the shiny stainless steel.

"Sorry," she gulped, her hands shaking. "I'll get you some more." She grabbed for the ice cube tray still sitting next to the sink.

Nick's hand covered hers. "Tessa, don't. I'll do it. But first, let's get this out of the way."

This? Her befuddled mind floundered, searching for an anchor. It found it in the touch of his lips on hers. She clenched her hands in the front of his shirt, hanging on as she gave in to the need that had been present all along but that she'd been afraid to acknowledge.

His mouth tasted hot and sweet as she remembered, faintly salty from the tears he'd cried. His arms tightened.

His body pressed against hers, hot and hard, aroused. No mistaking that.

She submerged herself in the pleasure of the kisses he distributed over her face with exquisite tenderness. Then he came back to her mouth, sending renewed heat to all the corners of her body. Made her remember how it had been last summer, sun spilling across the bed, his naked body covering hers.

Would they have that again, the perfect closeness? Was it possible? Once they found Andrew—

Gasping for breath, he tore his mouth away, and rested his forehead against hers. He ran one fingertip around her ear and across her cheek. "Tessa, I didn't know I could miss anyone the way I missed you," he whispered huskily.

She struggled back to coherent thought. Had she heard correctly? He'd missed her? She shook her head from side to side. "Then why didn't you keep calling?"

He slid his hands into her hair, tilting up her face. "I did. I left a message twice. After that I didn't try again. There was no point."

He kissed her again, effectively silencing any reply she might make. Not that she was capable of coherent speech. Her mind was in a turmoil. He'd called. Who had he called?

Then all thought fled as he gathered her closer. When they finally came up for air, they were both breathing heavily, hearts pounding like jackhammers.

"Tessa."

Nick's single word contained a wealth of feeling that echoed that in her heart. Tenderness, confusion, longing, regret.

Was there a chance for them? Would he stay around once Andrew was found? She would trust him with Andrew's life and welfare. She knew that as surely as she knew the sun would come up tomorrow.

Could she trust him with her heart?

Before she could examine the question too closely, the phone rang. They both jumped.

It rang again, a harsh jangle. "Will Millie get it?" Nick asked.

Tessa shook her head. "No, the phone in her room is a separate line." She disentangled herself from his arms and reached for the receiver. "Yes?"

"Larry here. I've got some news for you."

Blood drumming in her ears, she lifted her gaze to Nick's. She didn't know what he saw in her eyes, but he bent closer so that he could listen in, his cheek warm and rough with beard stubble against her face.

"News?" She forced an optimistic note into her voice, as if she could will it to be good news.

"Yeah," Larry said. She heard the creak of his office chair and could imagine him leaning back and raking his fingers through his hair. "I got hold of the secretary at the clinic. Dr. Benjamin Forbes doesn't exist."

Chapter Nine

"Dr. Forbes doesn't exist." The words rang in Nick's head. His breath hissed out and he jerked back from the phone. So there was something suspicious going on. It shouldn't have come as a surprise but having his suspicions confirmed jolted him.

He stared out of the window over the sink, his mind blank. A hummingbird hovered next to the feeder on the other side of the screen, its feathers iridescent as an opal. It fed, then darted away, borne on invisible wings.

Beside him, Tessa hung up the phone. She hugged her arms around her waist, shivering. "You heard, and it's just what you were thinking, isn't it? That the signature on the death certificate was forged."

"It's not an answer," Nick said tightly. "Only another indication that nothing about this is going to be easy."

Tessa's eyes looked like black holes in her stark white face. He placed his hands on her shoulders, but she stiffened her spine. "No, I'm not going to faint." Her breath rasped in her throat and she swallowed audibly. "Larry's going to let me know as soon as he finds out anything else."

The dishwasher swished and grumbled in the silence that fell between them. Finally Nick stirred. "I'll pour us some more coffee. Go into the living room."

"It's my house," she muttered, as she went in to sit down. He might be taking a lot upon himself, acting like he lived there, but she was too tired to argue. She massaged the ache in her temple with the tips of her fingers.

Nick handed her a fresh mug of coffee. She cradled it in her hands, clutching at the warmth as if it were the middle of winter instead of a pleasant evening in July. Sinking down on the sofa opposite her, he set his own mug on the coffee table.

Tessa took a sip of the coffee and nearly choked. "What did you put in it?" she sputtered.

"Some brandy I found in the sink cupboard. I suppose Millie uses it for Christmas cakes or something. Drink up. It won't hurt you. And the coffee's decaf. It won't keep you awake."

Tentatively, she sipped again. The alcohol seared her throat but subsided to a comfortable glow in her stomach. The incipient headache began to fade.

Nick crossed his ankles and leaned back in the corner of the sofa, giving every appearance of composure. Inside, he felt as if his guts were tied in knots. His stomach burned. He wondered if the ulcer he'd had two years ago had come back to life.

Still, he was sure what he felt was nothing like the hell Tessa was going through. She sat there, her knuckles white around the coffee mug, her eyes too big and dark in her pale face. She'd gotten thinner, weight she couldn't afford to lose. The bones under her skin seemed too fragile to support her body.

Only her breasts were more rounded than they had been last summer. He'd felt their fullness pressed against his chest earlier. He could only imagine the determination she used to hold back her despair, the courage it took to use the breast pump every day so that her milk would be available for her baby when she found him.

"We can leave this until tomorrow. You should be in bed."

"It's still light out."

"At this time of year, it's light out until after nine," he said dryly.

She raked her hand wearily through her hair, shaking back the heavy waves. "I can't go to bed yet. I wouldn't sleep anyway. Brain overload." She dropped her hands in her lap and stared down at her loosely curled fingers. "Who could have forged that signature? And why?"

"Yeah, why? That's the bigger question. Do you know any of the people who work at the clinic?"

"A couple of casual acquaintances, that's all. People I used to go to school with. I know what you're getting at. Would someone I know take Andrew and make it look like he was killed in the car accident? The answer is no. I haven't kept up with a lot of my school friends, but no one would do anything that cruel."

Scowling, he drank some of his coffee, then set the mug down. "What about some do-gooder who resents unwed mothers?"

"That's absurd."

He shrugged. "Stranger things have happened. And you said yourself that there was some gossip and even your father took a while to adjust. Understandable, of course."

"He loved Andrew as soon as he saw him." She smiled sadly, remembering.

"Yes, it's too bad he died," Nick said. He sat up straighter. "Look, we've got to look at all the angles, no matter how far-fetched. That missing will bothers me. If someone has it— Does Alexander know anything about your father's will? He's a lawyer. Wouldn't he have been the one who drew it up?"

"Not necessarily. Since he was a partner in the business, and I expect Dad would have left him some or all of it, it might have been considered a conflict of interest."

"Then your father must have had another lawyer."

Tessa frowned. "If he did, he never told me." She gulped the last of her coffee. Too fast. He winced as he saw her shudder. "Look, Nick, I was never involved in Dad's business. When he died, Alexander took over Dad's responsibilities as well as his own. It's worked out fine. I've got my own job."

"What about Andrew?"

Her eyes widened into startled blue-gray ovals. "Andrew? He's a baby. What could he have to do with the business?"

He gave up all pretense of relaxing. He got up and walked to the mantel, gazing at the excellent print of Monet's *Water Lilies* that hung over the fireplace. "Is it possible that Andrew inherits?" he asked, without turning around.

Her shocked breath sounded loud in the quiet room. "No," she said positively. "It's not. Dad had just come to terms with my having a child." She gave a hollow laugh. "My having a child in an unconventional way. Why would you even think such a thing?"

He turned to face her. "Because it would be a motive for getting rid of Andrew. Also for getting rid of you since you would probably be his trustee until he's of age."

Her face, already pale, turned as white as the porcelain mug in front of her. She swallowed a couple of times. Bracing her hands on the arms of her chair, she pushed herself to her feet. She swayed a little as she stood, but managed to regain her balance. She must be feeling the brandy. Even though she'd eaten a fair amount of dinner, the brandy carried quite a kick and she'd drunk it all at once.

He stepped toward her, ready to catch her if she fell. But she moved away from him. Her harsh laugh grated on his ears. "Nick, you're crazy. Either that, or you've got a very bizarre imagination."

"Have I?" he said coolly.

It only took her a moment to figure it out. She whirled round to face him, her cheeks flushing pink. Her eyes snapped fire. "You're implying that my accident wasn't an accident, aren't you? And since Alexander is the most logical person to inherit the business, he must be the one behind it."

He inclined his head, proud of her deductive powers on one level but sick with the implications on another. The risk he was taking scared him spitless. After this, she'd never speak to him again. She'd go straight to Roth, and tell him everything. Nick would be lucky if Roth didn't sue him for defamation of character.

Yet, it was the only thing that made sense.

"You've got an evil, twisted mind." Tessa practically spat the words at him. "And I think you'd better get out of here before I call Larry to throw you out."

"It would take more than friend Larry," Nick said mildly. "It's logical, though. You were driving Roth's car. He could have done something to sabotage it before he lent it to you. The weather cooperated as well, to cover it up."

"Oh, come on, Nick. You can't be serious. Alexander lent me the car the day before. My car showed an electrical problem on Thursday. With the weekend coming up, the dealer couldn't get it repaired in time."

"Did Roth know you were going up to the cabin?"

"Yes, he did, as a matter of fact," Tessa said. "I'd planned to leave earlier, but he came by after dinner for me to sign some papers. Company business. It took longer to go over them than we'd expected, but I decided to leave anyway. I didn't realize the storm would be that bad."

"Okay. Did anyone else know you were going?"

"Millie did. And I'd told her I planned to stay up there until possibly mid-week, so she decided to visit her sister in Vancouver. And Sophie knew. For that matter, so did the mechanic who was working on my Saab."

"And no one followed you?"

She stared at him incredulously. "Of course not. Naturally there was a certain amount of traffic on the road—several people overtook me—but no, no one followed me."

"Unless they were very skillful at it. Dark night, wind and rain. Easy to stay far enough behind."

"Why don't you just take your insinuations and get out?" Tessa said. "I think I've heard enough. Besides, if you can conceive of Alexander trying to kill me, I might just as well suspect you. Oh, not of trying to kill me, but of taking Andrew. You knew he was your son when you came here. Maybe you took him."

"He was already gone before I came. And if I took him, why am I still hanging around? Why haven't I flown out of here with Andrew stuffed in my briefcase or something?"

She smiled crookedly, ruefully. "I haven't figured that part out yet. It's all stupid anyway. The point I'm trying to make is that it's just as absurd for you to suspect Alexander or Sophie or Millie as it is for me to suspect you."

"I don't suspect Sophie or Millie."

Her shoulders slumped. "The most likely possibility is that someone took him from the clinic. Once we talk to the people there, we should be able to track him down."

Her voice broke and she sank down on the chair, burying her face in her hands. "Oh, please let it be resolved soon. I don't know how much more of this I can stand."

The muffled words tore through him like a serrated blade. He buried his fists in his pockets, wishing there was something he could do. Wave a magic wand and make Andrew reappear? How could he have been so stupid as to let this woman walk out of his life last summer? He must have been insane.

Yeah, come to think of it, maybe he had been, on some level, after what had happened with Laura and Andrea. They said the first year was the worst, and Laura and An-

drea had been gone only eight months when he'd met
Tessa. But he was totally sane now.

And helpless.

He crouched down in front of her and pulled her hands
away from her face. Gathering her into his arms, he rocked
her back and forth. "Cry, Tessa. You'll feel better."

She gave a strangled laugh. "Don't you think I know
that? But the tears are locked inside me. I can't cry."

"At least go up and sleep. I'll come back tomorrow and
we'll figure out what to do next." Her sweet scent filled
his nostrils and he wished he could suggest staying with
her, holding her and keeping the demons at bay.

But he couldn't. He knew himself well enough to realize
that he'd never be able to just hold her. He wanted her too
badly, despite the worry over Andrew, and the reserve and
distrust that stood between them. He didn't blame her for
the way she felt. He just hoped that when this was over he
had a chance to convince her he'd changed, that he'd been
a fool last summer.

As he had last night, he carried her up to her room,
laughing at her protests that he'd put out his back. "A
lightweight like you? You're going to have to start eating
more. A good stiff wind would blow you away."

She sighed as he laid her on the bed. He kissed his fingertips and pressed them to her mouth, the only contact he
would allow himself in the intimacy of her bedroom. "I'll
call you in the morning. Good night."

"Good night, Nick," she said. "And thanks."

IN THE MORNING her mind was clear and she knew what
she had to do. After finishing the waffles Millie insisted she
eat, she went out to the garage. The black paint of her Saab
gleamed from the washing Tim, one of Millie's nephews,
had given it the other day. She turned the key in the ignition, gratified to hear the throaty growl of the engine as it
immediately fired to life.

She hadn't driven since the accident, but no disturbing memories of the crash surfaced.

Going down the driveway, she pressed her foot on the brake a couple of times before turning onto the pavement. She didn't even think about what she was doing until she'd tested them for the third time. Blast that Nick for putting suspicions in her head. As if someone would break into the locked garage to tamper with her car.

Church bells rang sonorously as she drove toward the center of town. On impulse she turned into the parking lot of St. Luke's and got out of the car. The priest chanted as she entered. *Lord, have mercy.* She knelt in a back pew, inhaling the scent of candle wax. Bowing her head, she sent up a quick, impassioned prayer for Andrew's safety. Would God hear, or had He been busy elsewhere during the last nine days?

She crept out again before anyone noticed her, and got back into the car. Somehow the quiet moment had lifted some of the burden weighing her heart.

The Sunday silence of the office building enveloped her when she opened the outside door with her key. Upstairs, on the second floor, she walked through the deserted reception area to her father's private office. The door was locked. As far as she knew, no one, not even Alexander, had been in there since Joseph's funeral, three months ago.

Selecting another key, she unlocked the door. The spacious room held the musty, faintly damp smell of a space long unaired. Why hadn't she come sooner, she asked herself, to clean out the desk, if nothing else? She'd used the excuse of Andrew's care but deep down she knew it had been reluctance. If she cleaned out her father's office, she would be admitting that he was really gone. She hadn't been ready to do it before. But the greater crisis of Andrew's disappearance drove her to it now.

Going over to the window, she pushed up the old-fashioned sash. The squeal of dry old wood grated on her ears. Heat and the pungent scent of summer-soft asphalt rushed into the room, chasing away the mustiness.

She leaned for a moment on the windowsill, breathing in the fresh air. Across the street, the blinds of the ice cream shop snapped up, but she couldn't see anyone inside with the sun reflecting on the glass. A dog sauntered down the street, tongue lolling.

She knew she was wasting time, putting off the task she dreaded and anticipated at the same time. She hated the idea of finally putting her father's affairs to rest, but she had to look for any clue that might lead her to Andrew.

She was about to turn away from the window when she froze, a shiver crawling up her back. A shadow moved in the alley next to the ice cream shop. Chiding herself for her paranoia, she squinted against the glare, trying to make out who or what it was. Another dog, probably, loose in defiance of leash laws.

A man stepped out of the alley, his hands cupped around his face as he lit a cigarette. Baggy pants flapped around his ankles. Despite the heat, he wore a plaid flannel shirt. A baseball cap obscured his features but she recognized him.

Dorky Pete, a local character who made a precarious living selling junk at flea markets. He lived on a little farm outside of town, in a tarpaper shack surrounded by rusty car corpses. Gossip said he grew marijuana in the upper reaches of the acreage, a rumor fed by the presence of several vicious pit bulls he kept on the property.

As far as Tessa knew, he'd never been convicted of any crime, and his eccentricities were considered harmless.

He shoved the lighter into his shirt pocket and looked up. One finger tilted up the bill of his cap and she saw his face, thin and bony, bristly with salt-and-pepper beard stubble. His deep-set dark eyes seemed to meet hers for an instant. He lifted two fingers in what might have been a greeting, pulled the cap lower over his eyes, and shuffled down the street.

Tessa ducked back inside the window, shaking off her uneasiness. But the remnants stuck with her. The flea market was held on Sundays. What was Dorky Pete doing walking around the center of town when he should have been selling his dubious wares?

The question nagged her as she went to work.

The keys she'd brought opened the file cabinets and the desk. A small safe was fitted into the wall, hidden behind a picture of herself at the age of six. She wore a gap-toothed grin and her hair in two thick braids.

She stared at the picture before lifting it down to expose the safe. Had she ever been that young and carefree? She'd aged fifty years in the past week. She felt so old she was surprised when she looked in a mirror and saw her face still the same, tired, strained, but definitely not older than thirty.

Twirling the dial, she paused at each of the numbers she remembered. Her own birthday. Her father had used that as the combination.

The safe contained nothing except a bundle of bearer bonds, a few stock certificates dating back forty years, probably on long-defunct companies, and an old cigar box containing thirty-six dollars in coins and small bills. She closed the metal door and spun the dial to relock it. She rehung the framed photo, refusing to meet the innocent six-year-old's eyes. If she didn't find him, she'd never see Andrew reach that age.

She clutched her belly as a cramp ripped through it. Breathing shallowly, she willed the pain to subside. Could it be her period? Nursing the baby had suppressed her normal hormonal cycle, but it could begin again anytime, especially if she wasn't expressing as much milk as Andrew would have taken. And soon she wouldn't have any left.

She was sitting in her father's leather desk chair, staring

into space with dry, aching eyes, when a voice called her through the open window. "Tessa, let me in."

Moving stiffly, like an old woman, she got up and went to the window. Nick stood below, his black hair glossy in the sun.

He held up the white box in his hand. "I've brought pizza for lunch."

"What? It can't be lunchtime." Glancing at the clock on the wall, she gasped. A lost hour? More like two. The hands stood at attention. Noon, already.

"Let me in before it gets cold."

She gave a rusty laugh. "In this heat?"

He was insinuating himself back into her heart. Was she sure she wanted it? She asked herself that ten times while she ran down the stairs to the outside door. Even so, she couldn't stop the little skip in her heartbeat when she opened it.

His tanned skin was freshly shaven, and the spicy scent of his aftershave streamed through her, to settle warmly in her abdomen. She shouldn't let herself respond to him, but her body seemed to have a will of its own, separate from her brain.

"How did you know I was here? You couldn't have asked Millie. I gave her the rest of the day off."

"Logical deduction, my dear Watson. You weren't at home so I figured you might be here. I saw your car and I knew I was right. So I picked up the pizza for our lunch. Are you looking for the will?"

She moved ahead of him up the stairs. "Yes, but I've barely started. I don't know where the time's gone."

Another cramp doubled her over when she'd eaten two slices of pizza. Nick laid his hand on her back. "What's wrong, Tessa?"

She rubbed her stomach. "I thought it was my dot starting but it doesn't look like it. Must be something I ate."

"Or stress." His strong hands massaged her shoulders,

unknotting muscles she hadn't realized were tense. "Come on, eat some more pizza. Your stomach will feel better with food inside."

"You sound as if you're an expert." She picked up another wedge of pizza, forced herself to take a bite.

He grimaced. "Believe me, I am. I nearly had an ulcer once and spent a month on rice, poached chicken and antibiotics."

They finished most of the pizza. "Why don't you start on the file cabinets and I'll do the desk?" Tessa suggested, surprised that she felt better.

An hour later Tessa leaned back in the desk chair. "Nothing."

Nick's mouth turned down. "I wouldn't say nothing. We found enough paper in here to start our own recycling depot. Didn't your dad throw anything out? I found files going back to your grandfather's time."

Tessa laughed. "This is nothing. The archives are in the basement. There's masses more stuff."

Nick groaned.

"However," Tessa went on, "the good news is that we don't have to go through it. It's very unlikely his will would be among all those moldy files."

"Well, it's not here." Nick frowned. "How did he keep track of his appointments? On one of those computerized date minders, maybe, that he would have carried with him?"

Tessa shook her head. "Dad didn't believe in electronics. That's why there isn't a computer in here. He kept a desk diary in which he wrote down his appointments. Now that you mention it, I haven't seen it around here, and I know it's not in his desk at home."

She snapped her fingers. "I know. It's probably in Mrs. Pearson's desk. She would have had to cancel his appointments after he took ill. I just hope she didn't throw it away."

Mrs. Pearson's desk in the reception area was not locked. It held almost nothing other than a supply of printer paper, assorted pens and pencils and, surprisingly, a bottle of rather good brandy in the bottom drawer.

Nick whistled softly as he glanced at the label. "Medicinal? Or is Mrs. Pearson a secret drinker?"

Tessa grunted a negative. "Not Mrs. Pearson. It's likely my dad's. Probably kept it here so I wouldn't find it. He used it to deaden the pain when his angina bothered him. Against his doctor's orders. Aha."

Getting to her feet, she waved the leatherbound book she had discovered in the back of the drawer. "I think this is it."

Heads together, they leafed through it. Tessa's heart ached at the number of appointments he'd had with Dr. Ivers since January. He'd kept the severity of his illness from her. Of course, she'd been spending most of her time in bed, waiting out the pregnancy. She'd moved back home, unable to manage on her own. Millie had been only too happy to fuss over her. Tessa had felt Joseph's disapproval, but gradually proximity and their previous closeness had overcome the distance he'd put between them. When Andrew was born, one look into his deep blue eyes and Joseph was lost. He had redefined and enhanced the term "doting grandparent."

Sadly, though, he'd died a month later, fighting all the way and keeping up his office work to the end, even from his bed at home. Massive heart failure. Dr. Ivers had warned him repeatedly to slow down, but Joseph couldn't. It just wasn't his nature.

She shook off the dismal thoughts and refocused on the notations and dates. Fortunately most of the names were familiar to her, people and suppliers around town. She would go through again and write down those that weren't once they worked their way to the end.

The middle of March. *Andrew is born.* The square lettering stood out in red ink. Nick looked at her. "He was happy about Andrew."

"Not at first." Tessa bit her lip. "But he loved him as soon as he saw him."

Eyes burning, she flipped through the next pages. Routine appointments. Lunch with Alexander. Several dinner dates crossed out and new words substituted: Dinner at home. Stop at toy store. For Andrew.

She focused on a name. Roger Simmons. Two p.m. She was about to turn the page when Nick laid his finger on it. "Wait. Didn't I see that name before?"

They turned back. Twice more, once in February and again earlier in March, the name appeared. Moving forward, they saw the name again, after a week of blank pages, near the end of April. "That was only a few days before he died," Tessa said painfully. "He hardly went out of the house and he certainly didn't come to the office. I wonder whether he kept the appointment."

"If we can find out who this Roger Simmons is, we can ask him," Nick said.

They looked through the rest of the month and the first week of May but any appointments noted had been crossed out by Mrs. Pearson. "Those are the canceled ones. I called her to do it when he finally couldn't get out of bed. Just before his final heart attack."

"It must have been hard for you. Taking care of Andrew and your father."

Her nose burned with unshed tears. "Dad had a full-time nurse."

"Still, it's the hardest thing in the world to watch someone die."

"Experience again, Nick?"

"No, not really. Any deaths in my family so far have been quick and sudden." He reached into the desk drawer for the phone book he'd spotted earlier.

"Bingo," he said after a moment. "Found him. And guess what? He's a lawyer, specializing in wills and estates."

Chapter Ten

"Another dead end," Tessa muttered disgustedly ten minutes later.

They'd called Roger Simmons at home, interrupting his Sunday afternoon nap. He remembered Joseph Lee consulting him about a will, but he didn't recall the details. "Do you realize how many wills I draw up in a month, never mind in four or five months? Miss Lee, I'm really sorry but I can't help you. And he took all the copies with him. We don't have a facility for safekeeping for our clients. I'm very sorry."

"He sounds like a will mill," Nick said dryly. "Cranking them out with no more personal contact than is strictly needed."

"I'll have to talk to Alexander again. He must have some idea what Dad did with it." She went to the window, looking up and down the street before closing it. A few cars and pickup trucks going by, and a couple with three children coming out of the ice cream shop carrying loaded cones.

No sinister shadows in the alley. She picked up her purse. "Are you doing anything this afternoon?"

He made a mock bow. "I'm at your service."

"Okay. We're going to the flea market."

He glanced at his watch. "Bit late, isn't it? All the good stuff will be gone by now."

"We're not looking for stuff. I want to check something out. Come along."

THEY WENT IN TESSA'S CAR, leaving Nick's Peugeot parked on the street.

The flea market bustled with people, turbaned Indo-Canadians, small children, teenagers and adults in shorts and tank tops. Nick paid their admission and they walked through the gate. Tables laden with fruits and vegetables gave way to sellers of old toys, antique or junk dishes and outdated whirlpool machines for bathtubs. One seller dealt only in porcelain cows, another in plastic gadgets to fancy up curtains.

Tessa pushed her way through the crowds, towing Nick in her wake. "What's your hurry? You're not even looking at anything."

Tessa stopped so abruptly he crashed into her back. He put his hands on her shoulders to steady her when she staggered. "There. He's here now."

"Who's here now?" Nick peered around her.

She spun quickly around, turning him to face the other way. "Don't let him see you."

"Let who see me?" he demanded irritably. "Would you mind telling me what's going on?"

She ducked behind the next stall, pretending an interest in the sunglasses displayed. *Every pair five dollars. Buy them now for superior day and night vision.* "Dorky Pete, that's who," she hissed. "Do you recognize that van?"

He stepped out and looked. "Damn. He's the one who nearly ran us off the road."

The battered van stood behind a table laden with boxes of books, old bicycle parts, questionable electric motors and rusty garden tools. The van, its side door open, contained bicycles and more boxes. Pete, the inevitable cigarette dangling from his lower lip, was trying to convince a customer that an ordinary green bottle would soon be a valuable collector's item.

"I thought of it this morning when I saw him on the street, that he had a white van. See, he's only half unloaded. He can't have been here long." Tessa turned to the man selling the sunglasses. "When did the man over there come?"

The sunglass seller scratched his head and hitched up his trousers under his protruding belly. "'Bout an hour ago, I'd say. Dunno why he was so late. He's usually one of the first here every Sunday." He held up a pair of glasses with yellow lenses and lurid purple frames. "Sure you won't get one of these, lady?"

"Sorry," Nick said. "It clashes with her outfit."

He pulled Tessa to the end of the row of tables, and laid down a couple of dollars for a baseball cap advertising a beer company. "Wait here. I just had an idea. He shouldn't recognize me."

Putting his own sunglasses back on and pulling the cap low over his forehead, he walked over to Dorky Pete's table, scanning the items displayed. No car seat. He turned his attention to the van. "I see you have a high chair in there," he said. "You wouldn't have a baby car seat, would you?"

Pete rolled the cigarette from one corner of his mouth to the other. "Nope. Haven't got one of those." He eyed Nick narrowly. "You don't have a kid. Why do you need one?"

Probably knew who he was after all, Nick thought, cursing the small-town lack of anonymity. "I lost one the other day."

"Haven't seen any baby seats. Sorry." He turned to another customer looking at bicycle tires. "Help you?"

Nick shook his head as he rejoined Tessa. "No seat. Maybe he wasn't the one who took it from my car. But since it was his van on the mountain road, we'll be on our guard from now on.''

"He could have had business up there, buying junk," Tessa said, disappointed. She'd thought about calling Larry about the van but what would be the point? They hadn't been harmed. "And a coincidence that he was outside the office building this morning."

"What?" Nick yelled, drawing the attention of several passersby. He glanced at them and lowered his voice, taking Tessa's elbow in a firm grip and leading her toward the car. "You mean he was near your office building this morning? That scruffy-looking character?"

"He's harmless, you know." She leaned against the car door, struggling to get her breath back.

"Is he?" Nick said testily. "He's a dreadful driver, for one thing."

"That doesn't make him a criminal."

"No? Not even if he's been following us around for days."

"You don't know that, do you, Nick?"

"Okay, maybe not," he agreed, unconvinced. "Does he have any other vehicles that he drives?"

"I'm not sure. He's got plenty of old cars in his yard but I don't think any of them are fit to drive. I'd guess that van is the only one he uses."

"Not a black Mazda, then."

Tessa put the key in the door lock and turned it. "I wouldn't think so. He doesn't strike me as a fan of imports. Why?"

"I thought I saw it again this morning when I was driving to your dad's office." Nick shook his head and walked around to the passenger side of the car. "Whatever Sophie does for a living must pay well. It's a pricey model. If it was hers."

Tessa frowned. "I know she received a substantial inheritance from her grandmother a few years ago. And her family is well off. They own that motel complex on the edge of town, and a few other businesses.''

She drove back downtown and pulled in behind his car. ''There you are. You haven't been towed.''

He looked up and down the street for No Parking signs. ''Is that likely?''

Tessa laughed. ''No, not on Sunday, at any rate. Weekdays you only get two hours.''

Nick made no move to get out of the car. He slipped off his seat belt and turned toward her, resting his hand on the headrest behind her. His fingers played with a couple of strands of her hair. ''And where are you off to now? You haven't got some other scheme up your sleeve, have you?''

Tessa shook her head. ''Not today. I'd planned to clean out Dad's office but I think I'll leave the rest for another day.'' She rubbed the tender spot on her temple where stitch tracks formed a few rough bumps. ''My head aches a little. I never thought a simple concussion took so long to get over. It's frustrating that every time I try to do anything, I feel like I've been dragged through a hedge. I think I'll go home and have a nap.''

He stared at her. Was her tone too innocent? He touched a fingertip to the dark circles under her eyes and decided he was being overly suspicious. Also, overprotective. ''Go home, Tessa. I'll follow you and make sure you make it safely.''

''I'm sure I can find my own way home,'' Tessa said, but her protest lacked heat.

''Indulge me,'' he said, smiling. He leaned over and kissed her, full on the pink lips that parted in a startled gasp. Her breath held a ghost of tomato sauce, her skin cool against his fingertips, faintly damp. Her breasts pressed against him. He weighed one with his palm, feeling the nipple harden.

Stifling a groan, he kissed her again, a deep kiss rife with longing. How could he wait?—yet he knew he had to. He pressed a finger against her lips. "Don't say anything. I'll call you tomorrow. Are you all right alone?"

"Millie will be back this evening. I'll be fine."

He opened the door and got out, walking to his own car. Tessa signaled and steered the Saab into the street. Although she tried to deny it, she couldn't suppress the warm feeling of being cherished that filled her as he followed her home. When she turned into the driveway, he tapped his horn and made a U-turn, speeding back toward town.

THE HUNGRY WAIL of a baby filled her head. "Andrew," she whispered. "Where are you?"

The cries intensified, angry shrieks that ripped through her head. "Andrew," she cried, straining to get up. Unseen bonds seemed to hold her, trapping her in whatever place she lay. She struggled helplessly, crying her anguish into space.

The sound faded into a dark void that seethed with wind and rain. She rubbed her hand over her face. It came away wet. Was she crying at last? Her chest ached, and the constriction in her throat told her the tears had again dried up.

She rolled over and squinted against the slanting light from the window. No wind, no rain. Only July sunshine. She sat up abruptly, shaking her head against the wave of dizziness that sent the room spinning around her. She'd been asleep for hours; she'd only meant to lie down for a few minutes.

The phone rang. She snatched the receiver to her ear. "Yes?"

She heard only the hollow non-sound of an open line. "Say something, damn you."

A crackle of static, and then a weird, low voice making the words sound as if they were dragged through tar. "If you want to know what happened to your baby, come to the mill at ten tonight."

"What? What do you know about my baby?"

Before she finished the question, the voice interrupted. "Be there. Ten tonight. Come alone."

"Wait—" she cried desperately, but the phone went dead.

Her stomach cramped as if an eagle had buried its talons in her midsection. Clammy sweat popped out on her forehead. She ran for the bathroom. When her stomach was empty, she lay huddled on the floor. The tiles felt cool against her cheek, and for a moment she gave in to the urge to close her eyes and just drift.

Andrew. She sat up, struggled to her feet. Turning on the cold water tap, she splashed her face and rinsed her mouth. Water splattered against her nightgown. Clumsily she twisted the tap off.

She groped for her toothbrush. Most of the toothpaste she squeezed out plopped into the sink.

Her movements awkward and uncoordinated, she managed to stick the brush into her mouth and scrub it back and forth. She rinsed again, then drank a glass of cold water.

Alternate hot and cold flashes chased through her body. Her skin felt sticky, the nightgown clinging to her breasts and hips. Stripping it off, she stepped under the shower.

The stream of water temporarily drowned out her thoughts, but they flooded back as soon as she turned it off. Andrew. Where was he? Was the caller on the level? The voice had been creepy, like a recording played at too slow a speed. Fresh nausea roiled in her stomach.

No, she wasn't going to give in to it. She pulled on the robe hanging on the back of the bathroom door, bundling up in the soft velour.

She had to call Dr. Ivers. Praying he was home, she dialed his number. He answered at once, listening intently to her symptoms. "Sounds like stress, not a relapse," he said. "I'll come down and have a look if you want."

"I thought doctors didn't make house calls," Tessa said

in a halfhearted attempt at a joke. If she thought about Andrew and the caller, she would start screaming and never stop.

"Anyone I delivered gets special treatment," Dr. Ivers said. "I'll be there shortly."

Tessa went downstairs. The kitchen was deserted. Millie hadn't returned. Tessa opened the fridge door. Plenty of cold cuts, lettuce, tomatoes, green onions. Even though the thought of food made her stomach churn again, she knew she had to eat to keep up her strength. She would fix something once Dr. Ivers had examined her, if he gave her the okay.

The chime of the doorbell announced his arrival. She opened the door and let him in. He looked her critically up and down, placing his hand under her chin and tilting her face to the light. "A bit pale but at least you're on your feet. Though you probably shouldn't be. I told you that you had to take it slow, didn't I?"

"I have been."

He snorted. "Yes. And I suppose it's your double who's been driving all over town." He took her arm. "Come along, then. Let's see what's going on with your stomach."

She lay down on the living-room sofa while he listened to her chest, checked her head wound, and took her blood pressure. He grunted as he read the monitor. "A little elevated. No surprise, the tension you've been under."

He glanced around the room. "All alone, are you?"

"For the moment. Millie is due back later. Is there any reason why I shouldn't be alone?"

"Not as far as your injuries are concerned. But your state of mind, that might be another thing." He palpated her stomach and abdomen, nodding as she winced at a tender spot. "Just as I thought, too much stress. You'll have an ulcer if you're not careful. I can give you a prescription if you want."

She pulled the robe closed around her. "No. I need my mind to be clear."

He frowned slightly. "The meds won't affect your mind."

"Still—"

"You'd rather tough it out." He smiled gently, patting her shoulder. "Just try not to beat yourself up over Andrew. Whatever happened isn't your fault. I hear the police are looking for him, that he wasn't killed in the accident."

Please, God, let it be true. A pang of doubt stabbed her heart but she pushed it away, lifting her chin. "That's what we're hoping. That someone made a mistake that night."

"Are you still saving your milk?"

"Yes," she said, her tone a little defensive.

"I could tell you that when Andrew shows up, it won't hurt him to drink formula but I know you won't listen. Just don't break your heart over this."

The words twisted in her soul. "My heart is already broken. I need Andrew back."

"We all want Andrew back," Dr. Ivers said. "But making yourself ill is not going to hurry the process." He packed his stethoscope back into his bag and snapped it closed. "Rest and let Millie pamper you. And eat regularly. You're too thin. Let your friend Nick do the legwork. Even when you feel well, you have to be careful not to overdo. Concussions are no joke."

"Don't I know it," she muttered. She stood up and shook Dr. Ivers' hand. "Thank you for coming out."

"My pleasure." He paused at the door. "Just remember, eat and rest."

She made herself a sandwich and managed to choke down half of it. The rest she wrapped and returned to the fridge. She glanced at the clock. Nine-fifteen. The garden lay bathed in the golden light of sunset.

In half an hour she would leave for the mill. It was a ten-minute drive away, but arriving early would give her a chance to look for whatever vehicle her caller might be driving, which could identify him or her.

Come alone. The instructions were clear. She couldn't tell anyone. On the other hand, she wasn't about to run into danger like the reckless heroine of a Gothic novel. Pulling out the phone book, she looked up the number of the hotel. Her fingers shaking, she dialed it. "Mr. Marcopoulos's room, please."

"I'm sorry. Mr. Marcopoulos checked out several days ago."

"Oh." She stood there for a moment. "Uh, did he leave a number where he can be reached?"

"I'm sorry, madam. He didn't."

She swallowed down her disappointment. "All right. Thank you."

She called the two motels at the edge of town. No Nick Marcopoulos registered. Where was he staying?

Wait a minute. Hadn't he given her one of his business cards the other day? Going upstairs, she checked the pocket of the jeans she'd worn. There it was. Her heart sank when she saw the Montreal number. That wouldn't do her any good when he was here.

She was about to toss down the card when she saw the number scrawled on the reverse side, and recognized the local exchange.

Puzzling over where he might be staying, she punched out the numbers. Four rings and then his deep voice washed through her. *I'm not available at the moment but please leave a message.*

He wasn't there. For an instant, disappointment made her weak. But then she rallied. At least he couldn't try to talk her out of going.

She had to let him know, though. She held her forehead, thinking how she could word this. She didn't intend to be alone with a madman but on the other hand, she didn't want Nick to go charging in like an old-fashioned knight to interfere with the meeting, when the voice had admonished her to come alone.

She spoke into the phone. "Meet me at the mill at ten-thirty. Be careful." That seemed a reasonable compromise, she decided. She'd be finished with the caller by then. And if something went wrong, Nick would hopefully be there to bail her out if necessary.

She threw off the robe and pulled on jeans and a sturdy cotton shirt. She put her driving license and a handful of coins in her pockets. In case she had to run or fight, she didn't want a purse to get in her way.

Going back down, she shoved her feet into soft-soled sneakers and laced them up. The kitchen was dark and silent, and no light leaked from under Millie's door. She hadn't returned, which meant Tessa didn't have to explain this late excursion. No matter how convincingly she lied, Millie was bound to object.

Tessa went out to the garage and started the car, deciding to leave now, even if it was early, before anyone could stop her. After all, Nick might get the message at any time and come racing over to see what was wrong.

SHE PARKED HER CAR a block from the mill, behind an auto body shop, so that it was hidden from the street. Walking slowly along the perimeter fence, she kept to the shadows, avoiding the orange pools of light cast by street lamps. The industrial area near the river was deserted at this time of night. Although a pink glow still stained the western sky, overhead it was dark, an indigo expanse pricked with stars.

Reaching the gate, she paused. How was her caller planning to get into the compound, or had he meant for her to wait for him outside? The gate was locked, although she had a key. She ran her gaze up the eight-foot chain-link fence. Even a mildly athletic person could probably climb it.

On the other hand, perhaps he had counted on her to

leave the gate open for him. Thoughts of Andrew burgeoned within her. She had to meet this person. However risky it was, she couldn't let even the smallest clue pass by.

She inserted her key into the padlock and twisted it. The heavy metal loop fell open. She pushed the two halves of the gate far enough apart to slip between them, pushing them together again so that they appeared closed.

The yard was dark, the only illumination coming from security lights mounted on the outside of the sawmill building in the distance. She walked slowly between the stacks of lumber. The pungency of cedar filled the night. Nearby, a sprinkler hissed as it dampened piles of shakes, the sibilance drowning out any outside noise. A trio of bats swooped and dipped in front of her, their high-pitched squeaks piercing the air.

She moved closer to the buildings, pausing at the stairway leading to the offices above the work areas and warehouses. One of the bulbs on the double light fixture above the office door at the top was burned out, leaving most of the stairs in the dark. She sat down on the second step, crouched against the uprights holding the banister. The person meeting her would have to be very close before he would be able to see her in the dark clothes she wore.

The rumble of a car going by on the street carried to her above the hissing water. She held her breath, waiting to hear whether it would stop, come through the gates. No, the sound faded, leaving only the rhythmic swish of the sprinklers.

She moved her arm out into the light and squinted at her watch. Three minutes after ten. The sky was completely dark, moonless. The night had cooled, mist from the wet wood hanging in the air like fog and condensing on her face and hands. She shivered, hugging her arms around her.

Wait. She lifted her head, straining her ears. Was that

the squeak of the gate hinges? Damn the sprinklers, acting like white noise, deadening sound.

An indefinable rustle brought her gaze up to a high stack of lumber at the corner of the warehouse. Had she seen a shadow move? Why would anybody be up there?

A chunk of wood fell off the pile, thudding to the hard-packed ground. She jumped, her heart stopping, then going on at double speed.

She slid off the steps and ducked in behind them, her eyes peering fearfully through the pattern of light and darkness, trying to discern whether there was another human prowling the yard.

A cat squalled irritably and leaped down from the stacked lumber, stalking across the yard. It paused and looked toward her, eyes gleaming red. Gathering its muscles, it launched itself at another lumber pile, probably in pursuit of a mouse.

Ten minutes ticked by, marked by the hiss of the sprinklers and the low-pitched hum from the nearest security light mounted high on a pole.

He wasn't coming. Disappointment rose bitterly in her throat, and she gasped as another cramp knotted her stomach. She half rose from her hiding place, preparing to cross the yard to the gate when a sharp crack split the night.

Something whistled by her head, pinging against a shovel that hung on the corner of the building. Tessa threw herself flat on the ground, disbelief momentarily overcoming fear.

A shot. Someone was shooting at her. She lay still, hardly breathing. Was that the scuffle of footsteps across the yard? The scent of dust and creosote from the building foundations tickled her nostrils. She squirmed deeper into the shadows. Beneath her ear the ground vibrated. Machinery? Impossible, since nothing should be running at this time of night. More likely a car.

The gates clanged violently. Tires squealed and a car

engine revved to maximum. Tessa lifted her head. Head-lights stabbed her eyes. The car wasn't leaving as she had expected.

It was coming toward her, engine howling like a beast of prey.

Chapter Eleven

Tessa tensed in the deep black shadows, ready to leap out of the way if the driver spotted her. In case she was still a target. Overworked tires shrieked as the car spun around at the last possible second before it would have collided with the stairs. She'd never seen such a move outside of the movies. Tessa's mouth dropped open, amazement driving out her terror as she recognized the vehicle.

She scrambled to her feet, sprinting to the car and jerking open the passenger door. She launched herself into the seat, nearly hitting Nick who sat behind the wheel. Slamming the door, she unreeled the seat belt and clicked it into place.

"Boy, am I ever glad to see you," she gasped, finding the breath to speak at last.

He scowled at her. Oh-oh, she was in for it now. "How did you know it was me in the car?" he snarled. "You might have checked before you jumped in."

"I know your car. And I left you a message."

"Meet me at the mill?" he said sarcastically. "What kind of a message is that?" He slammed the car to a stop outside the open gate. "Give me your key."

She fumbled in her pocket, dragging the keys out. He snatched them from her hand. "What if there's still someone inside?" Tessa asked shakily, the adrenaline high fading.

"I doubt if he hung around. Don't move." Leaving the car running, he opened the door and got out. He left it ajar as he strode over to the gates, pulled them closed and snapped the padlock into place.

He dangled the keys from his fingers as he got back into the car. "Didn't need them after all. Where's your car?"

"Next street." Slumping down in the seat, she pointed to the left.

"Will it be safe there until morning?"

"What? I suppose so." She sat up, pushing away the fog in her brain. "I need my car. You can't leave it there."

"Wanna bet?" He shifted into a higher gear and sped down the street. "I don't see it."

"Behind the body shop. I'm not stupid enough to leave it in full view of the street."

"Not stupid." He gave a humorless bark of a laugh. "Not stupid? Going by yourself to a deserted lumber mill doesn't exactly show Mensa intelligence."

"I left a message."

"Yeah, a message. Lucky thing I got it before you were in serious trouble."

"Somebody shot at me," she said in a small voice. Suddenly feeling limp and washed out, she huddled lower in the worn leather seat.

"No kidding? Why do you think I slammed those gates open so hard? If they'd been locked I would have driven through them." He tapped her temple with a rigid forefinger. "Tessa, you must have been out of your mind."

Anger cleared her mind as effectively as a dash of cold water in the face. "I had a call. Someone who said they would tell me what happened to Andrew. I called you. You weren't there. And he said to come alone. I didn't want you coming around until after I'd talked to him."

"You're sure it was a man."

She shook her head, frowning. "No, actually it could have been a woman. The voice was distorted, as if they'd taped it and slowed down the tape. Sophie and I used to play with a tape recorder when we were kids. We could make ourselves sound like a man in a deep cave, which of course struck us as hilarious.'' She smiled a little at the memory. ''It's easy to do.''

She realized she was babbling when she heard Nick's impatient intake of breath. She snapped her mouth shut. ''So the instructions this person gave you could have been a recording?'' he asked.

''Yes,'' she said. ''I'm almost certain it was.''

''But he didn't show up. Or had he come and gone before the shot?''

''He didn't come. Unless—'' Her blood chilled at the possibility.

Nick took his eyes off the road long enough to give her a hard stare. ''Unless it was a trap to lure you where he could kill you.''

''Well, he missed,'' Tessa said smartly.

''This time. Next time you might not be so lucky.'' He turned down a side street and brought the car to a stop in front of a featureless three-story apartment building.

Tessa peered out of the window. ''Where are we?''

''My place.''

She gaped at him. ''You've got a place of your own? I thought you were staying at the hotel but they told me you checked out.''

''I rented this apartment.'' The hard edge in his voice puzzled her but she forgot it as he added, ''I'll give Millie a call, let her know where you are, but I think it's safer for you to stay here tonight. Whoever shot at you won't know to look for you here.''

TESSA GAZED around the sparsely furnished apartment while he made the call. Two leather chairs with matching footstools occupied the living area. In the far corner, next to the tiny kitchen, a table held a draftsman's frame, a number of rolled-up documents and a laptop computer. A pizza box rested beside the equipment, precariously balanced on the edge of the table. She went over and laid her hand on the box. Still warm.

The sound of the phone hitting its cradle brought her attention back to Nick. He stood leaning against the wall, his arms crossed over his broad chest.

"Your dinner, I presume," she said inanely. "You had pizza for lunch, too."

He shot her a look. "So? I like pizza. I was working and went out for a walk to clear my head, realized I hadn't eaten and waited while the shop down the street made a pizza. When I got back, I got your message and went straight there." He walked toward her, fists clenching and unclenching at his sides. "Tessa, why the hell didn't you at least call Larry?"

"Why didn't you?" Tessa backed away from the threat in his posture. Not that he would hurt her. No, it was more that she couldn't let herself give in to the urge to hurl herself into his arms and just hold on. Stiffening her spine, she warily increased the distance between them.

"Because I didn't want to waste time explaining. You know cops. They have to have a reason to call out a car. Besides, he might not have been on duty."

He came closer. Pressed against the wall, she had no place to retreat. "Eat your dinner, Nick." She nervously ran her tongue over her lips.

"Later." He stopped before her and braced a hand on either side of her head, flattening his palms against the wall. The spicy scent of him seeped into her pores and she let her eyes fall closed. She didn't want to hide anymore. She needed him to kiss her, to let her lose herself in his passion.

His mouth came down on hers, soft and tender, surprising her. The tension in him remained but it was firmly tamped down, as if he wouldn't allow it to break free.

"Don't you ever scare me like that again," he muttered, his warm breath feathering her lips.

Her eyes widened at the tremor in his voice.

She'd tried to ignore the delicious heat that ran through her when he kissed her, tried to deny the satisfaction of knowing he wanted her. Her lips parted in a sigh.

He took her mouth like a conqueror staking a claim. She sucked in a quick, shocked breath, and then gave in to the pleasure that was at once strange and familiar. Familiar because she remembered the taste and scent of him. Strange because he was subtly different from last summer.

He didn't hold back as he had then. It was as if the dam had burst during their separation, annihilating the restraints around his emotions.

Not that he hadn't been a wonderful, passionate lover. Quite the contrary. Physically, he'd been perfect, a man who wasn't afraid to show her a deep masculine sensuality, but she'd sensed that for him it hadn't gone much beyond the physical. Dazzled by her own instant infatuation—it must have been only that, she'd decided later—she hadn't stopped to analyze what was missing until later. But she knew that missing ingredient had been a factor in their final quarrel, the certainty that he wasn't ready to give her what she needed.

She wondered now whether it was simply that he hadn't come to terms with the deaths of his wife and daughter. Had he now? She struggled to think, but the feel of his lips moving hotly on hers, his tongue demanding entrance, stole her breath and drove out rationality.

She strained closer, angling her head to receive him, to taste him deeply, to forget.

And to remember.

Hot. Wet. She recalled the night they'd sneaked out to the hotel pool and gone swimming, just the two of them, near naked bodies touching and retreating, lazily circling, until they were both so crazy with passion they'd barely made it back to their room in time. Their passion had exploded, expanded until it encompassed both of them, fusing them into one and sending them soaring to a plane where only they existed. Coming down to earth to sleep, lying bonded in each other's arms.

That was the last night.

Cold reality drenched her. "No." Although the word came out as a breathless gasp, she pushed hard against his chest. "No, Andrew is still missing and we can't do this."

His eyes narrowed as he looked down at her. He kept his hands at her waist. She could still feel his arousal against her thigh. "Sooner or later we will," he said with such absolute conviction that she shivered.

She knew it, too. She wouldn't let him go before she experienced once again that rush to ecstasy that only he had awakened in her.

But not now.

"Take me home, Nick. I'll be okay."

His hands slid down, molding her hips before falling away. "Stay," he said. "Just for tonight. I wouldn't be able to sleep, worrying about you if you went home."

He took her hand and led her down the hall. To his bed, the only one in the flat. The bed was covered with a furry throw, slightly wrinkled, as if he'd made the bed in a hurry that morning. "All yours," he said. "I'll change the sheets if you like."

Exhaustion suddenly caught up with her, the adrenaline drain after the fear and tension in the lumberyard. She gave up. "No, it'll be fine. It's not as if—" She broke off, mortified. After all the trouble she'd gone to to avoid referring to last summer, she'd almost let it out.

"No, it's not," Nick said, his voice laced with satisfaction. The look in his eyes was dark and sensual, and she shivered again, wrapping her arms around her chest to hide the involuntary ripples that chased over her skin. "Good night."

She swallowed, unable to speak. "Wait," she finally choked out as he reached the door. "Where are you going to sleep?"

His mouth quirked up at the corner. "Why, are you telling me you actually care?"

"I—I don't want to put you out."

He came back, ran his knuckles over her cheekbone. "Don't worry. You won't. Just sleep now and don't worry about anything. We'll get Andrew back."

She closed her eyes, sending up a frantic little prayer. "I hope so. I hope so."

When she opened her eyes a moment later, he was gone. As she walked to the bathroom, she could hear the faint tick of his computer keyboard.

She hoped he would remember to eat.

AN HOUR LATER she still lay awake, her burning eyes staring up at the ceiling. She closed them but they popped open again, as if her eyelids were mounted on springs. Her body screamed with exhaustion, muscles aching and nerves twitching as if they were hooked up to a live wire. Her brain wouldn't let her rest.

Who had called her, and did they really have news of Andrew? Had the gunman scared them off? Or was her caller the gunman?

Gun man? Or woman? In their town, plenty of people owned hunting rifles, and were good shots, women as well as men.

Why had she been shot at? To kill her? Or just to scare her? Didn't they know she would be all the more determined to find Andrew if she thought he was in danger? Didn't they know that no mother would put her own life and safety ahead of that of her child?

Light slanted into the room through the half-open door. She turned toward it, comforted by the knowledge that Nick was out there. Her protector. She smiled. She didn't need a knight but she couldn't help embracing the feeling of being cherished.

The pillow smelled of him, clean man and spicy soap or shampoo. She shouldn't get used to it, but just for a moment she indulged herself. Last summer, she'd thought they had forever. Now— It didn't matter, as long as she got Andrew back. She would sort out this—this thing with Nick later.

She inhaled deeply, her mind calm at last.

THE RAIN BEAT against her face. An owl hooted, the sound hollow and lonely. She saw a white shape lying under a dripping tree and stumbled toward it. A blanket. "Andrew," she cried.

She lifted the blanket. Empty. It flapped in the wind.

She woke, tears on her cheeks, and a sensation of warmth at her back. "What? What are you doing here?"

Nick lay beside her, his arm around her waist as he tucked her back against his front. "You had a bad dream. Shhh, just let me hold you."

She wanted to tell him to get out, to leave her alone, but the comfort of his arms overwhelmed her. Just for a moment, she would let him stay. She drifted back into sleep, restful and dreamless.

SHE WOKE when the sun cast a hot beam across her face. Muttering irritably, she burrowed under the sheet. The scent of spice and Nick filled her head. She sat up abruptly, suddenly realizing she wasn't in her own bed.

Nick. Where was he? Tentatively, she moved her hand to the other side of the bed. Cold. She shook her head, trying to make sense of hazy memories. Had he really been there in the night, holding her against the demons that taunted her in her dreams? Or had the warmth and murmured words been just another dream?

She got up and dressed, grimacing as she pulled on her

eans and shirt from last night. A dark stain decorated one knee, sticky to her touch. Tar or creosote. She needed to get home, shower and change.

She found a note on the kitchen table, written in his broad scrawl. "Back soon. I'm getting donuts so don't eat. Nick."

She smiled. Just like him. No sentiment. Just straightforward business. The smile softened. He had come to her in the night, given her the gift of restful sleep. He had promised to find Andrew. What would happen after that he didn't know. The present moment was enough.

He came in, smelling of fresh air. "Wind coming up," he said. "I think it might storm."

The bag he carried gave off the heady aroma of hot oil, cinnamon, and honey. She peeked inside as he set it on the counter. "Oh, crullers."

A tiny smile played about his lips. "I remember." The deep timbre of his voice poured over her, sweet as hot syrup. A flush heated her face and she ducked her head to hide it, taking one of the crullers and biting into it.

She rolled her eyes. "Better than I remember."

"Oh, I don't know." Amusement sparking in his eyes, he kept his gaze fixed on her. Her flush deepened as she realized he was remembering one morning when they'd eaten crullers and then gone back to bed, the soft sheets having more appeal than going out into the rain. Of course they'd done very little sleeping. They'd been insatiable.

They'd been crazy. Or rather, she had, to believe they might have a future. The future had lasted exactly one month.

She supposed she should be grateful. She'd gotten Andrew.

A little hiccup hitched her throat and the amusement drained away. She'd lost Andrew.

Nick saw the pain that made her expression bleak. "We'll check out the clinic today."

The cruller turned to lead in her stomach. "Larry said he's going."

"I want to see for myself. We can't just wait for Larry."

"What about the shooting last night?" Tessa said. "We should have reported it."

"Yeah, then you would have been standing around there another hour while the cops searched the place and asked innumerable questions. And the gunman was long gone by then. From the lumber piles, it's easy to get over the fence and away."

He bit into a cruller, chewed, and swallowed as he poured coffee into two mugs. He brought her one, and pushed the sugar bowl across the table. Tessa dumped a couple of teaspoons into her cup and stirred it. She drank, welcoming the rush of caffeine and glucose. "We have to pick up my car."

"Yeah. We can swing by there on our way and drop it off at your house. I wouldn't mind checking out the yard."

"NOT MUCH TO SEE, was there?" Tessa said disgustedly as they walked back to Nick's car half an hour later.

"We know he used a real bullet," Nick said grimly. "You could see the scratch on the shovel where it ricocheted. I doubt if Larry's going to find much of interest."

"At least he didn't insist we wait for him."

They drove down the block to the body shop where Tessa had left her car. She nodded at the body shop owner whom she vaguely remembered from high school. "I was about to call you," he said. "Did you have trouble with it?"

Tessa shook her head. "No. I just needed a safe place to park. How did you know it was my car?"

He shrugged. "Everyone knows your car."

She guessed that was probably true, a mildly exotic European sedan in a world of Blazers and Rangers.

"You must know everyone in town," Nick observed as she unlocked the car door.

"I've lived here all my life. Which car are we taking to the clinic?"

"Mine, if you don't mind. I'll drive. You still need more rest than you're getting."

"Okay," she said, so calmly his gaze sharpened. She looked better this morning, more determined than ever. "Today. Maybe we'll find out today who took him."

AT THE HOUSE, Tessa hugged Millie, who'd been waiting anxiously by the door when she drove up. "Are you all right?" Millie asked, searching Tessa's face for signs of a relapse. "I was worried when I got your note. At least until Nick called."

"I'm sorry," Tessa said. "I should have explained."

"And you're off again, now?" Millie clasped her hands together against her chest. "Oh, I do hope you find the wee laddie."

"We'll find him," Nick said. He gave Tessa a little push. "Why don't you go change? The sooner you're ready, the sooner we can get going."

She'd showered and dressed in clean jeans and T-shirt when the phone rang. For a second she debated letting Millie pick it up but then she remembered her caller last night. "Yes?"

"Tessa, I finally got you. I've been trying to call you, to tell you I'll be out of town a few days longer, but either I get Millie or there's no answer."

"I'm sorry, Sophie," Tessa said contritely. "I should have called you."

"I guess that means there's been no news about Andrew." Sophie's voice shook, as if she held back tears.

"I'm afraid not," Tessa said gently.

Sophie made a sound that Tessa couldn't interpret. "You should have let me look after him that weekend instead of taking him up to the cabin in the storm. I wouldn't have minded."

Tessa frowned. Had they talked about her going alone when she'd seen Sophie that afternoon? She couldn't remember but they might have. But, she reminded herself, she wouldn't have gone up to the cabin alone. She wouldn't have left Andrew, not even with Sophie. "I'll get back to you later, Sophie. We're just on our way out now."

"With Nick, I suppose," Sophie said. "Watch out, Tessa. You know what I said last fall about rebound relationships. You can't trust them. But I know you won't listen anyway. Be sure you call. Leave a message if I'm not home. And good luck."

"That was Sophie," she said to Nick who waited by the door.

"I gathered that."

Tessa rubbed the healing wound on her temple. "You know what I want to do? When we finish at the clinic, I want to go up to the cottage. A lot of that evening is still a blank. Maybe if I see it, I'll remember something."

"Yeah, we can do that," Nick agreed. "As long as you feel up to it."

THE CLINIC, a small white stucco building, stood at the edge of a logging camp, bathed in afternoon sun. The waiting room was empty as they entered. A young woman in a white smock sat behind the desk, talking on the phone. Spotting them, she said, "Gotta go. Talk to you later."

She hung up the receiver. "May I help you?"

"Maybe," Nick said. "Were you working Friday before last?"

"Let me see." She paged back in the appointment book in front of her. "Yes, I was. Oh, that was the night we stayed open late. A schoolbusload of children coming back from a nature trip hit a fallen tree and some of the kids were brought here."

"There was another accident that night?" Tessa said incredulously. Why hadn't someone told her?

"Nobody was seriously hurt. Just cuts and bruises but it kept us going for a while, I'll tell you. And no one had time to write up everything in detail. That's why the records of that night are pretty sketchy." She looked up at them, her brown eyes round and ingenuous. "I already explained it all to Constable West. He came to my house yesterday."

So Larry had been on the job, Tessa thought gratefully, even though it was probably his day off.

"Do you remember someone bringing in a baby?" Nick asked urgently.

"A baby?" The girl frowned. "There were two babies here that night."

"Two babies?" Nick and Tessa looked at each other in disbelief. Was that how it had happened? Had someone taken home the wrong baby? No, there was still the phony death certificate and the obituary notice.

It couldn't be that simple.

"Yes. I thought they were both from the bus accident. Several parents were with the children."

"Was either of them hurt?" Nick asked. "Who looked after them?"

"I'm not sure." She glanced down at the book. "Probably Jane. She was on duty that night."

"And which doctor?"

"Dr. Pankratz."

"Is either of them in today?"

"Jane is. But Dr. Pankratz is on holidays."

"Could we see Jane?" Nick asked, the edginess in his tone doing a poor job of hiding his impatience.

"I guess." The girl looked toward the closed door at the back of the office. "Just have a seat and I'll call her."

Jane was a plump motherly woman in her forties, her round face surrounded by a mop of red hair. "Yes, we had two babies here that night, both boys, neither of them se-

riously injured. They were wet and cold and we did wha
we could.''

"Do you remember one of them wearing a silver bracelet?" Tessa asked anxiously.

Jane frowned. "I'm not sure. We were so busy—there
were two of us and Dr. Pankratz on duty, and a couple of
nursing aides we happened to have in for a training course
that day. After I checked the babies, I left them to one of
the aides. By the time I'd looked after the other children
both babies were gone, taken, I presume, by their parents.''

"You didn't see who took them?" Nick said.

Her brow wrinkled. "I'm really sorry. I heard one of the
mothers say she'd pick up her child and I saw her walk
out.''

New despair tightened Tessa's chest. "Have the police
contacted you?"

"Yes, of course," Jane said quickly. "Larry West called
about half an hour ago. I told him what I'm telling you
Your baby could have been brought here but I'm not sure
When Larry talked to me just now, that was the first I knew
about a car going off the road as well. It was a terrible
night. We were just praying the power wouldn't go off.''

"What about the log for that night?" Tessa asked. "You
do keep records, don't you?"

"They're a bit sparse for that night, I'm afraid. We didn't
get everyone's name. We were all patching up bruised children." She rummaged through a file on her desk. "No, the
babies' names aren't listed.''

She looked up, her eyes sympathetic. "The baby with
the bracelet was yours, was he? I'm sorry I can't tell you
more. All I know is that after the doctor checked him, the
woman who brought him in took him away.''

Tessa clenched her fists until her nails dug into her
palms. "He was all right then?" She could hardly force
the words through her tight throat. She glanced at Nick
when he took one of her hands, unclenched it and laced his

fingers through hers. She clutched at him as if she were drowning. "Was my baby alive?"

"Yes, definitely," Jane said. "In fact, when they came in, both babies were howling their heads off."

"Then you let some stranger walk off with my baby." Tessa's voice rang through the stark office.

Jane shifted uncomfortably. "It wasn't intentional, let me assure you. She brought him in. We had no way of knowing the woman wasn't his mother."

"She wasn't. I'm his mother," Tessa cried. Nick wrapped his arm around her shoulders and she gulped, struggling for control.

"Can you describe this woman?" Nick asked.

"As I told Larry, no. She was wearing a dark raincoat with a hood. I didn't get a good look at her. Wait, I'll call Lisa in and see if she remembers any more."

Lisa shook her head. "Dark raincoat with a hood. That's all I remember. Oh, something else. She seemed a very good mother. She was cuddling him and singing to him when she went out."

"What about the woman's car?"

Jane and Lisa exchanged glances. "I couldn't tell you," Jane said. "Once they went out the door, that was it." Her round face was creased with dismay. "I'm really sorry your baby's missing, but I don't know what we could have done differently."

"Yes, I can see how it could have happened," Tessa said slowly, the realization sinking in that someone had deliberately set out to take Andrew, although the abductor had obviously been concerned enough about his welfare to have him checked at the clinic after the accident. A small ray of hope to cling to.

"Is there any way we can reach Dr. Pankratz?" Nick asked.

Jane shook her head. "I'm afraid not. He left last week

on a hiking vacation up north. He won't be back until the end of the month.''

"Who was the other nurse on duty? You said there were two of you."

"That was Mrs. Pankratz. She often comes in to help out."

"And I suppose she's on holiday with her husband."

"I'm afraid so," Jane said regretfully.

What had she expected? Tessa thought dismally. She felt like screaming, but realized it wouldn't do any more good than her earlier outburst. "That must be what Larry meant when he said he couldn't get hold of the doctor," she said tightly. She turned to Jane. "Have you heard of a Dr. Benjamin Forbes?"

"Constable West asked me about him," Lisa said. "I'd never heard of him."

"Yes, it was before you started working here," Jane said. "Larry asked me about him, too. Forbes worked here about three years ago. He only lasted a month. He was a bit of a prig, just out of medical school. Didn't like being out of the city. Last I heard he'd moved down to Los Angeles." She laughed shortly. "I wonder if he now knows when he was well off."

She stepped out from behind the desk and impulsively hugged Tessa. "I'm really sorry about your baby. I hope you find him."

"So do we," Nick said soberly.

At the door, he turned back. "There's something else. Apparently someone from here called Larry and told him the baby had died and was transferred to the funeral home in town. Do you know who that could have been?"

Jane paled. "What a cruel thing to do. But no, no one here would have done anything like that. It's not possible."

Actually, the call could have been made from anywhere, Nick suddenly realized. "Okay, that's all, I guess. Thanks."

"WHAT WAS THAT about a silver bracelet?" Nick asked when they were in the car.

Tessa glanced at him. "It was a birth gift from my dad, with Andrew's name engraved on it. He was wearing it that night."

"So that could have been used to ID him," Nick said thoughtfully. "But it doesn't appear to be in the police report."

"It hardly seems to matter now. We know he didn't die." Elation should have filled her but instead she felt only intense frustration. "Some stranger took him. Now we'll never find him," she added bitterly.

"We know more than we did before. We know it was a woman. We know she's probably taking good care of him. And we know all the funeral stuff must have been to cover up the abduction. Which points to someone who wanted a child. To keep him."

"Well, I'm not going to let her get away with it."

Nick squeezed her hand. "*We* won't. We're in this together, Tessa. Don't forget it." He slowed the car at a fork in the road. "Do you still want to go up to the cottage?"

"Oh." Tessa looked at the surrounding forest as if she didn't realize they'd been moving. "Yes, it's not far. Turn right here, then right again. The cabin's set on a knoll in the trees; you'll see it in a moment."

Moments later he braked in front of a rustic log house overlooking the river. It was much more elaborate than the average summer cottage, Nick noted. And well cared for. The lawn, dotted with pink clover, had been mowed only days ago. Purple, blue, and yellow pansies tumbled over the edges of brick planters.

"Nice place," Nick said.

They got out of the car, inhaling the sharp scent of pine and the subtle, almost salty aroma of the river. A woodpecker drilled in the woods, a steady tap-tap-tap. Somewhere, far away, a dog barked.

A low rumble drew Tessa's attention toward the sky. A bank of angry, blue-black clouds massed in the west. Lightning stitched a jagged path across them.

She started at the clouds, an odd sense of déjà vu pervading her being. "I know why I wanted to come up here that weekend," she said slowly. "To look for Dad's will."

"Oh?" Nick's brows lifted.

"Yes. Now I remember. Alexander and I were talking the day before and we realized the only place we hadn't looked for it was here, at the cottage."

"Well, let's get at it," Nick said.

Despite the gathering storm, sunlight spilled through high windows as Tessa unlocked the door and let them into the cottage. Dust motes danced before them, shimmering like fairy dust.

Hot, muggy air rushed in after them, borne on a fitful wind that smelled of ozone and electricity. Tessa felt the familiar tightness at her temples and clammy sweat trickled down her neck.

She walked into the kitchen and turned on a tap, letting the water run cold. Soaking a paper towel she held it against her face, welcoming the coolness. She breathed deeply and cupped her hand under the tap to drink.

Wiping her hands, she flipped up the trash can lid to toss away the towel, and froze.

"N-N-Nick." The word caught in her throat. "L-l-look." He followed the line of her pointing finger to the bottom of the plastic bag lining the can.

In it lay the unmistakable bulk of a discarded diaper.

Chapter Twelve

"Who has a key to this cabin?" Nick asked tersely. He stared at her pale face, and wrapped his arms around her. Resting his cheek on top of her head, he softly nuzzled her hair. "Hold on, Tessa. You know what this means, don't you? Someone brought him here. This is the first real lead we've had."

She was shaking, a fine tremor that echoed in his own body. "You're sure it's his diaper," he added.

He felt her nod. "Pretty sure. The pattern of teddy bears. It may be common enough but who else's could it be?" She looked up at him, her eyes filled with anguish. "We have to find him."

"We will." He pulled out a chair from the table and pressed his hand on her shoulder. "Sit down for a moment." He carefully lifted the white trash bag out of the step-on can and dropped it into a clean bag, fastening the top with a wire twist tie. "Who has a key?"

"I'm not sure. My dad came up here much more often than I did."

"Have you ever brought Andrew here?"

Tessa shook her head. "That night the car crashed would have been the first time."

"Then who planted those flowers out front?"

"Oh, we have a yard service who come by to cut the grass and take care of the garden."

"But they don't have a key?"

"I don't think so, although the old man down the road used to have one to check that there weren't any leaks, that kind of thing, when we didn't come here for a while."

"We'll check it out."

A clap of thunder shook the cabin, rattling glass in the window panes. Tessa jumped. Nick steadied her, glancing toward the window. "Looks like we're in for it."

"We have to call Larry. Maybe he can get some kind of clue from the diaper."

"Maybe," Nick said without much conviction. He didn't think plastic would retain fingerprints. However, Larry would want to know about this.

He picked up the phone and started to punch out the number of the police station, stopping when he realized there was no dial tone. "Well, that tears it. Must be lines down. We'd better leave while we still can."

"But we haven't had a chance to look around. Maybe there's something else."

He studied her closely, gratified to note that color had returned to her cheeks and that her voice was stronger, steady. "Are you sure you feel up to it?"

Gusts rattled the eaves. The front door, through which they'd entered, flew open, crashing against the adjacent wall.

"Damn." Nick ran through the living room and pushed at it, bracing himself against the driving wind. Hard, cold pellets of rain battered his face as he forced it closed, throwing the dead bolt into place.

He turned to find Tessa standing in the middle of the room, eyes staring into some kind of horror only she could see. Heart clenching in his chest, he went over to her and shook her shoulder gently. "Tessa, what is it? What do you see?"

No response. Just those storm-colored eyes like dark holes in her dead white face.

"Tessa," he said urgently. Wrapping his arms around her, he pulled her against his chest. "Tessa, what is it?"

A shudder ran through her. "It's just like that night, thunder, lightning, wind and rain," she said in a low, stark voice. "The night Andrew died."

Nick rubbed his hands up and down her back, wincing at how thin she was, her vertebrae sharp points under her skin. "Tessa, Andrew isn't dead. That diaper proves it. We will find him."

"Yes, we'll find him," she said in a dreamy tone that alarmed him more. "We'll find him."

"We will," he said fiercely. "Someone took him. Someone knows where he is."

She gave a heartrending little sigh and slumped down against him. Exhausted. She'd done far too much today.

He swung her up into his arms and carried her to the long leather sofa, laying her gently down. Her eyes closed and a measure of peace came over her face although the tiny crease above her nose remained.

He knelt beside her and brushed her hair off her forehead. He traced the delicate line of her brow with his finger. Her eyelids were as translucent as shells, blue veins forming an intricate tracery across them. A pulse beat at her temple, more rapidly than he thought was normal. She moaned softly and raised her hand to cover the faint pink scar. Headache, no doubt, souvenir of the concussion.

An errant thought ran through his mind: had he ever just watched her sleep during that passion-drenched month last summer? He guessed not; he'd been too hot for her then. His mouth kicked up at the corner. *They'd* been too hot for each other.

He promised himself that once this was over he would take time to savor the quiet moments.

He was surprised to realize the thought didn't scare him anymore.

The interior of the cabin had cooled considerably with the onset of the storm. He opened doors, looking for spare blankets, at the same time familiarizing himself with the layout. The downstairs consisted of two bedrooms and a bathroom, as well as the kitchen, dining area and large living room. He took a blanket out of the capacious linen closet and covered Tessa with it. She sighed in her sleep and snuggled down on her side, her hands tucked beneath her cheek like a child's.

His throat tight, he left her and climbed the stairs that led to a loft above the kitchen/dining area. The outer section, a comfortably furnished library lined with bookshelves, overlooked the living room. Beyond it lay another bedroom complete with an attached bath that included a huge whirlpool tub. He permitted himself a brief, lush daydream of him and Tessa in that tub, with Andrew sleeping securely in the corner of the bedroom. Tessa happy again.

Shaking off the fantasy, he moved around the bed and looked out the large window toward the back of the house. The driving rain and low clouds gave the effect of an early dusk. The dense forest beyond the lawn selfishly held its shadows. He couldn't tell if there was anything out of place but the antsy feeling he'd had since they'd discovered the phone dead wouldn't leave him.

Going back to the other end of the loft, he flicked the light switch. Nothing happened. So both power and phone were out. They could, of course, still attempt the drive home but, considering Tessa's state of mind and health, he didn't fancy putting her through the trauma of negotiating the treacherous mountain road in a storm.

As if to confirm his decision, a gust of wind shook the house, and rain slammed against the window. No, better to stay put until morning.

The stove ran on gas, he found. He heated a can of soup

from the well-stocked cupboard and made tuna-melts under the broiler. They might as well eat before it got too dark although he discovered a supply of candles and a couple of large flashlights in a drawer.

Lightning slashed through the gathering darkness. The boom of thunder nearly deafened him. When his ears stopped ringing, he heard Tessa cry out.

He ran to her, pulling her against him. Another roll of thunder. Her eyes popped open, filled with comical surprise, not the glazed fear and horror of earlier. "Oh, did I sleep?"

He grinned back at her. "Yes, for several hours."

She struggled to sit up, shaking her tangled hair back off her face. "We have to get going. Get that diaper to Larry."

"Not until morning, I'm afraid," Nick said. "It's too dangerous. It'll be dark soon."

She slumped against the back of the sofa, clenching the edge of the blanket in one hand. "I suppose the phone still isn't working."

Nick shook his head. "And the power's out."

"There should be a lantern on the back porch, in the storage bin. You'll find the keys by the back door."

He went out and found the lantern where she said it would be. Before he went back inside, he stood for a moment on the porch, his eyes searching the woods. Rain pelted down, drumming noisily on the roof. Although it wasn't yet sunset, darkness enveloped the trees. Lightning flickered again, dimly, as if grudging the effort. Another flash of light, out past the trees, caught his eye, gone so quickly he wondered if he'd imagined it.

He remained where he was, straining to pierce the curtain of rain and dusk. Nothing moved except the sway of evergreens in the wind. He shivered as a gust dampened the front of his shirt. Chiding himself for being paranoid, he went inside, locking the door after him.

Tessa emerged from the downstairs bathroom as he came

in. She had washed her face and brushed her hair. The color had returned to her cheeks, although her eyes looked haunted.

"Tessa, is there another road back beyond the woods?"

She wrinkled her brow. "I think so. An old logging track. Off-roaders sometimes use it. Why?"

"I'm not sure. It's not the kind of weather for pleasure driving, but maybe somebody got stuck up there. I thought I saw a light."

"Could have been someone on the road we came up," Tessa said. "It's high here. In the dark, you can see headlights for quite a distance."

He forced the tension out of his shoulders. "Yeah, that must be it." He made himself smile, trying to pretend everything was normal, trying to make his nerves stop jumping.

Actually, if he were honest, he had to admit it wasn't only the possibility that someone might have followed them here that made him tense. It was the realization that he was alone with Tessa, isolated in the cabin. And he couldn't put himself through another night of torture like last night, when he'd slept with her, protecting her, but wanting so much more. Remembering how it had been and wishing they could have that again.

Yet how could he even think of pushing her?

"Come and eat," he said, his voice hoarse. He covered it up with a cough so blatantly fake Tessa gave him an odd look.

He was pleased to see her eat well. Afterward she insisted on washing the dishes. "Are you sure?" he asked. "I'd feel better if you rested."

"Don't make me into an invalid," she said with surprising spirit. "I'm fine now."

"Okay. I'll have a look around now that the rain has let up a bit."

He made a circuit of the cabin, shining the flashlight into

he shadows behind shrubs and planters. The only intruder
ie disturbed was a field mouse whose eyes glinted like
ireflies before it turned and scampered away.

Inside the cabin, he checked all the door and window
ocks, finally returning to the kitchen, satisfied that every-
hing was as secure as he could make it. Tessa stood by
he stove, heating milk in a small saucepan. She smiled at
iim. "Hot chocolate?"

"In July?"

"Why not, on a night like this."

They sat down on opposite sides of the table. Fragrant
team rose from the mugs of hot chocolate. Tessa cradled
iers between her palms, turning the mug this way and that.
Nick pushed his to one side and touched her hand. She
ooked up at him, her eyes soft with curiosity and trust.

Setting down the mug, she let him take her hands in both
of his. "What do we do now?" she asked.

"We find Andrew," he said simply. "We go to the po-
ice and have them put more men on it. I think we've got
nough proof now that he's alive to convince the most
keptical cop. Too bad the clinic records of that night are
o sketchy." He scowled blackly. "I keep thinking there's
omething here we're overlooking."

He pushed her mug closer. "Drink up. Time for bed.
We'll get an early start in the morning."

She gulped down half her chocolate, then set down the
nug. "There's something we have to do first. Since we're
.tuck here, we might as well look around and see if Dad
.tashed his will here. It has to be somewhere."

"Good idea." Maybe that would settle some of his rest-
essness. "Do you want the upstairs or down? There's no
:ellar in this place, is there?"

"No, but there is a small boathouse down by the river,
iot that there are any boats in it. It's used for storage."

"We'll save that until morning," Nick said. "Come to

think of it, maybe we should save all of it until then. The power might be back.''

"No, I don't want to wait. We've got plenty of flash-lights." She drained her mug and took it to the sink and rinsed it. "We'll start down here. You take the bedrooms and I'll do these rooms."

Half an hour later Nick emerged from his search of bed-rooms and closets to find Tessa sitting on the floor holding a photo album. She looked up at him, her eyes shimmering. "I found this upstairs. It's Dad's. It looks like he came here not long before he died. I thought he couldn't drive anymore, but he must have managed somehow. He put this together."

Nick took the book from her and paged through it, shar-ing her emotion as he hadn't when he'd looked through the album at the house. And he felt he knew Andrew so much better now. This was his child, his son. The sleepy-eyed baby wearing a little white toque in the hospital crib. Tessa holding the small dark head to her breast. Farther on, a toothless smile and bright blue eyes. Nick traced the photo with one finger. "He's beautiful, isn't he?" he said, awed almost beyond words.

"Yes, he has your eyes and your hair, black and thick and curly. In fact, the doctors were amazed that a baby so small could have so much hair."

He reached out to cover her hand with his. "I wish I'd been there."

She looked at him, several emotions crossing her face. Her eyes softened and she squeezed his hand. "I wish you had, too."

"So where do we go from here?"

Her gaze slid away. "I don't know."

He turned his attention back to the album. The last ten pages were blank. "He meant to continue this."

"Yes, I'd say so." Her voice hitched. "But he died."

Nick was about to close the book when he realized the last page was not lying flat. "What's this?"

A long white envelope was stuck under the heavy vinyl cover. "Could it be your father's will?"

Tessa took it, her hands shaking. The flap was not glued, merely tucked into the envelope. She pulled it out and extracted the folded paper inside. As she went to put down the envelope a small metal object clattered onto the floor.

"It's for a safe-deposit box," Nick said, holding up the flat brass key.

"That's all?" Disappointment flattened her voice.

She turned the envelope over and shook it. A small slip of paper fell out. She unfolded it, scanning the words. The name and address of a bank. She knew at once it wasn't the one where Joseph had kept his personal and company accounts.

"That must be where he put it."

"Okay. We can check tomorrow."

He rose to his feet, going to the window and adjusting the blinds so that they shut out the night. "I think it's time we were in bed. It's likely to be another long day tomorrow, especially when we're dealing with the police. I suppose you'll want the upstairs bedroom?"

She shook her head, pain in her eyes. "That was always Dad's room. I used one down here. I'm sure some of my things are still in it."

"Okay. You're first in the bathroom. I just want to check the doors and windows once more." He paced through the house, trying to ignore the sound of running water and the image of her naked in the shower. Water running off that silken skin and his mouth licking it up.

He sat on the edge of the sofa, clawing his fingers through his hair. He had no right. Or maybe he had every right. What should he do? He wanted her, needed her, and what better way to show her than to make love to her.

He was the lowest kind of rat. Lusting after a mother grieving for her child.

His child.

When this was over—

He realized the shower had stopped. Moments later he heard the bathroom door open and her bedroom door close. Pushing to his feet, he walked toward the bathroom, pausing briefly to listen outside her room. Not a sound. No light glowed under the door.

She'd left a candle lit in the bathroom, which smelled of soap and shampoo, the familiar vanilla scent that made him long to be with her, inside her.

He took a shower, turning the water to cold at the end, but it did little to discourage his rampant arousal. Wrapping a towel around his waist, he brushed his teeth with a new toothbrush she'd laid out for him.

He paused and listened to the sounds of the house settling when he came out. Rain pattered against the living-room windows. The wind had died as night fell and the storm passed. By morning it would be clear, a gorgeous summer day.

In the bedroom, a fresh sheet and blanket covered the bed. Tessa must have made it up while he'd checked outside the house earlier. The perfect hostess. His mouth twisted.

He opened the window, letting in fresh air scented with pine and rain-washed earth.

Hanging the towel over a chair, he flopped down on the bed, throwing his arm over his eyes. He knew he wouldn't sleep. Too wired.

Andrew was alive. His hunch had been right, but somehow it didn't give him the satisfaction it should have. Where was he now? And why was all this happening? Simple kidnapping? Then why hadn't Tessa been called to pay a ransom? And why had someone shot at her last night?

The questions ran around and around in his head. No answers.

"Nick, I need to be with you."

At first he thought he was dreaming. Blinking, he lifted himself up on one elbow. Tessa stood in the open doorway, ghostly in an oversize T-shirt. The sleeves hung to her elbows, the hem just above her knees. She moved forward and he saw why she had that funny little catch in her voice.

She was crying, shiny tracks of tears just visible in the dim light. His heart flipped in his chest and hung there, aching. He held out his hand, lifting the blanket.

As if she were afraid of second thoughts, she ran across the room and threw herself against him. Her hands clung to him, sharp nails digging into his shoulder. She buried her face against his chest. Her tears soaked his skin, hot as acid. He lay back, holding her as great, racking sobs shook her body.

"That's it, Tessa. Cry. Let it all out. It's about bloody time, isn't it?" His muttered words made little sense and he had to squeeze his own eyes shut to stop himself from joining in her grief.

He winced as she mashed herself to his body, as if she wanted to get inside his skin. One hand tangled painfully in his chest hair. He carefully pried her fingers open and kissed her palm. A forlorn little hiccup erupted from her throat. She pushed her face into the space between his neck and shoulder, her body shaking as if she were in a high wind.

More scalding tears. There seemed no end to them. And they were all the more terrible for being silent. She didn't scream her grief and anger. "This is stupid," he heard her mumble at one point. "First I can't cry. Now I can't stop."

"Doesn't matter. Doesn't matter." He repeated the phrase over and over as he rubbed his palms up and down her back and tried not to think of how she felt draped over his body, with her naked thigh wedged into his groin.

Don't let her notice. Don't let her notice. To distract himself he mentally recited snowload tables for roof joists. It worked, for about three seconds. He wondered how many people knew that Vancouver area houses were built to withstand greater snowloads than any other place in Canada even though snow didn't fall every winter.

Even thoughts of snow didn't cool him down.

The shaking lessened to occasionally shivers. She lay still, her mouth wet against his jaw. "I'm sorry. I shouldn't have come here. I had no right."

"You had every right," he said firmly. He slowly released her as she sat up, stifling a groan when her leg brushed his recalcitrant erection. He should have known that part of him never listened to what he told it.

Fortunately Tessa didn't seem to notice. She tucked her legs under her and used the ends of her voluminous sleeves to wipe her face. She even managed a watery smile.

Then, to his utter shock, she set her hands in the hem of the T-shirt and yanked it up over her head and tossed it to the floor. "Tessa, what are you doing?" he managed to gasp.

As if he didn't know. But he couldn't believe it. Nor did he want her to make a rash move, driven by temporary insanity, and regret it in the morning. "Tessa, you've got to stop," he said desperately.

"No, this time I won't stop." Her eyes, dark as the fleeing storm clouds outside, pleaded with him.

A plea he hadn't the strength to resist. Desire raged through him like an uncontrolled brush fire. Still, he paused and gazed searchingly into her eyes. "Tessa, are you sure?"

She nodded, her eyes glistening with fresh tears. "Yes, Nick, I'm sure. I was wrong. I should have tried harder."

"Tried harder?"

"To find you."

"Doesn't matter now."

All that mattered was the fire burning between them.

Nick pulled her down beside him, uttering a deep sigh as she snuggled against him. Skin to skin, rough to smooth, male to female. Tessa closed her eyes, savoring his texture, his tender touch as his hands began to move over her.

A sliver of moon peeked out from between the clouds and illuminated the bed. Tessa opened her eyes as heated pleasure sizzled through her. Now she could see him as well as feel him, that long, lean body covered in smooth, tanned skin and sprinkled with hair in strategic areas.

She laid her palm on his chest, felt his heartbeat speed up as she brushed her finger over his nipple, half-hidden in silky black chest hair. The heat of his skin seeped into her pores. He smelled deliciously familiar, as if his spicy scent had remained in her memory even after she'd tried to drive him out.

The bedside lamp flared on, bathing them in golden light. They both started, laughing nervously. "Guess I must have put it on without thinking," Nick muttered.

Tessa reached around to turn it off, but Nick stayed her hand. "Please. I want to see you. Leave it on."

For a moment she stiffened. To look at him was one thing, but did she want him to see her, to note the changes pregnancy and birth had made in her body?

He cradled her breast in one hand. Forgetting the light, she uttered a moan of pleasure. He stroked his hand down over her ribs and across her belly, one finger tracing a faint silver mark near her hip.

"From Andrew?" he whispered, leaning over to kiss the spot.

"Yes," she said, a catch in her voice.

"Don't worry. We'll find him."

They lay for a long moment, pressed tightly together, two parents concerned for their child. But soon the banked passion sparked back to life. Nick lifted himself on one elbow and looked down at her. Tenderness softened his eyes, turning them a misty blue. "Do you still want to do this? We can wait for another time if you like."

Tessa sighed. "I started it. I want you. Whether we make love or not, we won't get Andrew back tonight." She caressed the crisp curls at his nape. "Please, Nick, make love with me."

He studied her for a second longer, then nodded. His mouth came down on hers, hot and deep. Tenderness exploded into passion. Her breath grew ragged, her body soft and pliant. She suddenly understood the emptiness she'd felt since the last time she'd held him. No one could fill that void. Only Nick.

"Tessa," he groaned, raining kisses on her throat, her breasts, her belly, as if he couldn't get enough of her. He traced the faint silver stretch mark next to her navel.

Gently he laid his mouth upon it. Heat flashed through her. She shivered under his touch. "Nick, please."

Amusement lit his eyes. "Please what? Please stop? Or please go on?"

"Please go on." He hadn't forgotten a thing, the soft little touches that aroused her. As his hands and mouth roamed lower, she gasped, "Oh, please...go...on."

Long-forgotten rapture slid along skin slick with sweat. Time unraveled as he loved her, memories becoming the present, the past a gentle refrain in her mind. A jumble of emotions crowded her mind: sorrow, love, uncertainty, hope. A future?

It didn't matter. For now there was only love. Regrets were for tomorrow, not for this incandescent moment that seemed the only truth between them, the moment in which they were one and soared into the heat of the sun.

They lay at last in boneless lassitude, passion spent, bodies sated. Tessa watched out of half-closed eyes as Nick got up and went into the bathroom. She heard water running, and a ripple of goosebumps ran over her skin.

Through the open window, a cool wind carried in the smell of pine resin.

Nick came back. She gasped at the exquisite feel of the warm washcloth against her skin as he wiped away the sweat. He finished by drying her with a towel, then tucked the sheet and blanket around her. "Sleep now."

He returned the towel to the bathroom and turned off the light. Crawling in beside her, he snugged her against his chest, her bottom pressed into the cradle of his thighs. Moments later she knew from the steadiness of his breathing that he slept.

She lay wide awake, eyes staring at the thin path of the moon as it moved slowly across the ceiling. Doubts began to bite at her like nasty little terriers.

She was a fool for making love with him. But she had only herself to blame. She hadn't expected the long-plugged dam to burst tonight, right after they'd found almost indisputable proof that Andrew was alive. She should have been euphoric, but instead the tears had began. And once started, they wouldn't stop.

She should have remained in her own bed, weeping silently. But grief and fear had burdened her for so long, and Nick was the only one who understood, who could share it. The rapport between them last summer wasn't an illusion, not since he'd come back.

She'd had to go to him. As the tears flowed like a swollen river, she'd finally admitted she was still in love with him. There was no one else, whether he returned her love or not. Sophie and Millie had been wonderful support during the past year but they had their own lives. She couldn't burden them with her most profound sorrows and loneliness.

Nick was Andrew's father. Even without meeting Andrew, he understood what she was going through. He wanted their child back as passionately as she did.

But the nasty little voice in her head asked, what did

Nick want of her? It struck her that their conversations had revolved around the search for Andrew. She didn't know if he felt differently about commitment than last summer. They hadn't discussed the past or the future. He had given her no indication that there might be a future for them.

At least she knew Nick hadn't planned anything ahead of time. He'd come immediately after the call.

The call. Who had called him? Alexander? It had to be someone who'd had the resources to track him down.

She knew that it was unlikely he'd come with the intention of taking her baby away from her, since he'd only just learned of Andrew's existence. And now?

Fear dried her mouth. He might still decide he wanted Andrew and not her.

She couldn't allow herself to fall into the trap of thinking that making love meant he loved her.

Making love. She grimaced. A romantic term for an expression of basic need and want.

Having sex, Nick no doubt would call it, as he'd bluntly told her last summer during their final argument. If she was smart, she wouldn't let his tenderness and caring fool her into thinking it was anything more for him now. He'd been tender last summer, too. And passionate. At first they'd been so carried away by the heat flaring between them that they hadn't given a thought to consequences.

This time he hadn't taken any chances that she might get pregnant. He'd been prepared. But what did that mean, the fact that he'd been carrying a condom in his wallet? That he'd planned to seduce her? She hadn't exactly given him the chance, had she? She plastered herself against him and jumped his bones.

She gave a bitter, soundless laugh. The convenient condom. If he only knew the irony of it.

She turned her head. His breath drifted warmly across her cheek. His mouth was slightly parted, his features relaxed as he slept deeply. The lush black lashes fluttered faintly as he dreamed, and the corners of his mouth turned up.

Her eyes burning, Tessa turned her face back into the pillow. No, Nick wouldn't take Andrew. He couldn't.

NICK WOKE ABRUPTLY, jarred out of a dream in which Tessa lay in his arms. He pulled the dream woman closer and was surprised to find a real, warm Tessa lying next to him, her arms wrapped around him. He blinked, momentarily disoriented. Was he still dreaming?

No, she gave a little moan, then coughed. Alarm raced along his veins. The air in the room was hot and close, difficult to breathe.

Disentangling himself, he sat up, swinging his feet to the floor. He strode to the window but before he reached it, he knew.

Heavy smoke, tinted orange by the rising sun, billowed into the room.

Chapter Thirteen

"Tessa, get up." The urgent sound of Nick's voice woke her from a fitful sleep. She coughed harshly, an acrid smell filling her throat and nostrils.

"Wha-what's happening?" she mumbled, clawing her tangled hair back from her face. She coughed again. "Why is it so smoky?"

The sheet slipped down to her waist. Uncomfortable in the glare of morning after, she yanked it back up before reaching for her oversize T-shirt, which lay on the bedside stand. A cloud of smoke hung near the ceiling, growing denser by the moment. She stared at it, uncomprehending, her throat raw as she swallowed.

Nick tugged at her arm. "Come on, move. We have to get out of here," he snapped, pulling on his jeans and zipping them. He'd never heard of modesty, she remembered with mild resentment. "I think the house is on fire."

That got through the fog in her mind. "Fire?" She dragged the T-shirt over her head and jumped off the bed.

"Call the fire department, if the phone's working," Nick said as he went out.

Thankfully, the rest of the house seemed clear of smoke. Closing the bedroom door behind her, Tessa rushed down the hall. She heard a loud crash as Nick pushed open the back door, and her heart jumped into her throat. "Are you okay?"

"Fine. Forget the fire department and call the cops."

He took off running across the yard.

The cops? She pondered for a split second, then picked up the phone. Nothing. Still dead. So much for that. No cops. No fire department. She slammed it down.

Wisps of smoke drifted into the open door. Tessa unsnapped the fire extinguisher that hung over the stove. Outside she found why Nick hadn't dealt with the fire before running off. It was confined to a pile of sticks and dead leaves, which had blown into a corner of the porch during last night's storm. A lot of smoke, but the wet material hadn't ignited.

Abandoning the fire extinguisher, she ran to the garden hose. She aimed a stream of water over the smoking heap. The fire expelled a last belch of smoke and died.

A chill ran over her skin. She grabbed the broom and swept the mess off the porch, scattering the blackened twigs and leaves under the hydrangea bushes. Traces of soot remained on the floorboards. Lucky the leaves had been wet from the rain, or the whole house might have gone up.

She sank down on the step, her knees turning to rubber. The fire hadn't started by itself. Her skin crawled with revulsion at the thought of someone hanging around outside while they—

She stood up. Where was Nick? Cocking her head, she listened. Only birdsong and the quiet surge of the river. On the lawn she could see footprints in the dew-beaded grass. A lot of footprints. She walked down and studied them. The dew was drying rapidly but there appeared to be one set coming, fairly close together. The other prints pointed away from the house but they were farther apart. Two sets.

The arsonist's and Nick's, both of them running. She glanced at her watch, and saw that less than ten minutes had passed since he had told her to phone the police.

A crow cawed raucously and rose from the giant fir at the edge of the woods. It flew off, a black cinder against the blue sky. A moment later Nick emerged from the trees, striding across the lawn.

"You're all right," she exclaimed. "I was worried."

"Of course I'm all right," he said disgustedly. "I didn't catch him. He got away in that decrepit beater of a van."

Tessa frowned. "I didn't hear an engine."

"No. Apparently it wouldn't start but he let it roll down the hill until the engine caught. Even with that delay, I was too far away to catch him."

"You saw him, then."

"Not clearly, but I'd guess from the size and shape of him and the van that it's your old friend Dorky Pete."

Tessa's eyes widened. "Do you suppose it was him who tried to set the house on fire?"

"Well, he botched it, didn't he? Or maybe he just intended to smoke us out so he could pick us off with the rifle he was carrying."

"But why? Dorky Pete has never done anything like this before, that I know of."

Nick's face hardened. "Someone must have hired him."

IN THE CAR twenty minutes later, Tessa frowned as she stared out of the windshield. From time to time she glanced at Nick's uncompromising profile. The muscles in his jaw were knotted, his mouth set in a grim line. He hadn't spoken since they'd left the cabin.

Tessa let her eyes fall closed for a moment. She felt wrung out, both as a result of the excitement this morning and her almost sleepless night.

What was eating Nick? The near disaster of the fire? Or was he regretting last night? It hadn't been his fault, after all. Did men feel violated when a woman practically forced herself on them?

She opened her eyes. "Look, Nick, I'm sorry."

He shot her an astonished look. "What the hell for?"

Hot color swept up her cheeks and she cupped her hand around her face to hide it from him. "I shouldn't have come to your room. It was presumptuous of me."

He made a hard, derisive sound. "Whatever it was, presumptuous isn't the word I'd use."

"Then why are you in such a mood?" The words burst out before she could stop them.

He ground the gears downshifting, and swore under his breath. "Because I can't figure out what's going on here."

A measure of relief flowed through her, taking some of the bone-tiredness. "At least we checked the shed before we left."

"And found nothing," he said flatly. And judging by the layers of dust on every surface, no one had been in the shed since last fall.

"The police station first, I'd say." Nick's voice jarred her back to the present. "We'll drop off the diaper but I guess Larry'll want to go out and look for himself."

"AT LAST, A BREAK," Larry pronounced heartily after they'd explained about the diaper and the fire and Dorky Pete's van. "I'll bring Pete in for questioning. And send a crew out to fingerprint the cabin. You'll let me have a key?" he asked Tessa.

She detached it from her key ring and placed it on the desk. "Have you had any response to your bulletins?"

Larry shook his head. "Nothing concrete."

"Question," Nick said. "About your report on Andrew's supposed death, was there any mention of a silver bracelet he wore that could have identified him?"

Larry shook his head. "I was looking at the report only a few minutes ago and no, the only thing we had was that the doctor recognized him."

"Then we should have realized before that the call was phony." Nick crossed his arms over his chest. There was something about this situation he didn't like, but he couldn't put his finger on it.

Was Larry just a little too enthusiastic about a piece of evidence that he warned them wouldn't help identify Andrew's kidnapper? Or was it just his own dislike of the man—jealousy, he admitted—which colored his judgment?

He would run it by Tessa as soon as they were alone. Women were supposed to be good at interpreting nuances, and maybe it was time he stopped trying to protect her.

Larry leaned forward, his face earnest. "Tessa, I know we weren't going to alert the media but I think it's time we did. Would you give me permission to send Andrew's picture to both the local paper and the Vancouver dailies?"

She bit her lip, thinking. "Yes, do it," she said firmly. "Maybe it'll help. We've hit nothing but dead ends so far."

"Okay. I'll get on it right away."

"Is IT JUST ME, or did he act a little weird?" Nick said as soon as they stepped out into the hot sunlight.

Tessa's brow wrinkled. "What do you mean?"

"He acted as if we'd solved the O.J. Simpson case."

She gaped at him, and he felt like a fool. "Well, I'm sure he's as anxious to find Andrew as we are. Of course he'd be eager to follow up on any clue."

"That eager?" Nick knew he was pushing but he had to get it out.

Tessa glared at him. "Just because you don't like Larry doesn't give you the right to judge his abilities. You can't blame him for not picking up the bracelet thing. He wouldn't have known."

"It's not his abilities I'm questioning. I just think he knows more than he's telling. I'm convinced now that someone ran you off the road and took Andrew. Maybe he saw something at the accident scene that night after all."

"Then he'd tell me." She swallowed, visibly controlling her anger. "Maybe you've forgotten this, growing up in the

:ity, but I trust Larry. The people in this town are my friends. I've known them all my life. You've suspected Alexander and Larry of who knows what all along, without he slightest evidence."

"Tessa—" His hand on her arm, he tried to interrupt.

But she was like a runaway train. "You can't go around seeing what's not there. I won't listen to your suspicions anymore."

"But what other explanation is there?"

She shook off his hand. "Somebody took my baby from he car to the clinic and then left with him. That's what we have to go on."

"Yeah, and maybe Larry's involved."

The ice in her eyes chilled him to the bone. "I don't want to talk about it. And you don't have to see me home. I'll get a taxi."

Before he could stop her, she'd run down the street to the taxi stand and jumped into the cab waiting there. Fists clenched deep in his pockets, he watched helplessly as the yellow sedan disappeared around the next corner.

Hell! He'd really blown it now.

"Nick, where's Tessa?" The sound of Sophie's voice sent his heart into his throat. The heart he thought Tessa had taken with her.

"Oh, you're back," he said lamely. "How did you know where to find us?"

"I was up at the house and Millie told me you'd gone to the police station," Sophie said. "Have you seen Larry? Is there any news of Andrew?" The questions tumbled from her mouth.

"No news," he said tightly. "And Tessa's gone home in a taxi."

Her eyes and her mouth formed similar ovals. "Oh. Don't tell me. You two had a fight."

"Now why would you think that?" he asked, suppress-

ing his irritation. Maybe the secret to understanding Tessa
was getting to know her best friend.

His eyes narrowed as he recalled what they'd learned
yesterday. The irritation threatened to turn into anger.
"Yeah, Sophie, maybe you can tell me who might want to
steal Tessa's baby?"

She paled but stared brazenly back at him, her dark eyes
defiant. "What makes you think I'd know?"

"You're her friend. And everyone in this town seems to
know what everyone else is doing."

"It can't be anyone in this town. If anyone had myste-
riously acquired a baby, someone would have noticed,
don't you think?"

Yeah, that was true. Some of his anger seeped away.
"Tell me this, then. Who phoned me to tell me about Andrew?"

This time she eyed him narrowly before replying. "How
would I know? It wasn't me. Tessa was perfectly capable
of raising her child on her own."

"Yes, I suppose she is." The rest of his anger faded,
driven out by a wave of depression. Once they found Andrew, Tessa wouldn't need him. Why had he thought she
might?

"You might ask Alexander, though. I had lunch with his
secretary not long before Tessa's accident and she mentioned that Alex hired a detective to find you."

"Did Tessa know this?"

"Of course not. She'd washed her hands of you. She
was devastated when she couldn't find you. And then she
was so sick before Andrew was born. No, she wouldn't be
looking for you after that."

"She was sick? Before she had Andrew?" His guts
twisted, agony ripping through him. "What do you mean,
sick?"

"Oh, she probably won't ever tell you, but she spent the

ast three months of her pregnancy in bed. Her blood pressure was high and there were complications."

His head reeled and he thought for a moment he would faint. He must have turned green, because Sophie placed her hand on his arm, concern on her face. "Are you all right, Nick?"

"I will be," he managed in a strangled voice. "I need to talk to Tessa."

"Yes, I'd say you do." She squeezed his arm. "Nick, Tessa needs you, now more than ever. Especially since I'm thinking of leaving. I've had a good job offer in Vancouver." She looked directly at him. "That means I won't see Tessa as often. Which leaves only you. Don't hurt her."

"I'll try my damnedest not to," he promised.

"SHE'S IN HER ROOM." Millie, hands on hips, blocked the door. Protecting Tessa, which was laughable since he was twice her size. "She doesn't want to see or talk to anyone, except Larry West, if he calls with news about Andrew."

West's name did it. Putting his hands on Millie's shoulders, he set her gently aside. "I'm sorry, but this can't wait."

Taking the stairs three at a time, he stormed up to her room. She hadn't bothered to lock the door, figuring she was safe with Millie on guard, but he would have broken it down if he'd had to.

"Why didn't you tell me?"

His voice echoed around the room. Tessa jumped. She lay huddled on the bed, her hands over her face. She slowly rolled to her back and brought them down. Her eyes were red and swollen, her face streaked with tears. He'd seen her happy. He'd seen her angry. He'd seen her sad.

But he'd never seen her like this. Distraught, all her defenses down.

Pain clawed in his belly. He'd done this to her. And worse, abandoning her last summer to have his baby alone.

Because he'd been so wrapped up in his own anger and grief that he hadn't seen what she'd given him until it was too late. Until he'd thrown it away.

He sank to his knees on the floor and took her hands in both of his. "Tessa, why didn't you tell me?"

"Nick, you have to leave," Millie tugged at his sleeve. "Tessa needs to rest. I can't have you upsetting her."

He lifted eyes so anguished she stepped back a pace. He didn't care that every emotion he felt was displayed for her to see. "Millie, I have to talk to her. Please. Give me five minutes and then I'll be gone."

She hesitated for a long moment, mouth set primly. Then she nodded. "Five minutes." She went out, closing the door after her.

"And what was I supposed to tell you?" Tessa asked from the bed, her voice hoarse and muffled.

He toed off his shoes and lay down beside her. When his arms came around her, she stiffened, her fists clenched between them. After a moment he felt some of the rigidity leave her muscles. She didn't relax against him but she didn't push him away either.

Encouraged, he moved one hand up her back and threaded it through her hair. The long strands slid through his fingers, smooth, cool silk, the color of honey shot with sunlight.

"Oh, Tessa, I'm so sorry. If I'd known, I would have been here."

She punched him in the chest, struggling against his hold. "Known what? You're talking in riddles."

"If I'd known you were so sick when you were carrying Andrew, I would have moved heaven and earth to be with you."

Her breath hitched, then seeped out in a sigh. "Sophie's been babbling again, I suppose. I'm going to have to tape her mouth shut when I see her."

"I'm going to buy her a medal," Nick said. "When were you going to tell me, Tessa?"

She rolled onto her back, and he let her, keeping his arm beneath her shoulders. Shoulders that were far too fragile and slender to bear the burdens he'd inflicted on her. "It had nothing to do with you."

"I got you pregnant. I put your life in danger."

She said nothing. He waited, holding his breath. When the silence stretched and she didn't deny it, the truth hit him so hard his heart stopped. Her life *had* been in danger. And he was responsible.

"I'm sorry, Tessa." He found himself unable to speak above a strangled whisper. "Tell me about it."

"Only if you'll tell me why you disappeared so completely last summer."

"I thought Roth told you."

"He did, but I'd like to hear your version."

"I was in Greece," he said. "I had a phone call right after you left the hotel that day. The village my family came from was destroyed in an earthquake. I had to go and help out."

Fresh tears soaked through his shirt, scalding his skin. "Are they all right now?"

"Yes. Luckily, no one was seriously hurt. And they're all settled again, in new or rebuilt houses that I helped to put up."

She stirred, her vanilla scent beguiling his senses. "I don't know anything about your family. Are your parents alive?"

He shook his head. "They were killed in a plane crash some years ago. My brother lives in Montreal, but my grandmother and most of my cousins and aunts and uncles still live in the village." His arm tightened around her. "Enough of that. Tell me about Andrew and your pregnancy before Millie comes in here to kick me out."

She tensed again. "In the fifth month, my blood pressure

started to go up. Also, I was spotting slightly. Dr. Ivers was afraid I'd miscarry. He put me on bed rest.''

He studied her white face, the blue-veined eyelids, wishing he could see her eyes. "It was serious, wasn't it?"

"Yes." She didn't hesitate. "I carried him as long as possible. He weighed just over five pounds when he was born, a good weight for a preemie, and he was a healthy baby." She squirmed around until her back was to him. "Please, Nick, that's all there is."

His throat burned, his mouth so dry he had to swallow before he could speak. "I'm so sorry. It'll never happen again. I'll never put you through that again."

An icy knot wrung his stomach as he realized how close he'd come to forgetting the condom the other night. If she'd gotten pregnant again and maybe died....

The pain stole his breath but he knew what he had to do. As soon as he returned Andrew to her, he would leave. He couldn't take any chances with her. He knew himself well enough to be sure he couldn't live with her without making love to her. Too risky, no matter how careful they were. Better that she lived alone than that she died because of another pregnancy.

"Just so you'll know, I did try to call you," he said. "Several times. I left a message at Lee Enterprises when I couldn't get you at your own number."

"No one told me," she said in a small voice.

"Could have been some secretary screwing up," he said, trying to dismiss it. He slid his arm out from under her, and sat up. Pulling a tissue from the box next to the bed, he blew his nose.

Tessa sat up. A crease marked her face where she'd pressed it into the pillow. Her cheeks and lips were puffy and tears spiked her dark eyelashes. Wordlessly, he handed her a fresh tissue.

She used it to mop up, an occasional hiccup shaking her

body. Tossing the tissue toward the wastebasket, she swung her feet to the floor. "You need to rest," he said softly.

"I can't right now." Her voice was firm, determined, her chin set stubbornly. "I have to go to the bank and see what's in the safe-deposit box."

He'd almost forgotten about the key they'd found. "Okay, but when we finish that, you have to rest."

She made no reply as she smoothed her hands over her wrinkled skirt, finally throwing them wide. "They won't care how I look." She walked past him and opened the door.

AS TESSA HAD SURMISED, the bank was not the one in which her father had his accounts, but he had left instructions for her to have access to the box. Tessa followed the bank official into the vault, grateful once more for Joseph's foresight. Of course it would have been nice if he'd mailed her the key or something, not left it to chance that she would find it. But the whole situation about his estate should be cleared up now.

She was right. The box contained a single white envelope, unsealed but inscribed with the name and address of the lawyer she'd already questioned, Roger Simmons.

"So that's it," Nick said when she rejoined him.

She tapped the envelope against her palm. "The last will and testament of Joseph Lee."

"You didn't open it?"

"No. I'd rather have the lawyer do it, just in case."

SIMMONS LET THEM into his simple office as soon as they arrived. He pushed the files on his desk aside and took the envelope.

Tessa clasped her hands in her lap. "Is that the will you made up for my father?"

Simmons turned the envelope over in his hands. "I would say so. It's my handwriting on the outside. Would you like me to look it over before I read it to you? If there are other beneficiaries, they should be present for the reading.''

''Please look at it,'' Tessa said.

The heavy paper crackled as he unfolded the stapled sheets. Holding her breath, Tessa waited while he scanned the three pages. His expressionless face told her nothing. He looked up. ''It appears to be in order but I'd like Mr. Alexander Roth and Mrs. Millie McPherson to be present when I disclose the contents.''

Tessa stood up. ''If I can use your phone, I'm sure we can get them here in about ten minutes.''

MILLIE ARRIVED FIRST, out of breath and clutching her large leather purse to her chest. ''Tessa, what's this all about? You should be home resting.''

''I'll rest when this is over.'' She turned her head when the door opened once again. ''Hello, Uncle Alex. I'm glad you're here.''

''I hope this won't take long,'' he said, his brief smile abstracted. ''I was in a meeting with our Japanese buyers.''

''They'll understand about a family emergency,'' Tessa said calmly. ''We've found Dad's will.''

His brows shot up but he quickly regained his composure. His gaze fell on Nick, sitting silently next to Tessa. ''Hello, Nick.''

''Alexander.'' Nick glanced at Tessa. ''Do you want me to leave?''

She squeezed his hand. ''No, stay.'' She addressed the lawyer. ''Please proceed, Mr. Simmons.''

''By all means.'' He cleared his throat. ''This is the last will and testament of Joseph Lee....''

He droned on through the preamble. There followed a generous bequest to Millie and a request that she continue in Tessa's employ as long as the arrangement suited both of them. There were also bequests to St. Luke's Church and to a couple of charities. The house went to Tessa, no big surprise.

Finally Simmons came to the paragraph which began, "As for the bulk of the estate, half will go to my grandson, Andrew Joseph Lee, with my daughter, Tessa Elizabeth Lee, acting as trustee until Andrew reaches the age of majority. The other half I bequeath to my cousin, Alexander Roth, who will remain as CEO unless either he or Tessa deems the arrangement to be unsatisfactory. He will also receive outright the sum of $500,000 to be used as he sees fit."

Simmons looked up. "There are a couple of more paragraphs which I'll read but that's basically it. Are there any questions?"

No one said a word. After a weighted moment, Alexander stood up and took Tessa's hand, giving it a firm squeeze. "We'll talk later," he said quietly. He strode toward the door.

Nick jumped up and followed him out. "Alexander, could I have a word with you?"

"If you make it quick," Alexander said in his usual austere manner. "I've got people waiting for me."

"This won't take long," Nick assured him. "Did you call me after Tessa's accident?"

Alexander's eyes met his steadily. "Yes. I felt Tessa needed you, especially when we thought she'd lost Andrew. She kept calling your name when she was lying in the hospital. She probably doesn't remember."

"It didn't sound like you."

"What? Oh, you mean the voice sounded strange. That was my secretary. She had a bad cold at the time."

"How long had you known my number?" Emotion threatened to choke him.

"Only a few days. I understand it was a new listing."

"Yes. I'd just gotten back from Greece." He clasped Alexander's hand. "Thank you. I appreciate it."

Alexander looked embarrassed. "No problem. I hope it works out between you."

Chapter Fourteen

"At least I've got his blessing," Nick muttered as they got into his car a short time later.

"What do you mean?" Tessa asked.

"Oh, nothing," he said. "So you're going to be involved in the company after all. How do you feel about it?"

"Truthfully? Stunned. I can't believe he left half to Andrew." Her voice hitched, and tears blurred her eyes.

Nick touched her cheek, catching one that fell. "I know. It would be ironic if it wasn't so tragic. We'll find him, Tessa. Don't lose faith now."

She shifted, the leather seat creaking. "I'll have to keep it now. It's Andrew's legacy. Alexander won't have a problem with that. Nothing's going to change. I certainly don't want to be more involved in the running of the business than I've been up to now."

"I suppose you're on the board."

She glanced at him. "Yes, but it's mostly a nominal position. I only have to show up for meetings several times a year."

He put the car in gear and merged into the sparse traffic. "Where to?"

"Home, I guess. No, wait. I should go and see Alexander, talk to him."

"If he'll listen."

"I'M SORRY, MISS LEE, but Mr. Roth has left for the day," his secretary told Tessa. "He took the Japanese buyers out for lunch. I think they were planning to go into Vancouver."

Disappointment warred with relief inside Tessa's mind. She wanted to clear the air, but maybe it would be better to let a little time go by, give Alexander a chance to adjust to the news. "Thanks, Alice," she said. "If you hear from him, could you ask him to give me a call at home, please."

"That I will, Miss Lee." The gray-haired woman hesitated, then spoke again, in a diffident tone. "I just want to say how sorry I am about your baby. I mean thinking he had died in the accident and now, who knows where he is."

Tessa clenched her hand into a fist. "I'm sure we'll find him very soon. Goodbye, Alice."

"Not there?" Nick asked when she rejoined him in the parking lot.

Tessa shook her head.

"Do you want to stop by the police station, or go to lunch first?"

"Let's see Larry first," Tessa said. "Maybe he's found something."

To their disappointment, Larry had nothing to report. There were no usable prints on the diaper, nor had the forensic expert he'd sent to the cottage turned up anything. And the flyers he'd circulated with Andrew's picture had brought plenty of phone calls but no real leads. "I'm sorry," he said. "I wish I could hurry it up, too. I'm giving this top priority but we do have other cases and we're short-handed, especially with people on holidays."

"What about Dorky Pete?" Nick asked.

Larry shrugged. "I've sent a constable out to his place twice but he's not there, and neither is his van. I'm still not convinced that he's the one who followed you to the cabin. After all, you only got part of the license number and those three letters match dozens in the area. Pete's never done anything the police would be interested in.''

"Nothing?" Nick said skeptically.

"Well, there was the case of used books he was peddling at the flea market as new, but he had an invoice and we couldn't pin anything on him." Larry shifted in his chair, the metal spring twanging. "What I meant was that he's never done anything remotely violent."

"It was his van we saw following us the other times," Tessa said. "And that fire didn't start from a lightning strike."

"Wasn't much of a fire, was it? Maybe he or whoever was there dropped a cigarette butt."

"Did you check it out?"

"Yes. We raked through the burnt leaves beside the porch steps. We found several cigarette butts. And neither you nor your dad smoked." He leaned back, lacing his fingers behind his head. "Dorky Pete does. If it was him. Or it could have been kids hanging around, sneaking a smoke."

"Maybe," Tessa said doubtfully.

"I'll call you if there's any news," Larry said. "We could get responses to the newspaper article as early as tomorrow."

Another day to wait.

Tessa followed Nick out, feeling tired and dispirited. Getting into the car, she propped her elbow on the window frame and rested her forehead in her palm. Her thoughts slowed and dulled as weariness engulfed her like a suffocating blanket.

She pinched the bridge of her nose, massaging her forehead. What could they do now?

Nick slowed for a red light. He reached across and turned her face toward him, his fingers warm and gentle. "Tessa, you need to eat. It's way past lunchtime. And after you eat, I'm taking you home for a nap."

IT WAS AFTER SEVEN that evening when Tessa came downstairs to find Nick in the kitchen talking with Millie who was feeding him freshly made doughnuts. The fragrance filled the room, making Tessa's mouth water. "Any news?" she asked, reaching for a sugar-dusted doughnut.

Nick shook his head. "But I've been thinking."

"About what?"

"Alexander's response to the will. Millie agrees he didn't seem all that surprised."

"I thought he did," Tessa said. "But then with Alexander, it's hard to tell."

"Yeah." Nick let out an explosive breath. "What if he did know? What if he kept it hidden until he did something about it?"

Tessa's jaw dropped. "Are you saying what I think you're saying?" She shook her head. "No. No, you're wrong. Alexander wouldn't harm me or Andrew. He loves us."

"Greed sometimes outweighs love. And with you and Andrew out of the way, he could have it all. Do you have a key to his office?"

"Are you crazy?"

"Maybe." His expression softened. "For your sake, I hope so. But I'm thinking of motive. You have to admit Alexander's the only one with a motive."

"He wouldn't do it."

"Will it hurt to look?"

"Yes. It'll make me feel like a sneak."

"He's gone to Vancouver. If we don't find anything, he'll never need to know."

Tessa glared at him, setting down her half-eaten doughnut. "Okay, we'll do it. I'll prove to you he's innocent."

"I hope so. I really hope so." Nick said. "But we have to check."

Tessa set her jaw. "I suppose if I don't cooperate, you'll get in there anyway."

He passed his hand over his face. "Tessa, I have to. You have a right to know. Of course, maybe there's nothing. Maybe your dad discussed the whole thing with Alexander before he wrote the will."

Tessa seized on this, her expression lightening. "Yes, he must have. That's why it wasn't a surprise."

"But," Nick added, "then why didn't he tell you long ago instead of letting you wonder all this time?"

"Maybe he wanted me to get over Dad's death first."

Nick nodded. "Yes, I can see that, since it follows the pattern. Sparing you."

Something in his tone irked her. "Why do you think I moved out of the house when I started working? I was tired of being coddled. But at the end, Dad needed me."

Nick threw up his hands. "I wasn't criticizing, Tessa. I know how important family can be."

"You didn't last summer," she retorted, not caring that Millie was listening to every word. "You wanted to be on your own, not caring about anyone, wallowing in your guilt and grief."

"I had a reason, didn't I?" His voice softened. "Tessa, I've changed. Whoever said time heals was right. And what I saw this past year, everyone pulling together after a disaster, made me see that closing off your emotions doesn't work. I can't do it anymore. I had to risk feeling again."

She stared at him, stunned. Was this the declaration he'd refused to give her last summer? Did it include her, or was it only for Andrew?

Before she could form her scattered thoughts into words, Millie cleared her throat. "Do you want dinner before you go? An omelette won't take long."

Nick rubbed his stomach, giving her a broad grin. "After all those doughnuts, I think I can wait a while. What about you, Tessa?"

She gave herself a mental shake. "No, I'm fine." She

stood up. "Okay, Nick, let's get on with the breaking and entering."

"It's not breaking and entering when you use a key," he argued. "Even Larry admits that."

"It's still sneaking behind my uncle's back."

"Just be careful," Millie called after them as they left the kitchen, still arguing.

"GOOD THING it's still daylight," Nick muttered as they climbed the stairs to the executive offices in the deserted building. "We won't need the lights on."

"I still think it would be more honest to ask him," Tessa insisted.

"And have him lie to you?"

"Alexander wouldn't lie to me."

"Wouldn't he, for your own good?"

They opened the outer office door, slipped inside and relocked it. The only light came from the hall and from an open door behind the reception desk, making the area dim and shadowy. The scent of roses in a tall vase on the desk wafted around them.

Tessa, her heart hammering against her ribs, led the way through the maze of offices until she reached the suite in the corner. She opened the door, stepped around the secretary's desk, and inserted a key into a wooden door carved with native symbols.

"His office certainly is the fanciest one in here," Nick commented.

"Years ago it was Dad's, but Alexander redecorated after Dad moved down the hall and gave this office to him. The last few years since he appointed Alexander CEO and made him a full partner, Dad was taking it easier. For all intents and purposes, Alexander ran the business. In fact, he lives for this business."

"That's what I was afraid of," Nick said.

"Afraid?" Tessa crossed the Oriental rug to adjust the curtains to let in a little more light.

"His ambition," Nick explained. "Makes me wonder how far he'd go to hang on to it."

"Nick! I told you Alexander would never hurt me."

"Okay. We won't talk about it." Nick scanned the room and groaned. "It'll take forever to search all those book shelves. Doesn't he even have a filing cabinet?"

"They're in the outer office. The paneling lining the walls is a series of doors."

"What about a safe?"

"The only safe is in Dad's office."

Nick pursed his lips. "And you've already cleaned it out." He crouched down behind the desk, pushing the deep leather arm chair out of the way. "Of course, with a desk like this, who needs a safe? I wonder how tricky the locks are."

"You won't have to use your lock picking skills," Tessa said dryly. "I know where he keeps his spare desk key."

Nick's brows flew up. "You do?"

"Sure. Don't forget my mother died when I was little. Dad used to bring me to the office all the time. I had the run of the place. Oh, Alexander may have changed his habits over the years but—"

"Looking at Alexander, I'd say not," Nick put in.

A group of healthy indoor trees occupied the corner near the windows. Tessa groped around in the saucers under the pots. "Should be the third one." She grunted as she tried to shift the heavy pot.

"Here, let me." Nick lifted the pot slightly.

"Got it." She uttered a cry of triumph as she dug a small brass key out of the saucer. "Those trees have grown since I was a kid. They didn't use to be so heavy."

"What are you doing in here?" A quiet voice asked from the doorway.

Startled, Tessa lifted her head, banging it painfully

against Nick's. Rubbing the spot, she stood up, her face burning. "Uncle Alex, you're back early."

He strode around his desk and separated a key from the ring he carried, using it to unlock the desk. From the bottom drawer he took out an envelope and tossed it to her. "Here, read it. But believe me when I say your father discussed everything with me. I was completely agreeable to the way he arranged the new will. And I didn't want to hurt you."

"Hurt me?" Tessa asked.

He gestured at the envelope. "I should have burned it rather than let you see it. But maybe it's better to have it out in the open."

Tessa picked up the envelope and held it as if it were a bomb in imminent danger of explosion. Roger Simmons's return address and the words "Last Will and Testament of Joseph Lee (Copy)" were neatly typed on it.

Gritting her teeth, she ripped open the flap. Her heart pounded in her throat, choking her as she unfolded the stiff paper.

The form was familiar from this morning's session in Simmons's office, the content vastly different.

An icy chill ran up her spine as she read the words leaving her half a million dollars and the house, with the business going to Alexander, free and clear. She scanned down to the bottom and saw the date, October last year, just around the time she'd told her father she was pregnant.

So Joseph *had* been angry. He'd given no outward sign except to display an uncharacteristic reserve. He'd always been open and affectionate with her, even during the sometimes turbulent teenage years, but this time he had withdrawn. And he'd never yelled at her, as he'd often done during disagreements over hair and clothes when she'd been in high school. She suddenly understood how deeply she'd hurt him.

She would have noticed it before except that the strain between them had been great enough that she'd avoided seeing him, which was easy since at the time she had her own apartment.

Joseph must have been ill then already, and she closed her eyes for a moment, grieving for the time they'd lost. After New Year's, when Dr. Ivers had recommended complete bed rest and she'd moved back to her childhood home, they'd drawn close again.

She looked up at Alexander who stood by the door, his arms crossed over his chest, his face impassive. "When did he formulate the new will?"

"Around Christmas we talked about it, worked out the details."

"Even to using Andrew's name."

A tinge of color crept up Alexander's cheeks and he shifted uncomfortably. "Your father assured me your baby was a boy, that the ultrasound was clear."

Tessa's chest felt tight and hot. "So he forgave me even before I got sick and moved back home," she whispered.

"He never blamed you, Tessa," Alexander said, his voice surprisingly vehement. "At first he was angry, thinking that someone had taken advantage of you, someone who might be another fortune hunter. He did it more to protect you than anything. But around Christmas, when he saw the ultrasound, I think the baby became real to him. That's when he made the new will we heard today."

Tessa nodded, her mind whirling. "Did you have a copy of the new will?"

"No, I believe the copy in the bank was the only one." He frowned.

"So you really didn't know where the will was, all this time?" Nick asked.

"No, I didn't," Alexander said. "He probably kept it in his safe at first but then when his heart got worse, he must have put it in the bank. Maybe he forgot to give one of us the key, or that last heart attack came so suddenly he never had time."

Tessa shook her head sadly. "We'll probably never know but it doesn't matter now. The important thing is to find Andrew and get him back."

"Yes, it is," Alexander said soberly. "Is there anything I can do?"

The honest concern in his voice touched her. She gave him a tremulous smile. "No, not right now."

Alexander picked up the briefcase at his feet and set it on the desk. He walked around the desk and awkwardly hugged Tessa. "Call me, will you?"

"Yes, I will."

She was glad of Nick's arm around her waist, guiding her down the hall. Her eyes blurred. One tear escaped and rolled down her cheek. Nick wiped it tenderly away with his thumb. "I guess I owe you an apology," he said as they headed for the stairs.

"Apology?"

He cast her a sheepish look. "I was thinking all kinds of nasty things about Alexander. I was wrong." His arm tightened. "I'm glad."

"So'm I," Tessa said fervently. But her relief lasted only until they reached the outside door. Andrew was still missing and they had no leads at all.

THEY WALKED AROUND the building to the back alley where they'd had to park the car. The movie theater across the street did a booming business on Cheap Tuesday and they'd been unable to find a parking space earlier.

Night had fallen, mercury lamps casting an orange glow over the street. The alley, dimly lit by a yellow bulb on the back of the building, smelled of rotting cabbage. Bits of paper tumbled past them, driven by a light, hot wind.

Nick's keys jingled as he pulled them from his pocket.

"Hold it right there."

"What the hell?" Nick's muscles tensed as he pushed Tessa in front of him, before slowly turning his head.

Dorky Pete, a greasy baseball cap stuck on his head, stepped out of the shadows, holding a sawed-off shotgun which he aimed directly at them.

Chapter Fifteen

"Get in the van."

Tessa moved like a robot with low batteries, her mind reeling. Dorky Pete? He couldn't have taken Andrew. The clinic staff said a woman had brought him in. Dorky Pete had never been involved with a woman, not in the twenty years since his wife had left him. It was well known that he hated women, considered them the scourge of the earth.

What was going on here?

Beside her, Nick swore softly and steadily. "Shut up," Pete snarled, gesturing with the gun. "Move. Ain't got all night."

Nick climbed up over the back bumper into the van, turning to give her a hand up. Pete jumped nimbly after them.

The acrid odor of spilled paint thinner on the floor of the van swam into Tessa's nostrils. Nausea rose in her throat, hot and bitter. She stumbled, bracing her hand on the side of the van to keep her balance. For a second she debated whether she could create a diversion by throwing up.

Pete swung the shotgun over toward Nick, aiming at the middle of his chest. "Any funny stuff and he gets it." He gave a cackle she assumed was meant to be a laugh. "You wouldn't believe what a big hole this'd make."

"Why are you doing this?" Tessa choked out the words.

He laughed again, showing misshapen, tobacco-stained teeth, and gave her a painful poke with the shotgun. She staggered forward, swallowing to control the queasiness. Nick steadied her, his hand on her back conveying reassurance, however brief the touch. She felt his breath feather her ear as he whispered, "Stay cool. We'll get a better chance later."

"Hey, no talking," Pete said. He motioned them to a couple of old car seats bolted to the side of the van. He kept the gun pointed at Nick while he pulled a strap around Tessa, pinning her arms at her sides. He clipped it behind her back. The snug webbing bit into her bare arms and constricted her chest, making it difficult to breathe. Her eyes flashed defiance but Pete only smirked at her.

He moved to the other side to bind Nick.

"Law-abiding citizen, I see," Nick said coolly. "Making sure we wear our seat belts."

Pete poked the shotgun into Nick's midsection, hard enough to cause him to grunt in pain. "Cut the smart-ass remarks, or I'll shoot you right here."

Nick shook his head, a half smile on his face. "I wouldn't, if I were you. Blood is awfully hard to remove and the smallest drop would be enough to convict you."

"Not if the van is at the bottom of the lake, like that damned baby seat."

"So you're the one who took it," Nick said. "And I suppose it was you who forced Tessa off the road in the storm."

Pete's eyes narrowed craftily. "Why should I tell you anything, smart guy?"

He turned away and slammed the rear door of the van closed. Threading his way between the front seats, he sat down behind the wheel, and laid the shotgun across the passenger seat.

Too far away to grab even if they could get loose, Tessa realized. She saw that the door handles were missing on all but the driver's door. No escape. Even if she managed to work the strap loose, the doors would be impossible to open from the inside.

The engine coughed to life. A moment late they were moving down the alley and onto the street leading out of town.

Cold seeped deep into her, penetrating the marrow of her bones. If Pete killed them, what would happen to Andrew? She could only pray that whoever had him would take good care of him.

She looked across at Nick, wishing she could touch him, wishing she could tell him everything in her heart. He met her gaze and smiled faintly, encouragingly. "Thank you," she mouthed. It was little enough.

She let herself drift mindlessly for a time. She knew she should be planning their escape but when she let herself think, pictures of Andrew came into her mind and she wanted to cry.

She had no intention of giving Pete the satisfaction of seeing her fear or despair. Besides, she still had Nick. He would help her find a way out of this.

"I wonder who's in on this with him," he murmured, pitching his voice below the roar of the engine.

Tessa shook her head. "Maybe he's acting on his own."

"Not likely. He doesn't have the brains for it. And I can't think why he would."

"Shut up, back there," Pete yelled.

The gears ground as he downshifted to climb another hill. New chills ran through Tessa as she realized where they were. On the approach to the cabin she and Nick had left—was it only that morning?

The van lurched to a stop. Tessa turned her head to look out of the windshield but all she could see was darkness. The engine died. In the abrupt silence Tessa heard the plaintive cry of a night bird.

Pete came back between the seats but instead of releasing

them, he opened the back door of the van and stood there, gazing back down the road as if he were waiting for someone.

Headlights flickered in the trees. A moment later, a car drew up, spraying gravel and raising a cloud of dust that lingered in the still night air. Beside her, she heard Nick swear pungently. "What is it?"

"I know that car," he muttered. "A black Mazda. It followed me a couple of times."

"What?" Tessa tipped her head back against the hard metal wall, closing her eyes. "No, it can't be. It can't be."

"Sophie?" Nick muttered in disbelief. "Your friend Sophie."

Sophie stepped from the car. The white silk shirt she wore over black leggings fluttered in the breeze. She walked to the back of the van, her sneakers crunching in the gravel.

Her dark brown eyes skipped over Tessa without remorse or apology and lighted on Nick. "Why did you have to come back? Your snooping spoiled everything." She turned to Pete. "Release them and bring them to the cabin."

Keeping the shotgun in one hand, Pete unfastened the straps holding Tessa. She swung her fist at him but he easily ducked the clumsy blow. Her arms prickled with pins and needles as the restricted blood flow rushed back.

"Move," Pete said when both Tessa and Nick stood beside the van.

Nick took Tessa's hand. She clasped her fingers tightly around his, needing his touch while she tried to absorb Sophie's betrayal.

"How charming," Sophie sneered, tapping her foot impatiently. "Two lovers tragically dying together."

"We're not dead yet," Nick snapped.

Tessa swallowed the icy lump in her throat. "Where is Andrew, Sophie?"

"How do you know I took him?"

The wind blew Tessa's hair across her face. She pushed it back, feeling unutterably tired. "You wouldn't be doing this unless you were the one."

She suddenly freed her hand from Nick's grasp, and lunged at Sophie. Pete grabbed her arm and jerked her back. Her hair flew wildly around her head as she tried to scratch and bite him. "Where have you taken Andrew? What did you do with my baby?"

She kicked at Pete's shin, pain shooting up her leg as her toe, in soft sneakers, hit the bone. He grunted and flung her at Nick who caught her against his chest. She braced her hand on his shoulder, rage surging through her. "Why, Sophie?" she screamed. "You were my friend." Her voice broke in a sob. "Why? Just tell me why. And tell me where he is."

"He's safe enough," Sophie said, her own eyes glittering. "Don't worry. I'll take good care of him. We're moving to Vancouver where no one knows us. He'll be all mine."

"He's mine, not yours," Tessa yelled.

"He's mine now." Sophie turned to Pete. "Get them out of here. You know what to do."

Pete gestured menacingly with the gun but Nick stood his ground. "Just a minute. I want to get a few things straight here. Did you have anything to do with Tessa's car accident?"

The arrogant smirk slid off Pete's face and he glanced at Sophie. She shrugged. "What difference does it make now?"

"I didn't mean for her to go off the road with the baby in the car," Pete said sullenly. "I was supposed to stop her and take the baby but the truck I was driving skidded in a puddle and crashed into the car."

Sophie took a step toward Pete, fixing him with a killing

stare. "So that's what happened, you blithering idiot. You could have killed Andrew."

Sophie slapped him across the face. His head jerked to one side but he recovered quickly, muttering, "You bitch. If it wasn't for the money, I'd do you, too."

Tessa cried out in helpless rage as she clenched her fists in the front of Nick's shirt. "Tell me where he is."

Nick stroked her hair, his mind working. If he could create a diversion— Or cause dissension between the players. The seeds of it were there already. Sophie angry. Dorky Pete looking rebellious. Only one gun between them.

"How much is she paying you, Pete?" he asked, making his voice as sardonic as possible. "I'll double it."

The man's eyes, small and dark as pebbles, narrowed and he licked his thin lips. The greed in his face faded as he met Sophie's glare.

"Afraid of her, are you?" Nick taunted. "Tell me, are you the one who shot at Tessa at the sawmill?"

Pete gave that eerie cackling laugh. "Yeah, that was me. Would've finished the job if you hadn't come along." He looked at Sophie defiantly. "I don't know what you'd want with a brat anyway."

"My baby isn't a brat," Tessa retorted. "Yes, Sophie, why did you take my baby?"

Sophie clenched her fists at her sides. "You had everything. All your life, you got what I couldn't have. It was so easy for you. Good marks you hardly had to study for. I had to work like hell to keep up. Then Scott. He saw me first but one look at you, he didn't want me anymore. Of course you had more money. He wanted it. When you broke up with him and went away on holiday, I thought he'd turn to me. But I lost again. He left town instead. And then you came back, glowing and pregnant."

She gave a bitter laugh. "Well, I won after all. I've got the baby and you have nothing."

Tessa clapped her hand over her mouth, sure she would be sick. "You could have had your own children."

Sophie made a derisive sound. "I saw how it was with you, no picnic, for sure. I've got one now, without going through a messy pregnancy and childbirth."

Renewed anger cut through Tessa's shock and despair. "I suppose you're going to kill us and make it look like an accident," she said, keeping a tight rein on her temper.

"Accident or suicide, what's the difference?" Sophie pursed her lips, considering.

"Suicide would probably be more convincing," she continued. "The grieving mother who's lost her child and who knows she can't have another, nothing to live for anymore."

Tessa thought she heard Nick make a sound but she didn't dare meet his eyes, keeping hers fixed on Sophie's face. "What about Nick?" She drew in a ragged breath. "Give it up, Sophie. No one's going to believe that, especially after my other accident." A new thought struck her. "I suppose I should be grateful that at least you took Andrew in to have him checked by a doctor after the accident."

Something softened in Sophie's face. "Of course. Thanks to Pete's bungling, he could have been hurt. But then I had to forge the death certificate and call Alexander about the funeral. Good thing Mr. Faversham was away. It was easy to arrange since I still had keys to the funeral home from the time I did some temp work there. All you really need is the appearance of truth. Follow procedure and nobody double-checks."

"And you also did temp work at the clinic at one time, didn't you?" Tessa asked. The mechanics of Sophie's deception were coming clear. "That's why you knew the routine. Weren't you afraid they'd recognize you?"

"It was so long enough ago that I worked there, they

wouldn't remember me anyway. And nobody I'd worked with was on duty that night. It was easy.''

"What about Larry?" Nick asked.

"Larry? No, Larry had nothing to do with anything. And he'd never suspect me anyway. We've gone out a few times and we understand each other.''

"You've gone out with Larry?" Tessa said. "You never told me.''

"I didn't tell you everything, *friend*.''

"Obviously not," Tessa muttered, kicking herself for not seeing through Sophie before this, especially not interpreting her eagerness to care for Andrew as an unnatural possessiveness. It had been there all the time, but she'd trusted Sophie.

"Tell me this, Sophie. How did that diaper get up here in the cottage?''

"I had a key. You gave me one last year, remember, when you went to Victoria. Pete drove off, like the coward he is, after the car crashed. I took Andrew to the clinic and then waited out the storm up here since I knew you weren't coming.''

Next to Tessa, Nick tensed. "You mean you just left Tessa in the overturned car?" he said, his voice icy and deceptively soft. "You little bitch, she could have bled to death.''

He leaped forward. Pete, his attention more on the conversation than on covering them, tried to bring up the gun. Too late. Nick knocked it out of his hands, and charged at Sophie. She dodged around him and dived for the gun, bringing it up in one motion and fired at them.

A deafening blast shook the air. Ears ringing, Tessa shook her head, amazed to realize she was still alive. Before she could take a breath, Nick was at her side.

"Quick, let's go," he hissed urgently. "This may be our only chance." He grabbed her arm and dragged her behind the van, into a pool of darkness. Adrenaline surged through her, and the numbness faded. Her mind cleared; her feet flew over the ground.

Behind them, Sophie screamed something. But the headlights now worked to her disadvantage. Blinded by the glare, she couldn't see Nick and Tessa in the darkness beyond.

Tree branches slapped at Tessa's face as they ran into the forest. She tripped on an exposed root, and nearly fell. Nick's arm dug into her waist, keeping her upright. Another shot cut through the trees above their heads, spraying them with leaves and twigs.

"Keep your head down." They tumbled down a small embankment, landing in a tangle of blackberry bushes. The thorns caught their clothes and tore at their skin. Nick grunted with satisfaction. "She can't see us here. Just stay low and don't make a sound."

Her heartbeat roared in her ears, nearly drowning out his whispered words. Beside her, his chest rose and fell like a bellows. She hung gratefully on to his hand, not moving.

Unable to move, she realized. Her hair was tangled in the thorny branches. She just hoped Sophie and Pete didn't see it if they came searching with a flashlight.

Beams of light cut through the trees. "Let's get out of here," she heard Pete pleading. "We'll never find them in the dark."

"Stop your sniveling," Sophie said harshly. "We have to find them."

"It wasn't supposed to be like this," Pete whined.

For a long moment nothing moved, the woods silent as even small night animals cowered in the underbrush, disturbed by the humans tramping through their domain. Then Pete spoke. "I've had it. I'm outta here."

Twigs cracked as he turned and ran toward the van. Tessa held her breath, waiting for the shot that would bring him down. Nothing happened. A moment later the roar of the van's engine cut through the night, echoing off the trees before receding in the distance.

The flashlight beam strafed the forest, once cutting above their heads so closely that Tessa could see the reflection in Nick's eyes. "You might as well come out," Sophie said. Her voice dropped, became cajoling. "I'm sure we can come to some sort of agreement."

"Like hell," Nick muttered beside her. "She's crazy, totally insane."

Footsteps squelched over ground still damp from last night's storm. Suddenly Tessa realized Sophie was only a couple of meters away from them. Could she see them? Nick wore a white shirt although after the tumble down the hill, it must be less than clean now. Would it be visible, or had they burrowed far enough into the blackberries to be safe?

She heard Nick's breath hiss out when Sophie's footsteps moved away from them. "Wait here," he said. "I'm going to get her. We'll end this once and for all."

Crouching low, he wriggled out from under the thorny vines, brushing sticks and leaves out of his path before he crept forward. Tessa jerked her hair free of the hooked thorns, stifling a cry of pain as several strands pulled out of her scalp. The scratches on her arms stung like ant bites.

Silently, belly to the ground, she crawled after Nick. Once they reached the top of the embankment, they stood up, keeping behind the heavy trunk of a hemlock. Nick glanced at her, his eyes hard in the dim light, but he must have realized it was useless to scold her for disobeying him.

She squeezed his hand. "You might need my help."

Sophie had gone deeper into the woods, the wavering flashlight beam giving away her location. That and the ghostly paleness of her white shirt. Tessa heard Nick's breathing speed up. The hunted had suddenly become the hunter.

"We'll hit her from two sides." Nick spoke so close to

her ear she felt as if she read his thoughts rather than heard his low voice. "You go that way. Stay behind the trees. She could turn around at any time."

He looped his arm around her waist and caught her against him. His mouth covered hers in a searing kiss that was over almost before she registered it. "Be careful," he said.

Stunned, her fingers touching her tingling lips, she watched as he seemed to melt into the shadows. The flashlight still gleamed intermittently in the distance.

Carefully, she slid her feet over the ground. No twigs here, only a mat of fallen needles beneath the towering evergreens. She slipped through the trees, keeping the thick trunks between her and the flickering light. Her eyes strained to penetrate the dense shadows. Where was Nick? She heard nothing, only the ghostly flutter of wings and a low hoot as an owl flew over her head.

The light grew stronger. Tessa froze, her fingers digging into the rough bark of a tree. Sophie was coming back. She made no effort to be silent, footsteps crunching in the undergrowth.

Tessa heard a low whistle that sounded like a bird but she knew it wasn't. What should she do? With the clearing in front of her, there was no way to get behind Sophie. And she might spot her as she drew closer, since the trees around her were sparse and thin. Not to mention that Tessa's own shirt was pale yellow, almost as visible as white. If Sophie saw her, they'd lose the element of surprise, and she still carried the shotgun, fully reloaded no doubt.

Tessa crouched down, dragging her hand over the ground to find something to use as a weapon. Her fingers closed over a palm-sized rock. Not big enough to do any damage and she would have to get dangerously close to use it. Better to try something else.

Praying that Nick was alert and in position, she stood, drew back her arm and threw the rock as far as she could

eyond Sophie. It thunked against a tree trunk. Sophie
hirled, her shoes slipping in the damp leaves on the
round.

Nick, like a hungry predator, leaped from the shrubbery.
essa's heart jumped into her mouth as she saw Sophie
cover with remarkable speed. Just as Nick reached her,
ae brought the shotgun up, bracing it on her hip and aim-
g at Nick's chest. The flashlight bobbled and steadied.
ick skidded to a stop.

"Where's Tessa?" Sophie asked.

"Far enough," Nick said shortly.

"Tessa," Sophie called. "You can come out now. Or
ou can watch me blow a hole in your lover. The sainted
ther of your child," she added sarcastically.

"Stay where you are," Nick yelled. "For Andrew."

His leap forward was so sudden Sophie staggered under
e blow that landed on her chest. She couldn't bring the
aotgun to bear at once, but as he fell back, Nick overbal-
aced and almost went down. Sophie laughed as she swung
e gun back into position. "You realize you've signed
ur death warrant."

Tessa, scrabbling over the ground under the trees, finally
und a tree branch sturdy enough to use as a weapon.
Not if I can help it," she screamed, rushing forward.

She swung the branch with all her strength, bringing it
own on Sophie's head. She dropped like a rag doll. "Good
ork, Tessa," Nick said, his voice shaking. "I thought I
as a goner for sure and that she'd get you next. Do you
alize if she'd turned her head only the slightest bit she
uld have seen you?"

"Yeah, like you," she said, adrenaline making her
ddy. "Make a note, the next time we go on these break-
d-enter jobs, we wear darker clothes."

Nick scrambled forward and rolled Sophie over. Tessa's
aees suddenly sagged, and she fell to the ground. "I didn't
ll her, did I?"

"No, worse luck. Just stunned her. She's got a knot th
size of an egg on the back of her head, but she's alread
coming out of it."

Nick picked up the gun and ejected the shells, tossin
them into a clump of blackberry brambles. He prodded So
phie with the barrel. "Hey, time to wake up."

Tessa played the flashlight over Sophie's face. Sh
moaned and opened her eyes, squinting against the ligh
Her faculties hadn't been dulled, she saw. She took in th
sight of Nick holding the gun and sank back down, closin
her eyes.

Nick grabbed her wrist and jerked her to her fee
"Enough of that. We have to get out of here."

Tessa opened the back door of the house, noting the gra
fingerprint dust on the door frame and counter surfaces i
the kitchen. She'd have to clean it up later, once they foun
Andrew.

Nick asked her to fetch cord from the pantry and h
efficiently tied the groaning Sophie to a kitchen chai
"Call the police."

Tessa picked up the phone. The reassuring sound of th
dial tone hummed in her ear. "Must have been the stor
after all, and not Pete who put the phone out of commissio
last night," she muttered as she punched out 911.

She gave their location and a brief rundown of the si
uation, then hung up. "They're on their way," she said.

"Good," Nick said, his voice hard. He pressed th
sawed-off shotgun against Sophie's temple. "Now you'r
going to tell us where Andrew is or you're dead. What wa
that little scenario you dreamed up? We can vary it. Woma
involved in attempted murder and kidnapping takes he
own life rather than face prison. Yeah, they'd buy it."

Tessa felt the blood drain from her face. Had Nick r
loaded the gun? She knew he'd removed the spare shel
from Sophie's pockets but had he used them? Would h
really pull the trigger?

Sophie's shrill laughter rang around the room. "You can shoot me if you want. It won't do you any good."

She laughed again, so hard she almost choked. "Don't you get it? I'm going to use Andrew's location to plea-bargain a shorter sentence. And if you kill me, you'll never find him."

Chapter Sixteen

Nick woke suddenly in the middle of the night. He sat up. Had he heard a sound or was it a dream? Pulling on his jeans, he slipped out of the guest room and into the hall. The house was dark and silent but then he heard it again, a low humming.

The hair at the nape of his neck stood on end. He tiptoed down the hall, passing Tessa's room. The door stood open. He glanced inside. The bed was rumpled but empty.

He continued down the hall, drawn by a thin sliver of light under a closed door. His heart thundered in his ears as he curled his palm around the cool doorknob. He turned it and pushed the door open.

Only a dim nightlight illuminated the room but it was enough to let him see Tessa sitting next to a crib, rocking slowly back and forth, a teddy bear hugged to her chest. He had an impression of sunshine yellow walls with apple green trim as he crossed the room.

She looked up, tears tracking down her cheeks in silver rivulets. "Nick." Her mouth soundlessly formed the word.

She made no protest when he lifted her from the chair and sat down on it with her on his lap. He hugged her and the furry teddy bear close, rocking them both, his own tears

aking into her hair. "Tessa, we'll find him. We will, if
takes forever."

HE STORY WAS ALL OVER the front pages of the city papers
e next morning—Daughter of Prominent Brownsville
amily Arrested for Kidnapping and Attempted Murder.
aby Missing. Details on page A5.

Tessa flipped over to A5 and found herself staring at a
ainy photo of Andrew. She must have made a sound be-
ause Nick lifted his head and glanced at her across the
tchen table where they were eating Millie's special
rench toast. "What is it?"

She looked over the paper at him, her eyes meeting his
silent communication yet with a faint uncertainty in
em. Did she still not trust him? A pang of disappointment
ifed through him. Surely after last night—or rather, early
is morning—in Andrew's room— They'd slept together
terward, holding each other like lost children, but in the
orning he'd woken in her bed to find her gone, already
essed and downstairs.

Dropping her gaze, she handed him the paper. "That's
e photo I gave Larry. I suppose he also used it to make
 the flyers and send them out."

"He did," Millie said. "I saw one on the grocery store
lletin board."

"That means she kept him hidden or took him out of the
mediate area." Tessa sighed. "Let's hope she tells the
lice this morning, once she'd got a lawyer there."

"'Baby still missing,'" Nick read aloud. "'Although we
ve been unable to get a statement from Sophie Marsden,
is believed that she is involved in the disappearance of
ndrew Lee, grandson of the late Joseph Lee, founder of
e Lee business empire. Police departments around the
ower Mainland have asked all citizens to be on the look-
t for the four-month-old child. Anyone with information
 asked to call the Brownsville police department or this

newspaper. Tessa Lee, the child's mother, is in seclusio at her home.'''

"In seclusion." Millie sniffed. "If those reporters woul only leave a body alone. This morning the answering ma chine tape was completely full of messages."

"Did you play them back?" Tessa asked. Last nigh after the phone had rung constantly for an hour, they ha turned off the ringer and let the machine take messages.

Millie shook her head. "No, I just put in the spare tape It's probably still taking messages."

Tessa frowned. "Maybe we should play them, or answe the phone. There might be news about Andrew."

She gulped down the last of her coffee, and went int the living room to check the answering machine. "I sup pose we'd better turn on the phone again."

She lifted it to slide the button into position, jumpin nervously when it rang. She picked up the receive "Yes?" She listened briefly. "No, I'm not interested i making a statement. I have nothing to say. Goodbye." Sh hung up the phone with an abrupt little click.

"Vultures," she muttered.

"Freedom of the press and all that," Nick said with wry smile. "Let's hear the tape."

The messages on the tape were mainly from radio, T and newspaper reporters asking for details on the sens tional story. Only one was different, an offer from a psych who had heard about Andrew still missing. She would hel them find him if they could supply her with an item Andrew's clothing. She left her number.

"Might be legitimate," Nick commented. "The pap isn't printed until about 3 a.m. That message came in half past one." He pushed the eject button on the answerir machine. "Let's see what we've got this morning."

The first message was from a reporter, calling at 6:4 obviously working on the early-bird theory. The secor was from Larry, saying he'd found a truck hidden behir

Dorky Pete's shack, which had dents in the fender and bumper and paint scrapes that matched the wrecked Volvo. Pete was still missing, however.

"They'll find him," Nick said bluntly. "And nail him." Larry went on to add that Sophie was waiting for a lawyer although she had admitted to trying to get Nick to leave by surfing him out of the hotel, which happened to also be owned by her family. Larry promised to get back to them as soon as he had anything else.

The next call brought them to attention. Even Millie held her breath as they listened to the female voice. When the machine beeped to indicate the next call, Nick hit the rewind button. As the tape hissed and stuttered, he laid his hand on Tessa's head, smoothing her glossy hair, praying as he'd never prayed in his life. *Please, let this be the one. Let this be on the level.*

He pushed play again, waiting impatiently through the first call. He turned up the volume. The woman's voice came into the room, the call timed at seven. "I think I have your son." They heard a little catch in her voice as she paused. "I didn't know he was your son. Please call me." She gave the number.

Nick pushed stop. In the silence, Tessa wondered that he couldn't hear all three hearts pounding. Nick cleared his throat. "That could be it."

The clock on the mantel chimed eight o'clock. Tessa grabbed up the phone. "We've already wasted an hour." Her voice broke on a sob. Covering her eyes with one hand, she handed Nick the receiver. "You do it. I don't think I can talk."

Nick swiftly punched out the numbers, including the area code. He waited while it rang. On the third ring someone picked it up. "Hello?"

Elation filled him as he recognized the voice as the one on the tape. "This is Andrew's father. We got your mes-

sage." His own throat closed and he had to swallow har
to clear it.

"She said he needed a foster home for a few days.
didn't know who the baby was until I saw the story in th
paper this morning. He's wearing a bracelet with the nam
Andrew on it. I'm so sorry but I just didn't know."

Nick was about to interrupt the stream of words whe
he heard the soft sound of a baby babbling in the back
ground. The woman moved her mouth away from th
phone. "Hush, Andrew," he heard her say quietly. "You'
see your daddy soon."

He couldn't have uttered a word if his life depended o
it. His son. He'd heard him for the first time. Tears spran
to his eyes, and he couldn't stop them from overflowing.

"Mr. Lee, are you still there?" the woman's voic
flowed into his ear.

Not Mr. Lee, he thought, but it seemed useless to corre
her. "Can we come and get him?" he said in a strangle
voice.

"Of course." She paused for a heartbeat. "You'll hav
to bring some proof that you're really his parents. I can'
just give him to anyone."

Nick closed his eyes, wiping them with the back of hi
hand. "Your address?"

He wrote it down as she gave him the numbers and di
rections for getting there. It wasn't far, less than an hou
away, he figured. He thanked her and hung up.

"Well?" Tessa sat looking up at him, her heart in he
eyes. He felt like crying again, a great lump clogging hi
chest.

"It has to be him. His name is Andrew and she says sh
recognized the picture. He's wearing the bracelet. I didn
ask her for details but her name is Sally Smith."

Elation surged through Tessa. Tears of relief ran dow
her cheeks. Laughing shakily, she swiped at them, an
scooped up Nick's car keys from the coffee table. "I thin

you'd better drive. I'll probably have us off the road in the first block.''

He smiled ruefully, his own eyes still misty. ''What makes you think I won't?''

Running to the hall closet, she paused as she opened it. ''I suppose we should call the police and tell them we've found Andrew.'' Even as she said the words, she knew she wouldn't, no matter how much flak Larry gave her afterwards.

Nick looked at her as if he couldn't believe she'd suggested such a thing. ''No way,'' he said forcefully. ''Wait for them to fill in endless forms—forget that. We're going now.''

Tessa nodded. ''Yes, we're going now.''

She pulled a loaded cartoon-printed bag from the hall closet, her hands trembling. ''We'll have to take diapers and fresh clothes.''

Caution crept into Nick's mind. Her eagerness nearly broke his heart. What if it turned out to be a hoax? Of course, wasn't he in just the same state of joyous anticipation? He hardly dared think what would happen if this baby wasn't Andrew.

SALLY SMITH LIVED in a modest neighborhood in a town halfway to Vancouver. Her house was distinguishable from its neighbors mainly by its color and the wheelchair ramp leading up to the front door. The lawns were well-kept green rectangles separated by concrete driveways. Yellow and bronze marigolds bloomed around Sally's front doorstep.

''This is it,'' Nick said, his palms sweating. He wiped them on his jeans thighs as Tessa hoisted the heavy diaper bag over her shoulder.

He rang the doorbell, scarcely breathing while they waited. Beside him, Tessa looked pale, her mouth set in a grim line. Only the sparkle in her eyes told him she wouldn't allow the thought that they might be disappointed enter her mind.

The door opened. A small blond woman stood there but he scarcely noticed her as he fell into the deep blue pools of his son's eyes. "Andrew," Tessa whispered, her voice trembling. "Andrew, come to Mommy." Dropping the bag, she held out her arms.

The baby screwed up his face and he seemed about to cry. But when she cradled him against her, he calmed, nuzzling her shirt as if he'd come home.

"He's yours, all right," the woman said quietly. "He knows your scent. Babies always recognize their mother."

Tessa ran her palm over his soft dark hair, gazing into his little face, her heart so full she couldn't speak. She could only murmur incoherent little phrases. Andrew gazed back at her, and then he gurgled contentedly and broke into a wide smile. Tessa clasped him closer, covering his face with kisses, inhaling the sweet baby fragrance of him.

Sally Smith pulled the door wider. "Why don't you come in? We'll be more comfortable than standing out here in the hot sun."

Nick picked up the diaper bag and guided Tessa inside with a hand on the small of her back. Behind them, Sally closed the door. As they crossed the entrance hall, a toddler came out of the living room, rosy mouth framing a wet thumb. "Auntie Sally, bafroom," he mumbled around it.

She scooped up the child, gently removing the thumb from his mouth. "Excuse me, please. He's toilet training. I'll be right back."

Tessa sank down on the sofa as if her legs had given way. Nick knew how she felt, as he sat down on a chair opposite. Toys lay scattered over the floor. Two small children played with little plastic cars in the corner of the room, paying no attention to the visitors.

Nick glanced at them. A boy and a girl, both blond. If he and Tessa had another child, would it have her hair?

Then he remembered Sophie's cruelly spoken words. Had she meant what he thought? That Tessa couldn't have more children. It didn't matter; they had Andrew.

She held Andrew tightly, one hand roaming over him as if she had to keep reassuring herself that he was really in her arms. "He's grown since I've seen him last," she said, her eyes shining.

"It hasn't been two weeks," he said. "How could he have grown?"

"I don't know but he has. Babies grow very quickly. At least I can see that Sophie took good care of him."

"Sophie and Sally." Feeling awkward but unable to stop himself, Nick got up from the chair. He sat down beside Tessa. "May I?"

She nodded. His hand shaking, he laid it on the baby's head. Andrew twisted his head around and stared at him. The blue eyes were achingly familiar. "You're right. He has my eyes." A bubble seemed to invade his chest, expanding until it filled his whole body. He'd never known he could feel this—this mixture of pride and love and a desire to be part of this child's life.

He moved his hand, fingers touching the black curly hair. It was soft as dandelion fluff but much thicker. He ran one fingertip down the baby's cheek. His skin too, was unbelievably soft, firm yet resilient.

"Do you want to hold him?" Tessa asked hesitantly.

Alarm stopped his heart. Could he? It had been so long since he'd held a child. What if he did something wrong, damaged this fragile little creature?

As if understanding, Tessa smiled. "You can't hurt him. Babies are very tough. They have to be. Hold out your hands."

She placed the child in his hands which suddenly felt too large and ungainly. The baby's head fit in one of his palms. He was surprisingly heavy as he gazed trustingly up at Nick's face.

Nick arranged him so that he lay comfortably, inhaling the baby-powder smell. It was all coming back to him, he realized, the skill of holding a baby. In the years since his little girl had been this young he'd gotten out of practice, but he hadn't entirely forgotten.

Andrew gave a little whimper and nuzzled his face into Nick's chest. Nick laughed. "Sorry, kid. Your mom's got the right equipment, not me."

Not finding what he wanted, Andrew wrinkled his face and let out a small wail of protest. He waved his chubby arms, the little silver bracelet jingling. "You'd better give him back," Tessa said. "I can tell he's hungry, and when he wants to eat, he means right now, or he'll bawl the house down."

She reached down and took a small blanket from her bag, draping it over her shoulder. She took the baby from him, and started to unbutton her shirt, discreetly tucking him under the blanket. She sighed, closing her eyes as a deep sense of rightness swept through her when he began to nurse.

Nick couldn't take his eyes off them. She gazed down at the baby, her face serene, with a tender, inward look. He felt his heart expand until it seemed too big for his chest. No matter what happened with him and Tessa, seeing her reunited with her baby was worth everything. He could only pray she would let him be part of them, let them be a real family.

Sally came back. The little boy with her hung back shyly, one fist gripping her pant leg. "I'm sorry. It took a little longer than I expected."

She stooped and whispered something into the child's ear. He nodded and scampered off to join the other two children. "They're foster children," Sally explained. "And Miss Marsden told me Andrew was also a child who needed care for a couple of days. She even had papers from social services."

"Probably salvaged from one of her temp jobs," Tessa said, too happy to think about Sophie right now.

Nick wasn't inclined to be so charitable. "She sure got around, didn't she?"

Sally clasped her hands together, a worried frown creasing her brow. "It was a shock to pick up this morning's paper and see Andrew's picture. Really, I had no idea he could have been kidnapped."

Tessa smiled at her. "It doesn't matter. I have him back now. It's all over." She glanced across the room at the children. "You don't have children of your own?"

"No. My husband is in a wheelchair. His disability is extensive enough that it's very unlikely that he'll father children." She said it matter-of-factly, and her face lit up as she mentioned him. Her marriage was obviously strong.

What about her and Nick, though? The worry that Tessa had woken up with early in the morning came back, and she bit her lip. What would happen between her and Nick?

Nick glanced down at Andrew, realizing he hadn't heard the soft slurping noises he made for the past few minutes. The baby slept, long black lashes lying like miniature fans on his rosy cheeks.

Tessa shifted the baby in her arms. Nick leaned over. "Let me take him."

Andrew stiffened at the shift in position, his arms flailing briefly. He snuffled, frowning, then settled down, a little snore escaping from his rosy pink lips. Nick cradled him against his chest, filled with a love he hadn't expected to ever feel again.

Tessa wasn't like Laura. Tessa would never neglect a child, especially the only child she'd ever have. She would treasure him, nurture him, and yet she wouldn't smother him. He'd seen it in the past days, the anxiety, the absolute refusal to give up even when she thought Andrew was dead.

What a shame that she couldn't have more children. Unless— His breath died in his throat. Maybe it wasn't true at all. Maybe Sophie had used it as a shot to wound them both.

He would have to ask Tessa.

Holding the baby, he stood up. "We should probably go. Millie will be anxious to see Andrew as well."

Tessa held out her hand to Sally. "I can't thank you enough for what you did."

Sally's pretty face still wore a troubled frown. "You're very generous. Most people would have been angry. I should have questioned her more carefully, especially since Andrew seemed so well cared-for, not like most of the foster children I get."

Impulsively, Tessa hugged her. "I'm just glad it's over, and that I have Andrew back. Come down and visit sometime. We'd be happy to see you."

"Thank you, I will." Sally walked over to Nick and touched Andrew's cheek. "You be good now."

The baby sighed and continued to sleep.

NICK GLANCED in the rearview mirror, adjusting it so that he could look into the back seat of the car. He could only see the top of Tessa's head, the crooked part in her tawny hair, as she bent over Andrew. He couldn't see the baby, securely strapped in the rear-facing infant seat they'd stopped to buy on the way to Sally's this morning.

Tessa hadn't said a word since they'd left Sally's and the few times he'd met her eyes in the mirror, they'd looked sad and oddly wary.

"You haven't said much about Sophie," he ventured. "You're probably feeling like you want to kill her. She was your best friend, after all, and she put you through hell."

"Was, all right," Tessa said, but her voice lacked heat. "I don't want to think about her yet. Maybe later."

She fell silent once more. Not Sophie. So, what was eating her then? He couldn't figure it out; she should have been bubbling over with joy. Andrew was safe, back in her arms. And he'd just heard on the radio that the police had picked up Dorky Pete. That meant that Sophie must have talked.

Tessa shouldn't have a worry in the world.

They had nearly reached Brownsville. Soon they would be back at her house. Millie would make a fuss over her and Andrew, and he would be left out in the cold. Oh, he was willing to give her some time but he wanted to be part of Andrew's life. And hers. She couldn't shut him out.

Abruptly he pulled over to the side of the road, braking under a tall chestnut tree. He turned the key and killed the engine. Tessa looked up. "Why are we stopping? We're not home yet."

"I want to talk to you," he said, and was instantly sorry when the words came out more harshly than he'd intended. But he'd seen the look in her eyes as they met his, a mixture of fear and defensiveness. Was she afraid he'd tear Andrew away from her?

It suddenly dawned on him that that might be exactly what she was thinking. "We have to talk," he said more gently. "Leave him here. It's cool enough, and we can sit there under the trees and watch the car."

She fussed a little with the blanket she'd put over Andrew, then opened the door and got out. Nick had to shove his fists into his pockets to keep from touching her.

Oh, Tessa, don't you trust me at all?

Pain knotted his guts as he realized she had no reason to. He'd told her last summer he only wanted a temporary fling with her. She had only his word that he had changed, and after all the lies she'd been told lately, why should she believe him?

In the shade off the road, Tessa lowered herself to the ground and rested her back against a tree trunk. She plucked a blade of grass and began to tear it into shreds. Nick said nothing, not knowing how to start.

She finally spoke into a silence filled with the drone of a bumblebee sampling the clover blossoms that sent their sweet perfume into the still summer air. "When are you leaving?"

He watched the iridescent blue-green shimmer of a dragonfly as it landed on his raised knee. "Leaving? I'm not leaving."

"You're not?" Surprise laced her voice.

"No. Why do you think I rented an apartment instead of just staying at the hotel?"

"You mean you're not going to try to get custody of Andrew?"

He reached over and lifted her face so that she could meet his eyes. "Tessa, I would never take your baby away from you."

To his utter horror, she burst into tears. "Oh, Tessa," he said helplessly. "I didn't mean to make you cry." He gathered her into his arms, absorbing the shudders that racked her body, rocking her back and forth. "Oh, Tessa, how could you think that? I love you too much to hurt you ever again. It kills me to see you crying."

She tilted her head up, tears spiking her lashes. "What did you say?"

"I don't want you to cry anymore."

"No, before that."

Heat crept up his face. "Oh, that. I love you, Tessa. I want us to be a family. That's why I took the apartment. I know I really screwed up last summer but as soon as you left I realized what I was throwing away. When I saw you again, everything just seemed right. I planned to court you."

"Court me?" A faint smile broke through the tears, like a rainbow after a storm.

"Yeah. I figure in a month or two we could get married. Maybe you don't trust me enough to love me after what I

id, but I know you like me a little or you wouldn't have
t me help you with Andrew."

She began to cry again, huge silent tears running down
er face. "Oh, Tessa," he said miserably. "Please don't
ry anymore. You're soaking my shirt."

"Nick," she sobbed. "I thought you were going to leave
gain and take Andrew. That would have been the end. You
eard what Sophie said."

"That you can't have more children? So it's true."

"Yes, it's true. I'm sorry."

"Why should you be sorry?" he asked incredulously. It
nly hit him now what profound anguish she must have
uffered when she'd learned that Andrew would be her only
hild. She was a wonderful mother and deserved more chil-
ren. But if it wasn't to be, he could only help her to live
ith the pain.

"It's not your fault," he said. "And why should it di-
inish me in my eyes? I've never thought of women as
roodmares. I just wish I could have been here when you
ere going through that agony. I'll regret it for the rest of
y life."

She laid a finger across his lips. "Don't, Nick. Please
on't. I love you. We have a second chance."

A second chance, he thought, holding her tightly against
im. And this time he was going to do everything right.
e held out his hand. She took it. "Let's go home."

The three McCullar brothers once stood strong against the lawlessness on their ranches. Then the events of one fateful night shattered their bond and sent them far from home. But their hearts remained with the ranch—and the women—they left behind. And now all three are coming

HOME TO TEXAS

Gayle Wilson has written a romantic, emotional and suspenseful new trilogy and created characters who will touch your heart. Don't miss any of the cowboy McCullar brothers in:

#461 RANSOM MY HEART
April

#466 WHISPER MY LOVE
May

#469 REMEMBER MY TOUCH
June

These are three cowboys' stories you won't want to miss!

HARLEQUIN®

I N T R I G U E®

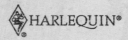

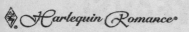

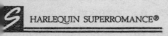

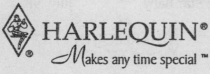

DEBBIE MACOMBER

invites you to the

HEART OF TEXAS

Join Debbie Macomber as she brings you the lives
and loves of the folks in the ranching community
of Promise, Texas.

If you loved Midnight Sons—don't miss
Heart of Texas! A brand-new six-book series
from Debbie Macomber.

Available in February 1998
at your favorite retail store.

Heart of Texas by Debbie Macomber

Lonesome Cowboy	February '98
Texas Two-Step	March '98
Caroline's Child	April '98
Dr. Texas	May '98
Nell's Cowboy	June '98
Lone Star Baby	July '98

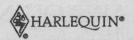

HARLEQUIN®

HPHRT1

MEN at WORK

All work and no play? Not these men!

April 1998
KNIGHT SPARKS by Mary Lynn Baxter

Sexy lawman Rance Knight made a career of arresting the bad guys. Somehow, though, he thought policewoman Carly Mitchum was framed. Once they'd uncovered the truth, could Rance let Carly go...or would he make a citizen's arrest?

May 1998
HOODWINKED by Diana Palmer

CEO Jake Edwards donned coveralls and went undercover as a mechanic to find the saboteur in his company. Nothing— or no one—would distract him, not even beautiful secretary Maureen Harris. Jake had to catch the thief—*and* the woman who'd stolen his heart!

June 1998
DEFYING GRAVITY by Rachel Lee

Tim O'Shaughnessy and his business partner, Liz Pennington, had always been close—but never *this* close. As the danger of their assignment escalated, so did their passion. When the job was over, could they ever go back to business as usual?

MEN AT WORK™

Available at your favorite retail outlet!

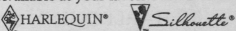